THE
AMAZON
CONSPIRACY

S.J. PHILIPS

ISBN: 978-1-7358057-1-9 (Paperback)

ISBN: 978-1-7358057-0-2 (eBook)

Library of Congress Control Number: 2020918424

This is a work of fiction. The story, characters, and events are entirely made up. A few public institutions, locations, and countries are mentioned, but the characters involved and the events described are imaginary. Names, characters, businesses, places, events, locales, and incidents are the products of the author's imagination. Except for a few historical facts, any resemblance to actual persons, living or dead, or actual events is unintentional and purely coincidental.

Cover and book design by Damonza

Published by S. J. Philips

Annandale, Virginia, USA

www.sjphilips.com

To Helena and Henrique

PROLOGUE

EARLY ARRIVALS WERE starting to trickle in at the Truman Building, headquarters of the world's largest diplomatic corps. The morning air was cool and crisp, but the forecast called for a warm day as summer fought its way into the ever-shorter spring season of the mid-Atlantic.

Third-generation diplomat Andrew Everett sat at his desk on the fourth floor, slouching toward his window with a despondent look, watching a tall woman wearing a green-and-orange dress and high heels stumble up the barricades in front of the building, negotiating her way to the sidewalk.

Everett smiled at the scene because he welcomed the distraction from the unfolding international crisis. No one, including himself, could gracefully climb over the ugly concrete planters permanently obstructing the right lane on Twenty-Third Street.

Still, he was a big advocate for those barriers, having seen up close the carnage car bombs can produce. It had happened during his first assignment, in the fall of 1982, when a van loaded with two thousand pounds of explosives blasted the American embassy lobby in Beirut, killing sixty-three people. It was in the grief following the brutal and senseless loss of so many lives that he had found his calling: to fight the proliferation of weapons of mass destruction.

The offices next to Everett's were still empty, just as they had been the entire weekend while he had worked around the clock on a resolution about to be put to a vote at the United Nations Security Council.

Timing was critical, which was why he had not slept for more than a few hours in the past several nights. Reliable intelligence indicated that scientists from the Republic of Alashrar were nearing a technological break-through that would put the regime on a short path to developing nuclear weapons.

American intelligence officials estimated that without the approval of a stiff economic embargo, Alashrar would master the capacity to weaponize uranium in a matter of months. After that, sanctions would be of little use.

Aware of reports that the existing regime had already provided terrorist groups with arms and money, the veteran diplomat knew it wasn't a stretch to fear it would share more powerful weapons too.

The embargo was not a permanent solution. The intent was to delay the nuclear program by at least a year while American diplomats pushed for a comprehensive deal that would allow independent inspectors to monitor the country's nuclear program.

Up until now, Everett and his colleagues at the State Department had expected the resolution to pass, following intense negotiations with key members of the UN Security Council. With their companies profiting tremendously from lucrative exports to the regime full of petrodollars, some countries stood much to lose from the agreement. It had been a diplomatic coup to bring them around to support the American proposal.

Now they had just been presented with the perfect excuse to walk away.

Driven by their ambition to show that the two Latin American giants had a role to play on the international stage, Brazil and Mexico had just announced, with great fanfare, a deal to stop the Alashrari regime from developing nuclear weapons. The two countries would supply non-weapons-grade uranium to the Republic of Alashrar, which would in turn stop processing the mineral.

In theory, this would prevent the country from developing the know-how to weaponize uranium and produce a bomb. But despite Brazil's and Mexico's best intentions, Everett and other American officials believed that the Alashrari regime would just use the deal as an excuse to forgo international inspections by an independent agency.

"We believe that with this new deal in place, the international community can rest at ease. Going forward, all nuclear research will be conducted solely for medical purposes and to provide electricity for the people," the charismatic Brazilian president had professed during the announcement a few moments before, with the heads of Mexico and the Republic of Alashrar standing in the background.

Absent from the South American leader's remarks was the fact that Alashrar was awash in cheaper and readily available energy sources like oil and natural gas, not to mention an abundance of land and sunshine that could sustainably power its economy with solar panels.

The French government had reacted quickly, welcoming the deal and expressing optimism. The foreign secretary of China requested the UN vote be postponed so they could review the deal and "give diplomacy a chance."

Everett feared that delaying the vote and the economic sanctions by several months would give ample time for the ongoing tests that would bring the regime—and the terrorist groups it supported—closer to having a nuclear bomb.

He sat back in his chair with a sick feeling in his stomach. Weeks of intense negotiations, which had finally convinced key countries to agree on measures designed to slow down the advance of nuclear proliferation, seemed all but wasted.

The career of a diplomat is filled with travels, meetings, and negotiations that seem boring and pointless most of the time. But a few of those can change the course of history.

This looked to be one of them.

CHAPTER 1

ALTO RIO NEGRO INDIGENOUS TERRITORY, BRAZIL
APRIL 4

L UNCH WAS RICE, beans, flour, and chicken.
Sometimes it was fish, sometimes beef, occasionally a wild animal, like turtle, caiman, capybara, or armadillo. But every day, without fail, the cook would make white rice, black beans, and fried manioc flour.

The wild-caught meat was illegal, but it mattered little in this remote corner of the Amazon basin, where there were no roads and the nearest town was hundreds of miles away.

Except for water and a cereal bar in the middle of the morning, tropical ecologist Henry Foster had eaten nothing since leaving at daybreak for his daily rounds in the jungle. When he returned to the research camp's base at noon, sweaty and itchy from mosquito bites, he looked forward to this daily portion of rice, beans, flour, and whatever meat was on the plate. No conceivable course at the fanciest restaurants of New York or Paris would ever taste as good as that ordinary dish and a glass of cold water after a hard day's work.

The rustic building where the food was served was the heart of the Pitiri Research Station. A cabin made of uneven wood planks and a thatched roof, it served as cafeteria, meeting room, community center, and hangout for the researchers who gathered on the porch in the late afternoons, swinging on hammocks attached to the wood columns as they talked about the exploits of the day.

The old thermometer on the wall by the door showed 102 degrees. Perennially close to 100 percent, the humidity levels were always too high for anyone to bother keeping track.

Henry embraced the stupor that came after a full meal on a hot day, heading to his dorm for a short nap before getting back to work. After his siesta, he would transcribe his notes into the laptop, charged daily in the camp's solar-powered generator, and run a few preliminary analyses of the data collected for his research on rain forest fragmentation.

Walking toward his dormitory, across the open sandy square surrounded by wood plank buildings, he heard his name being called. Pausing and looking back over his shoulder, Henry saw Marcelo Pereira, the camp manager, raising the palm of his hand and signaling for him to wait.

"I just talked to Teresa on the radio," the short, broad-chested man said in Portuguese as he approached. "We have a film crew coming, and we need you to take them to go see the cave."

A cathedral-like natural wonder, the cave was just starting to get international attention. It was half the size of a football field, with a river flowing under its high ceiling. The sunlight coming in from the large entrance and the gaps at the top allowed an underground forest to grow inside, an otherworldly sight that could have inspired Jules Verne's *Journey to the Center of the Earth*.

To top it all off, the cave walls were adorned by rudimentary drawings estimated to have been painted millennia before. The Pitiri Research Station being the closest settlement to the cave, its researchers occasionally doubled as guides to the visitors who came from far away and paid good money to see it.

"Does it have to be me?" Henry asked, knowing he had little choice in the matter. The prospect of dropping his work to serve as a tour guide did not appeal to him. "Can't someone else do it? Joaquim would be perfect for this."

"Teresa asked for you. Your English is better and you know the area well. You know we are short staffed for a few more weeks," Pereira replied.

Most of the scientists who carried out research at the station were college professors or graduate students who would not arrive for another month, during the summer break, when they could leave their classes behind to do fieldwork. Having been expelled from his PhD program, Henry didn't have any such inconveniences. The only native English speaker working on the site during the school year, along with a team of local Brazilian scientists, he was a natural fit to lead a crew of foreign filmmakers to the cave.

He liked Pereira, an energetic and eager-to-help Amazon native born in a small village tucked in the rain forest. As a young boy, Pereira had left his home to live with relatives so he could go to school in Manaus, the metropolis of almost two million that served as the region's eastern hub, and became the first in his family to read and write fluently. Henry, born and raised comfortably in a Philadelphia suburb, admired that.

"How long is this going to take? I have a lot of work to do," Henry said, going through the motions of protesting, though he knew the value that helping camp visitors could bring. Maintaining a working research base in this remote and unforgiving region was not cheap, and part of his job was to support his team with fundraising and management. That included the occasional PR stint and being a host to public officials, donors, politicians, and the occasional celebrity *doing their part to save the Amazon*, which somehow always included bringing a good photographer.

The attention could also expedite funding and formal recognition of the cave as a World Heritage site, helping to protect it.

"Don't worry. I'll get you some help," Pereira continued. "It will be just a few days. You meet them in the Baniwa village, bring them here, and then head over to the site."

"I have to pick them up at the *village*? Why can't I just meet them here?"

"We don't want them getting lost trying to find our camp, especially since one of the filmmakers is the daughter of someone who helped raise a lot of money for the foundation. Come on, Henry, they are paying us, and the documentary will bring good exposure to our research and the cave."

It was futile to argue and not in Henry's nature to prolong a discussion when he already knew the outcome.

"Okay," he resigned himself. "When are they coming?"

"You should leave for the village tomorrow morning."

CHAPTER 2

THE FOURTEEN-FOOT ALUMINUM boat rocked gently on the black waters of a tributary of the Amazon River, deep into the Alto Rio Negro Indigenous Territory. The immense, remote protected area at the northeast corner of Brazil and inside the world's largest rain forest was larger than the average European country.

Henry gripped the throttle on the steering handle of the outboard engine. He rolled the accelerator, thrusting the boat downriver toward the Rio Negro, Portuguese for *black river*, to the small village of the Baniwa, one of the many indigenous groups that lived in the reserve.

The rivers of the Amazon basin began either in the tall mountains of western South America or in the rain forest's highlands. Those coming from the Andes Mountains to the west collected an abundance of sediment during the descent, making their waters muddy and white. In the forest-born rivers, without the balancing effect of the sediment load from the mountains, the decay of leaves, fallen branches, and other organic matter leached tannin compounds that turned the water acidic and dark.

Both types of rivers teemed with aquatic life, though the white waters were richer, thanks to their lower acidity and the presence of nutrient-rich sediment. Their banks were also more fertile and suitable for farming, making their margins more populated and thus afflicted by a higher rate of deforestation.

The encroaching farms and logging around the Andes-born rivers explained why the Pitiri Research Station was in such a distant corner of the Amazon, in dark-water territory. The acidity of the black rivers had the added benefit of being a poor breeding ground for mosquitoes, a welcome relief to the local inhabitants, scientists, and visitors alike.

∽

Henry docked the aluminum shell at a small pier on the riverbank, next to several dugout canoes and another powerboat. Flipping a small switch, he killed the fif-teen-horsepower engine and walked the few hundred feet from the river to the village.

The children ran to greet him, and Henry could not help but be heartened by their excitement and happy smiles, even when it became clear that many of them expected candy or gifts, neither of which he had thought to bring.

The cacique, the tribe's chief, welcomed him excitedly. According to tradition, the title was given to the eldest male descendant of the settlement's founding family.

Contrary to stereotype, the village leader was dressed not in traditional indigenous garments but in blue soccer shorts with three white stripes on the side, the signature Havaianas rubber flip-flops, and a worn-out green T-shirt with the phrase "Batteries Not Included" in bold yellow letters designed in the shape of a lightning bolt.

He was pleased to meet the new visitor, offering Henry a personal tour of the village before the arrival of the other guests. The warm, friendly reception was a trait Henry found everywhere in the region.

Only about 150 people lived at the site. Most other Baniwa were scattered in small settlements along the area's rivers and across the border, in Colombia and Venezuela. Many lived in small urban areas, the largest one being the little town of São Gabriel da Cachoeira, a couple of days by boat from the village.

The Baniwan language was a variation of an ancient dialect called "Arawak," common in the Caribbean and the northwestern Amazon, a version of which was spoken by the first Native Americans encountered by Christopher Columbus. Thankfully for Henry, his hosts spoke Portuguese as well, a tongue he was now fluent in after a couple of years in Brazil.

The village was laid out as a long rectangle. A community center with a zinc rooftop stood at the end, the only cinder block structure within a fifty-mile radius. It faced an open square delineated by a single row of huts on each side.

With no stores or any form of commerce, the villagers subsisted on hunting and fishing, manioc farming, and provisions brought in by the Brazilian government's

Bureau of Indian Affairs, which in addition to the community center also maintained the dock and the airstrip. The rudimentary runway provided the only quick link to the outside world for the nearby communities and settlements, making the village the area's main hub.

An open-wall shed for processing manioc into flour was the most notable part of the tour. It had an elementary hammer mill, operated by hand, used to grind the roots of the cassava grown around the village. The coarse flour was then sifted through sieves weaved with palm leaves and baked on a large iron bowl over a wattle-and-daub circular oven. This process had been the same for centuries, improved only by the iron bowl, a modern upgrade provided by the Brazilian government.

For Henry, the mix of the old ways with an infusion of modern civilization was one of the remarkable things about the village. It was best illustrated by none other than the cacique himself, who would often wear feather headgear and face paint while dressed in a T-shirt and flip-flops.

The villagers were no different. Instead of the traditional longhouses that used to accommodate several families, made with pitched roofs of thatch, poles, and reeds, they now preferred the single-family wattle-and-daub huts that dominated the rectangular plaza.

While Henry was fascinated to see the huts and the ages-old flour-making technology, the chief was most proud of the masonry-built community center, with its radio equipment, generator, and computer. Thanks to a blackboard, desks, and teaching props, the building doubled as a school for the children, offering the opportunity of a future beyond village life.

It wasn't too long after arriving in the Amazon that Henry learned that the *caboclos*, as the local peasants were known, as well as the indigenous peoples of the region, were proud of their traditions but also craved the comforts of modern civilization, not the idealized idyllic life revered by academics.

∽

While he waited another hour for the arrival of the film crew, Henry dozed off as he sat on the floor against a wall at the community center's porch. He was awakened by excited squeals coming from the main square. Getting up slowly, he walked with curiosity to the middle of the plaza and found the reason for the uproar. Jumping children giggled and pointed to a small plane on the horizon above the dark green canopy.

As it approached the village, the small turboprop flew around them three times, the kids shrieking and waving frenetically. Knowing the aircraft carried a film crew, Henry gathered they were taping the scene below. It would make for great footage.

The children ran toward the grass-covered runway, the adults yelling and gesticulating at the boys and girls, trying to keep them from getting in the aircraft's way.

Henry followed.

The plane bounced ungracefully from side to side as it got closer to the ground but landed smoothly, zipping by the crowd that waited on the side of the runway before coming to a stop. The children rushed to greet the passengers, engines still running. Henry cringed, but the captain was quick to kill the propellers.

Four people disembarked before the pilot, welcomed by a flock of children and a few adults, including the cacique. The enthusiasm was palpable. Visitors of any kind, let alone a TV crew, were not a common feature in the village.

Henry waited until they started walking toward the plaza before approaching the group and introducing himself.

A man with a square jaw and undulating dark hair showing the first traces of gray stepped forward to greet him.

"Good to meet you, Henry. I'm Aidan Green." They shook hands, and Aidan pointed to his companions. "These are my colleagues: Clare Andersen, Bill Powers, and Liam Nguyen."

They waved.

"Thanks for meeting us here," Aidan finished.

Henry recognized Aidan and Clare as the hosts of a TV nature show about remote, unexplored places. It wasn't bad, he remembered, feeling a little more positive about his forced assignment.

Henry wondered if Green was an assumed name. It was far too convenient for his profession. The host spoke in a British accent, one of the key attributes for gaining credibility as a TV personality in America. He was older than Henry and a bit shorter, an inch or two under six feet, but had the handsome features, physique, and charisma of a seasoned celebrity explorer.

Clare, his Australian cohost, was a younger version of Aidan, tall and fit, with natural charisma and dark, curly hair, light-blue eyes, and freckles around her nose. A well-seasoned explorer himself after a couple of years in the Amazon, Henry could tell both seemed at home in the jungle. This wasn't their first excursion to a remote area of the planet.

Bill and Liam were a study in contrast, compared to their two colleagues. Scruffy looking and long haired, they were behind-the-camera types. Bill, the lone American on the team, was muscular and sported a short, dark beard and the tattoo of a marine sword next to the letters USMC on his left forearm. Liam, heavily tattooed with a towering but skinny frame and straight, dark hair, addressed Henry as "mate" and carried an unmistakable Australian accent.

Henry related better to the pair in the supporting role. Like them, he had the job of setting the stage for the stars of the show to shine—in his case, the university professor who was the coordinator of his research program.

"It's good to meet you all," he replied. "I have a boat waiting for us at the dock. We should get going as soon as possible to make it to the research station before it gets dark."

The filmmakers looked at each other with vexed expressions. Henry realized he would not be leaving the village today.

"I'm afraid we have plans to spend the night here," Clare said firmly, and Henry detected a hint of entitlement in her tone. "We made arrangements to see a traditional ceremony and have dinner with the Baniwa. We thought you knew," she added.

The positive change in mood he had been starting to feel vanished. He considered raising the fact that he had real work to attend to but remembered that one of the filmmakers was the daughter of someone linked to the foundation that managed the research camp. With his position not exactly secure, he grudgingly let it go.

Twenty-four hours earlier he was merrily trudging along with his research. Now, in addition to having his work interrupted, he realized the filmmakers expected him to be at their disposal. He also felt embarrassed by the lack of communication from Pereira before he had sent Henry on this task.

"Okay," he replied in a low voice. "Can we leave tomorrow morning then?"

"That's the plan, mate," Aidan replied in a conciliatory tone, likely noticing Henry's disappointment. "Bright and early."

Henry nodded and retreated to the community center's porch, trying to shrug it off as the misunderstanding it was. But with the chip he carried on his shoulder since being kicked out of his graduate program, it was hard to let it go. Once an ambitious scientist, he was now an assistant to the same PhD students and college professors that used to be his peers. Being expected to wait around and cater to the needs of the filmmakers made him feel as he did around his former research colleagues: not an equal but a subordinate, a role he was still struggling to get used to.

He sat down on the floor and watched the crew at work. Although they didn't speak the language, the two hosts built an instant rapport with the children and many of the adults. The villagers congregated around them, happily posing for pictures and delighted to show everything their guests wanted to see.

A little girl approached Clare hesitantly, pulling her by the hand and pointing to a small wooden bowl containing a red dye extracted from the seeds of the *urucum*, a small native tree known to the tribe for hundreds of years and now the source of a food colorant used around the world. The TV host sat cross-legged and smiled while her face was painted by the young girl and Bill captured every detail with his camera.

∽

The Baniwa offered a banquet of boiled fish and manioc cooked with water from the river, served with flour, on the long table at the community center.

Although the food was not as tasty as that from the research base, Henry enjoyed the chance to share a meal prepared in the same way of the Baniwa ancestors. The experience improved his mood, reminding him that life was about more than career and rank. While his colleagues back in Pennsylvania stressed over deadlines and bowed to the pressure of constantly publishing to stay relevant, here he was, immersed in a centuries-old culture with no distractions or concerns aside from his own insecurities.

After dinner the villagers changed into their traditional regalia. The men wore white loincloths, and the women donned long beige skirts of weaved dry-leaf threads hanging from a band around their waist. Some were bare breasted while others, perhaps more self-conscious since contact with modern civilization's customs, wore bikini tops.

They danced in a single row, going around in a big circle while swinging their upper bodies from side to side.

The men played long flutes made of leaves from the paxi-uba, a palm tree that stood on aerial roots like a house on stilts. The song was off-key and primitive, yet there was something special about it, providing a unique peek into the distant past. It was by far the oldest music Henry had ever experienced.

As part of the ceremony, the Baniwa offered a thick ritual drink that looked like eggnog. Aidan Green tried it with blissful curiosity and passed it to Henry.

"This is called *caxiri*," Aidan explained.

Henry took a sip. The soupy beverage was plain and starchy, neither sweet nor bitter, though he could taste the alcohol.

"It's made of fermented manioc," Aidan continued. "Only the women can make it, and they must prepare it away from the men, who can't even see them doing it. It should be strictly for religious purposes, but these days they also do it to amuse fools like us. And some people make it for just drinking, of course, though these days liquor is well available." The filmmaker had clearly done some research on the customs of their hosts in preparation for the documentary. No wonder they were so keen to spend the night at the village.

"Funny how every culture on the planet manages to develop their own form of booze," Henry commented, sharing Aidan's fascination.

"This dance is not exactly *The Nutcracker*, to be sure, but this drink and this dance have been unchanged for thousands of years!"

"I'll take this over a ballet any day."

"This is as close as you get to time travel. The caxiri

recipe is the same as it has been since before the birth of Jesus. It sort of changes your perspective on things, doesn't it?"

"Sort of explains why it's so bland also," Henry replied with a grimace and an attempt at humor after trying another sip. The religious and historical significance, while not lost on him, didn't make the drink taste any better.

Aidan gave a polite smile, but Clare seemed incensed by Henry's sarcasm, shushing them and casting a disapproving look.

The dancers were now in a different formation, with rows of five people following a couple at the head of the line, who went around in a circle before bringing along the rest of the group. Aidan explained that the couple was following the tradition of checking whether the surroundings were safe for the celebratory dance. The men had switched to short flutes and played a different tune, just as off-key as the first one. They moved together as a column, taking a step forward, bowing, and then another step.

Henry hadn't studied or thought about it quite as much as Aidan, but the timelessness of the experience did change his perspective. This was what had drawn him to the Amazon in the first place.

CHAPTER 3

AMAZON RAIN FOREST, BRAZIL
APRIL 6

AN AIRCRAFT APPROACHED the landing field before sunrise, with all its lights turned off. The fog above the tree line made for a challenging landing, but the military pilot was accustomed to those conditions. The plane touched down without incident, assisted by the beacon lights at both ends of the grassy runway, stopping near a storage pavilion.

The predawn air was cool for the tropics, though that would not last for long.

A man in jeans and a red T-shirt stood waiting on the porch of a wooden cabin at the western end of the airstrip. Short and slim, he had a receding hairline and sported a thin, dark beard that shaded the contour of his sharp jawlines.

After hearing the engines shut off, he walked down the steps of the cabin and toward the plane.

An officer in military fatigues, sporting the stripes of a colonel, stepped out of the jet. He climbed down the airstairs and waited while the pilot helped a frail-looking old man, with thin, gray hair and a pencil mustache, down the steps.

The man in the red T-shirt, the head of this clandestine compound hidden in the world's largest rain forest, approached and addressed the elderly man.

"Welcome back. The site is ready for inspection."

The compound boss had noted that despite the man's apparent fragility, he commanded deference from the other passengers, including the colonel. They called him "The Engineer."

The colonel exchanged glances with The Engineer and greeted their host with a short nod. He spoke Spanish with a strong accent, not bothering with pleasantries, not even a "good morning."

"Did you prepare according to our instructions?"

"Yes," the compound boss replied.

"Good. The Engineer would like to start right away."

The compound boss shouted something in Spanish to one of his associates, a young and obliging lieutenant dressed in uniform. Four men in fatigues emerged from the pavilion at the head of the runway. They carried a large camouflage tarp and stopped next to the aircraft, waiting for additional orders.

The visitors unloaded their equipment from the plane as The Engineer waited in silence. While the four soldiers covered the airplane to disguise it from spy satellites, the compound boss and the young lieutenant joined the old scientist and his team as they set out to inspect the facilities.

The Engineer moved slowly with his clipboard, stopping frequently to make notes. Despite his advanced age, his small eyes were sharp and alert, missing nothing. No detail seemed too small to escape his attention.

The inspection took a little more than three hours. By midmorning the group had finished the walk-through.

"Everything appears to be in good order," the colonel said at the wrap-up meeting. "But we are disappointed by the pace of progress. We need to increase productivity to meet our targets. I trust that you will implement a few recommendations, including an extended number of working hours," he concluded, handing over a piece of paper with some handwritten notes.

The compound boss nodded. "We will get it done."

The young lieutenant did not look so pleased. He was the one who would have to tell the men, and he knew they were bound to complain. His soldiers were already lacking motivation after working months on end at this isolated corner of the jungle. But he did not speak up. He had orders from the very top of the chain of command to cooperate fully.

"I trust that you have encountered no problems? No outside visitors?" asked the colonel.

"No," responded the lieutenant. "No incidents."

"I don't have to tell you how important the secrecy of this operation is. If any word of this compound gets out, it will be an embarrassment to our countries."

"We are prepared to deal with any unwanted visitors,"

the compound boss interjected. "I can assure you that no word will get out." His tone left no doubt he meant it.

In the afternoon the soldiers working at the compound helped load the plane with heavy boxes carrying a week's worth of the site's production. With the recommendations made by The Engineer, they might load almost twice as many boxes when the aircraft returned in a week.

None of them knew where the plane came from, where it was going, or who the visitors were. They were under clear orders not to ask questions or speculate among themselves, though many often did the latter.

After loading the plane, the visitors retreated to the compound's cabin for the remainder of the day, resting before the long return trip.

They left after nightfall without delay, taking off as they arrived, with all lights off and under cover of darkness.

CHAPTER 4

AFTER SPENDING THE night at the Baniwa village, Henry and the film crew left shortly after sunrise. Going upriver, against the current, the trip back to the research station usually took twice as long, and Henry wanted to avoid the thunderstorms that would gather early afternoon. Though he had traveled safely through rain before, it was far more comfortable to make the journey in dry clothes.

Liam Nguyen set a waterproof camera at the bow, then sat in the middle of the boat next to Bill Powers. Each man carried a high-definition camcorder, showing they were serious about getting good images for the show.

At the stern, Henry controlled the engine. The ride was noisy, but he managed to carry on a conversation with Aidan Green, sitting slightly ahead of him, directly on the boat's floor. The conversation was frequently interrupted by "Wow" and "Look at that" as the river turns revealed small islands covered by emerald-green forest, fresh views of the wide river, and giant trees partially submerged near the margins. Pink dolphins made an occasional appearance, while flocks of blue-and-yellow macaws flew by in the distance.

"This is our fifth location this year," Aidan explained. "We were in the USA, Mexico, and Central America. After this we go to southern Brazil and Patagonia. It makes sense for logistical and budget reasons to work our way through the continent."

The TV host had been to many exotic locations in every continent, including Antarctica, and carried a contagious enthusiasm, speaking of each place he had visited as if it had been the best.

"How long have you guys been working together?"

"A couple of years. I've been with Bill and Liam for longer, but Clare just joined the show last season. We poached her from an Australian variety news show. She had a promising career in broadcasting, and maybe will still end up doing just that, but we're lucky she caught the bug for traveling and exploring and decided to join us. She's a biologist too, you know? Double major in biology and journalism."

"What did Bill and Liam do before?"

"Bill was in the military, including a tour in Afghanistan. Liam has a business degree but burned out after a few years' trying to climb the corporate ladder. They both traveled the four corners of the planet on their own before turning to making films."

Aidan paused as Henry turned around a bend, and the boat grew silent at the sight of the horizon, made of uneven strips of color. Shades of lush green emerged from the margins of the black river, with tall trees spearing irregularly and reaching toward the blue sky, which was starting to fill with clouds.

"So what exactly do you do here?" Aidan asked Henry.

"I manage a research project for an American university. I'm also trying to learn soccer. The former is going well, thankfully. The latter not so much, though it seems to amuse my colleagues at the camp."

Aidan smiled, letting Henry continue.

"We are studying how to best manage the fragmented areas to maintain their health in the long term in the face of increasing deforestation."

"Sounds important."

"It's repetitive work, and the conditions are challenging to say the least. But it beats working in an office. And hopefully, what we learn here will help preserve some of the jungle remaining in the areas being developed."

They passed by a lone house sitting on the riverbank, next to a pasture or a manioc farm, and the conversation was interrupted again.

"Is that a satellite dish?" Clare turned around and asked, gasping.

Henry laughed at the confounded look on everybody's face. He had been surprised, too, the first time he had seen one of those six-foot-wide devices next to a humble wood plank building, an out-of-place sight in the serene remoteness of the rain forest.

"It's their only link to the world," he explained.

"Besides, Brazilians can't live without their *novelas*, the Brazilian soap operas. Some nights, most people in the country are watching them. They are a big part of the culture, and the folks around here find inventive ways to watch. I can't blame them. There's not much else to do here in the evenings. People power their TV sets with car batteries since they are nowhere near the power grid."

He saw a collective smile as the property shrank from view. They had been navigating through some of the most glorious views on earth, but it was the unexpected ways and ingenuity of the local peasants that had drawn the biggest reaction.

Arriving at the research camp right before the afternoon storm, the crew was once again greeted by local children, the sons and daughters of the research camp's local support staff.

A little girl named Ana Maria rushed to Henry, leaping into his arms. She was a seven-year-old *cabocla*, the daughter of a local farmer who also did odd jobs at the camp. Her mom worked as a cook and a cleaner, good jobs to have in an area where work outside subsistence agriculture was scarce. The girl had taken a particular liking to Henry, who found it impossible not to reciprocate.

The Pitiri Research Station was run by Fund-Ama, a nonprofit research institute headed by Teresa Oliveira, a prominent scientist with deep political connections. She had raised millions of dollars from international universities and other donors, thanks to strict regulations that required research projects by a foreign institution be developed in partnership with a government-sanctioned Brazilian organization.

Pitiri was one of several projects located in the immense indigenous reserve that also hosted Brazilian army outposts, religious missions, and other research camps. When he had first arrived, Henry had fit right in with the locals: a mix of Brazilian student volunteers, folks from the Baniwa tribe, and the caboclos, the non-Indians—though many of them had mixed blood. The caboclos who lived in the forest were some of the kindest people Henry had ever met: hardworking, nice, and always smiling, as if the hardship of living in the jungle was nothing to them.

"Welcome to Pitiri," he said, gesturing toward the camp while Ana Maria hung on his arm.

✎

"Tell us about the cave," Aidan said the next morning, surrounded by his colleagues and enjoying a cup of strong coffee at the breakfast table set in the research station's main building.

The main course was *beijú*, a fried manioc-flour pancake. It was bland on its own, but Henry found it tasty when served warm and covered with salt and melting butter on top.

"I've only been there once," Henry replied. "But it's one of the most beautiful places I've seen. Well worth the trouble to get there."

"It seems incredible," Aidan suggested. "I've seen a few pictures, but not a whole lot. There aren't very many good ones available as far as I can tell. I suppose it adds to the site's mystery. One of the world's last hidden gems."

"I doubt better pictures would do it justice. You have to be there to take it all in. When you're looking at photographs, it's hard to understand the magnitude of that place. You can't hear the sound of the water or inhale the cave air mixed with the forest smells that blow in . . ."

"Is it true that there is a waterfall inside the cave?"

"Yes." Henry had hardly believed it the first time he saw it. "The underground river enters the cave at the top of a big wall, and the water just drops, creating a little lake and then a meandering creek that leaves through the large opening until it disappears under the rocks again. It's quite a sight, like it was imagined by one of the great landscape painters."

"In my experience, nature often exceeds the imagination of the best artists," Aidan noted philosophically.

"Very true," Henry agreed. "We had a geologist visiting a few months ago, and he explained that they think this cave formed much faster than normal. Usually, the limestone is eroded by rainwater seeping through the ground; but in this case, the underground river helped to wear it down, so the process happened faster. And since the water here is more acidic, it dissolved the limestone even quicker."

"I can't wait to see it. Does it get many visitors?" Liam Nguyen asked, joining the conversation from the far end of the table.

"It's too remote and inside an indigenous reserve, so access is not easy. Getting there is difficult enough, but the hardest part is getting all the permits. You need one from the Bureau of Indian Affairs to enter the reserve, one from the environmental agency, and another from the Ministry of Culture because of the archeological value. The hike is a cakewalk compared to the Brazilian bureaucracy." Henry paused and shook his head with a mix of laughter and sighing, remembering his own nightmare with the Brazilian authorities.

"How about the cave paintings?" Clare asked.

"Apparently, they are from thousands of years ago. Just in case the amazing natural beauty of the site is not enough for you."

"I can't wait to see this place!" Liam repeated with even more enthusiasm. "How was it discovered?"

The entire film crew was leaning forward, their eyes wide with curiosity.

"I was told there used to be an iron mine nearby decades ago, and the site was discovered during the surveys. Of course, the local natives knew about it all along, so 'discovered' is not quite the right word. The research station actually gets its name from the fact that the Baniwa referred to the cave as 'the place of the bats,' since they have no word for 'cave.' *Pitiri* means 'bat' in Baniwa. It didn't get any attention for a long time, until a team from the University of Amazonas library was digitizing its archive and noted the mention of a cave in the old mining surveys."

"Did you say 'iron mine'?" Clare pressed. "We read all about the cave but did not see any mention of a mine."

"It hasn't been active for a long time. It must have been abandoned like so many other failed megaprojects."

"This I've heard about. There were all sorts of big projects in the Amazon that were defeated by nature," observed Bill Powers. The marine's curiosity about the

Amazon region seemed to be growing with every new bit of information. "Didn't an American tycoon sink a billion dollars into trying to set up some sort of factory in the middle of the jungle?"

"That's right," Henry confirmed. "The Jari project. An entrepreneur bought an area the size of Connecticut in the eastern part of the Amazon, near the Atlantic, for paper-tree plantations. He ordered a paper mill be built in Japan and towed it by sea from halfway across the world. But it didn't go well. The workers started dying of malaria, and the trees were destroyed by insects. There's a reason you won't find the same tree species less than a few hundred feet apart in the Amazon. It's their protection against disease. The tree diversity works as a buffer. Since the bugs usually affect only one species, they can't spread. But once you get all the same trees together . . . If only someone had consulted a tropical ecologist. I could have saved the guy a lot of money."

They laughed.

"Didn't Henry Ford also lose money over here?" Clare asked.

Henry had studied that, too, when preparing for his assignment. The famed American businessman had built an industrial town from scratch, in the middle of the jungle, to supply rubber to the shiny new cars coming out of his assembly lines.

" 'Fordlandia,' they call it in Brazil. This was around the 1930s. Same problem with pests. Put all the rubber trees together and all you are doing is creating a feast for the bugs that prey on them. Ford also faced competition from Asia. Once the rubber trees were smuggled over there, they did much better without their natural predators. But my favorite part is that the Brazilian workers revolted because they were tired of eating hamburgers."

He paused wistfully, trying to remember the last time he had tasted one.

"That's a tough environment," Liam observed, bringing Henry back from his longing for American fast food.

"There is no shortage of doomed-from-the-start projects here," Henry continued. "They also tried to build a railroad in the early 1900s, and a more recent attempt to build a trans-Amazon highway didn't go too well either. There's no match for the so-called Amazon factor, a combination of poor soil, pests, heat, humidity, torrential rains, and tropical disease."

The morning was already muggy. They had been up since sunrise, but the crew took their time listening to Henry and eating the hearty breakfast before the long hike to the cave. The visitors seemed to enjoy their exotic breakfast, but Henry was well past that phase.

After so long in the jungle, he craved eggs and bacon. And, of course, cheeseburgers.

CHAPTER 5

ENRY REMEMBERED THE way well, and the modern navigation equipment made things easier still, though the GPS reception was spotty under the dense canopy. He and the film crew made good time on the way to the cave, despite the heat and humidity. They were experienced hikers, and the demands of their jobs ensured all of them stayed in good shape.

Henry wondered whether their guests were expecting to see dramatic vistas in the interior of the forest. The animals were always well hidden, and the vegetation on the ground was sparse, the tall canopy blocking most of the light that would allow plant life to grow below it. That made for easy walking, though there was not much to see except by the trained eye.

When he first arrived in the Amazon, Henry had been disappointed at how hard it was to see the celebrated fauna of the jungle: jaguars, tapirs, capybaras, macaws, monkeys, anacondas. All were masters of camouflage. But he soon came to appreciate the other never-ending riches of the forest. The variety of trees alone could keep him entertained forever. There were more tree species in one square mile of the jungle than in Aidan Green's entire native England, not to mention the diversity of the majestic bromeliads and vines hanging from them. Accustomed as he was to the sights of the rain forest, he didn't think he would ever grow tired of it.

To a layman, the forest didn't seem to change much, an endless variation of tall trees and decaying-leaves-covered ground. To the locals and scientists, however, the scenery changed constantly.

Henry noticed the flora along the way, admiring an imposing Brazil nut tree, which could reach as high as 160 feet, and keeping track of the smaller plants he saw, like the curious monkey cup, a carnivorous species sporting pitcher-shaped red leaves that accumulated rainwater drunk by the forest monkeys—at least according to local folklore. He also picked up on subtle terrain changes and variations in the array of vegetation along the way. To the skilled observer, the jungle was different and unique at every step, just as downtown city blocks filled with the same style of boring glass buildings could be easily distinguished by those who lived there.

After about three hours of fast-paced hiking, they found that the terrain became more rugged, with the inclines getting progressively steeper. The trekkers were starting to get to the rocky formations the cave belonged to.

Although the topography of the Amazon looked flat on a map, it was anything but. Occasional escarpments shot out of the jungle, resulting in some of the most beautiful landscapes on the planet.

The cave the five explorers were heading to was one such wonder. Thousands of years before, on the terrain that gently ascended toward Brazil's largest peak, in the far north of the country, one of the Amazon tributaries carved a hole in the yielding limestone, finding its way underground and slowly dissolving the rock into a large cavern.

After a long day of walking through the jungle, the group descended the last slope, to the bottom of a valley covered in tropical forest. It was late afternoon, and the thunderstorm that showered the jungle with astounding regularity at this time of year was dissipating. The sunlight was perfect, bathing the forest in a golden hue accentuated by the moisture of the air in the after-showers.

The cave entrance was hard to find from the ground, covered by the forest and disguised by thick vegetation sprouting from the edges of the opening. But once they reached the small body of water streaming out of it, the tall gap leading into the cavern was unmistakable.

The crew stood in awe, looking at the large opening. The underground river that had originally helped carve out the chamber thousands of years before now dropped fifteen feet to the ground from a hole on the tall cave wall, creating a pond inside the jaw-dropping site. A stream emanated from the small lake, flowing past the entrance for half a mile until it finally went back below the forest floor. A few gaps in the ceiling let the sunlight in, allowing small trees and several tropical plants to grow around the lake inside the cave, creating an eerie underground garden that appeared to be out of a fantasy movie or a fairy-tale landscape.

The site must have been magical to the early settlers of

South America as well, who went through the trouble of adding to its beauty by decorating some of its walls with their own artwork. Their paintings were now the main driver of the efforts to raise funding for protecting the site.

Henry could see the excitement taking over everyone on the team. They were laughing out loud like children, the fatigue of the strenuous walk overshadowed by the exhilaration of the new discovery.

Henry sat near the edge of the lake and watched the crew get to work. Clare and Aidan quickly put on some makeup, adjusted their clothing, and went in front of the camera, introducing the cave to their viewers and bringing the amazing place—in high definition—to the comfort of living rooms.

As night fell, Bill lit up the small camping stove, and Henry joined the crew for dinner. The menu, dehydrated pasta and sausages, was not quite as exotic as the banquet they had experienced at the Baniwa village or the fresh meal they had eaten for breakfast, but it tasted superb to the five exhausted hikers.

Clare started writing copiously in her notebook after dinner, while Aidan stood next to her. He seemed deep in thought, probably just soaking it all in. Liam and Bill stepped outside to set up camera traps. If they were lucky, a jaguar would come roaming around and trigger the equipment, making for a great picture.

But they were lucky enough as it was. From their campsite on the shore of the underground lake, they could see the sky through the big opening above the creek flowing out of the cavern. It was cloudless and filled with stars.

CHAPTER 6

THE CREW SPENT the next day filming. Henry offered to help, but there was little for him to do. He spent his time exploring the cave and watching the production at work. The quartet worked in almost perfect synchrony, sometimes together, sometimes individually, identifying the spots they wanted to film, finding the best angles, scripting the scenes and shooting. Aidan and Clare would share some shots, then film another scene on their own with Bill or Liam behind the camera. Occasionally the crew would ask Henry a question, which made him feel useful, but mostly they had done their homework, explaining to their viewers the site's geological origins and commenting on the mystery surrounding the people behind the paintings, of whom archeologists knew next to nothing.

As they wrapped up filming and prepared for a second night at the cave, Clare suggested extending their trip. She badly wanted to see the iron mine Henry had mentioned.

Inspired by the tales of Jari and Fordlandia, the two failed enterprises of American billionaires attempting to tame the Amazon, she argued how great it would be to see and document one of those large ventures that could not flourish under the harsh conditions of the jungle.

"We have to check it out," she pleaded. "It'll be such a nice piece for the show, to highlight how the jungle can be so beautiful and brutal at the same time."

Her colleagues briefly resisted the idea, concerned by the limited time they had left to finish their episode. But everyone was curious about the site—including Henry—and the discussion quickly turned to *how* instead of *whether* they should go.

They agreed that Henry would take Clare and Bill to the abandoned iron mine while Aidan and Liam would split from the group, so they could do a story about the research station as they had originally planned.

Henry felt a dash of resentment that they took for granted he would lead them there. But this time he didn't let it bother him. He had come to this remote part of the world because he shared their thirst for exploration. While his sense of responsibility called him to get back to work, it did not take much to convince him to add a couple of extra days to their excursion. It helped that his boss was thousands of miles away, in an office in Pennsylvania. Besides, he told himself, it had not been his idea to be the guide for the film crew.

Their supplies were limited, but they could make it work with the reserve food they had brought. Henry had the coordinates of the iron mine on his GPS, just as he had the locations of dozens of other sites in case he ever got lost. He calculated that he could get them to their destination in one day, back in another one or two.

Changing their plans in this inhospitable region was not a decision to be taken lightly, especially considering Aidan and Liam's limited familiarity with the area. But the two of them were experienced explorers. A day's hike back to the Pitiri Station, with modern navigation equipment, didn't seem so daunting.

The next morning, as they packed their belongings, Henry gave the pair detailed directions and handed them the satellite phone despite their protests.

"I know the region far better and can get around just fine," he said. "And I'm already breaking the rules by letting you two go back to the camp by yourselves."

There weren't really any rules. But if something bad happened, Henry knew he would be blamed for agreeing to leave the visitors on their own in one of the most punishing environments on the planet.

"In case you can't find your way, the numbers for both the station and the Fund-Ama office are programmed. If anything happens, call them. Someone will be able to help. Even if your GPS has poor reception, like mine, you should still get a connection enough times to find your way. Just remember that if you don't hit flatland in three or four hours, you're probably lost."

"We won't get lost," Aidan reassured him. "This is not our first time in the jungle. Please be careful out there. You never know what you are going to find in an abandoned mine. There could be explosives or other dangerous stuff around."

"You got it."

"And you won't get in trouble for this," Bill added. "Whatever happens, we'll say we forced you to lead us to the mine."

They all nodded.

Henry appreciated the sentiment. But he knew that if something went wrong, the crew's support would matter very little. It would be strike two. This not being baseball, there would be no third chance.

Bidding goodbye to Aidan and Liam, Henry and the other filmmakers turned north, hacking their way into the dense bushes, moving away from the cavern and into the jungle. As they penetrated deeper into the forest, the terrain started to change again.

"The abandoned mine is supposed to be on the other side of this ridge," he explained as the ground got steeper. "We should reach it before nightfall."

They pressed on, scaling the top of the rise a few hours later, though their view of the valley ahead was blocked.

"It should be that way," Henry said, stopping at the hillcrest and, after checking his compass, pointing to the northeast. "But I want to see the valley to try to spot the exact location. It will reduce the chances of us getting lost."

"How are you going to do that? We can't see anything beyond the vegetation," Bill noted.

"We climb." Henry smiled, pointing at the trees.

He was taught the technique by the workers at the Pitiri camp, who would climb the acai palm tree to harvest the dark purple berries that were now all the rage in smoothie shops and health stores in America and Europe.

It required nothing but a rope. And a lot of endurance.

Henry searched for the right tree on the edge of the ridge, one that would afford a clear view to the valley ahead and that had a narrow trunk. He gazed at a *pau mulato*, a tall and slender species with a graphite-colored trunk so silky that it looked as though it had just been polished. It was more slippery than the trunk of the acai tree, but Henry felt confident the rubber soles of his boots would provide enough grip. The pau mulato was rare and beautiful, its wood so strong and valuable that it made the tree even more endangered than the mahogany sought after for upscale furniture pieces. Henry took a few seconds revering the beauty of this specimen, aware it remained untouched only because it stood where no chain saws could get to it.

He took a rope from his backpack and tied a circle around the tree, leaving just enough room to slide his feet between the rope and the trunk. It was a simple and ingenious technique. With the right amount of slack between the rope and the tree, flexing his feet toward his shins tightened the rope enough for him to lock his shoes in place and push against the bark with his legs, propelling his body upward. He then hugged the tree, loosened the rope by stretching his feet, and folded his legs, sliding the rope toward his chest. After tightening his grip again, Henry extended his legs and hugged the tree once more, moving up the tree like a caterpillar. It was a strenuous effort, but he had harvested enough acai with the caboclos to be up for the task.

At the top, breathing heavily from the effort, he found a branch that seemed strong enough to support him, where he stood and moved the leaves in front of him to take in the view.

He never tired of the sight of the rain forest from above. The carpet of trees below was gentle and undulating; one could see the diversity even from a distance. Although the cover was entirely green, even the casual observer could distinguish all sorts of shapes and color shades. Two and a half acres of the Amazon jungle contained more than three hundred different species of trees. *Imagine how much of all other life forms,* he liked to wonder.

He carefully scanned the landscape, from the hill where he stood all the way to the horizon, regretting he did not have his binoculars with him.

Smoke rose in the distance, probably from a slash-and-burn clearing for subsistence farming. Henry noted the color, white from vapor released from the water in the vegetation as it burned. In the dry season the forest retained less water and the smoke was light yellow, indicating increased fire danger.

Reassured the fire risk was low, Henry turned his attention to the valley and saw a strip of uniform green at the bottom. He guessed it was the old landing runway used by the miners. It appeared to be in better condition than he would have expected for an abandoned site. Next to it was a large patch of dark green and brown, which he suspected to be contaminated soil that prevented the vegetation from growing.

"I can see some abandoned buildings from the old mine," he said as he moved off the tree, panting heavily and sweating from the effort. Getting down without falling was almost as hard as going up. "That's the direction we'll go." He pointed. "We're a few miles out. We should be there in a few hours."

"Great, let's go," Bill said before Henry could catch his breath.

"Aidan and Liam should be arriving at the camp soon, hopefully," Henry said, looking at his watch. He reached toward his water bottle and took a long swig, tilting his head backward and closing his eyes.

He put on his backpack again and led the way down the north side of the ridge. The path was rockier than the terrain Henry was accustomed to, and he guessed they were walking on top of whatever mineral formation had been exploited years before.

While they couldn't see very far ahead, Henry had mastered the art of navigating under the canopy. The GPS and compass were a big help, of course, but he had come to know the jungle's features so well that he had learned to keep a straight line intuitively, based on the light patterns and times of day. He knew enough about the forest by now that when they went back to the research station, he could probably find his way without the help of instruments.

The crunching of leaves as they walked had become a comforting sound. His mind wandered away, forgetting for a moment where he was and who he was with. His thoughts landed back home and on everything he had left behind for the past couple of years. He missed his family, hanging out with friends, dating, the food, and the privacy of having his own place as opposed to sleeping at a dorm. He didn't miss living in the city as much as he thought he would, though he wouldn't have minded going to a coffee shop or a bar every now and then. But Henry was grateful for a chance to explore the jungle, as he had dreamed of since childhood, and he looked forward to seeing the iron mine and all the new sites that fate may present him an opportunity to visit.

Coming back from his wandering thoughts, he noticed that the ground had flattened. They were at the bottom of the valley and should be getting to the mine soon.

He thought he heard unfamiliar voices.

"Wait, stop!" Bill called in a hushed tone. "Do you hear something?"

Could there be other people around?

"Yes, what . . ."

The three of them stopped, but the crackling sound of dead leaves and sticks being trampled on continued.

"We've got company," Bill whispered.

The abrupt sounds of something moving around in the forest grew louder, until they saw a group of armed soldiers emerge from behind the trees.

Within seconds they were surrounded.

Chapter 7

"*O* QUE VOCÊS ESTÃO fazendo aqui?" *What are you doing here?* asked a skinny, short man with a receding hairline and a thin, dark beard that shaded the contour of his sharp jawlines.

Henry, Clare, and Bill had been brought into a large clearing in the valley where the abandoned iron mine was supposed to be.

Henry remained calm, to his own surprise. He had never been in any position remotely similar to this. But in reaction to the stress, his mind cleared of everything else, developing an uncharacteristic focus.

He turned and looked at the others. Clare's face was white, the blush in her cheeks from the strenuous walk fading as the rush of adrenaline constricted her peripheral vessels.

Bill's expression was more collected, his dark beard masking what was likely the same change in skin tone as Clare's. Henry suspected his face had turned just as pale.

He decided to give away as little as possible. The slower the situation unfolded, he calculated, the better the chances of finding a way out.

Unlike the soldiers who had brought them into the compound, the man asking the questions was not wearing a military uniform, just jeans and a red T-shirt that looked to be unwashed for days. He had addressed the question to all three captives, but Henry was the only one who understood it.

He pretended he didn't.

"Eu não falo português. Eu não falo." *I don't speak Portuguese,* he lied, hoping it would buy them some time. "We were just looking for birds. *Aves,*" he concluded, flapping his arms like wings in a scene that would be comical under better circumstances.

It wasn't a good excuse, but it was the first that came to mind. It seemed safer than to admit that they were filming a documentary and that one of them was a journalist.

"Sorry to bother you. No one needs to know we were here," he told the man who had addressed them.

The plain-clothed man who had asked the question stared at Henry with a humorless expression.

"We will just leave, okay? We won't tell anyone and we'll never come back, we promise," Henry pleaded, turning around slowly, keeping his hands raised.

One of the guards stepped in Henry's direction and raised his weapon, pointing the barrel straight to Henry's chest, coming within inches. Henry froze, paralyzed with fear and making a conscious effort not to faint.

The man in the red T-shirt mumbled something to one of the soldiers, gesturing toward the backpacks that the visitors were carrying. The guard who had pointed his machine gun at Henry held his position, while another reached for the bags.

The soldier spilled all the contents on the ground and leaned over them on one knee, looking for clues as to who the visitors were and what they were doing there.

"Why the camera?" the red-T-shirted man yelled at the captives in a rudimentary English. The soldier examining their belongings was holding a high-tech, professional digital video camera, not a typical amateur camcorder.

Henry, an assault weapon still inches from his torso, was too scared to answer.

"Birds," Bill intervened. "We film birds. That's why we are here, just looking for birds," he explained slowly, trying to make sure their captors could understand him.

Henry was reassured to see that Bill backed his story. But conspicuously absent from their possessions was a pair of binoculars, the one device bird-watchers never leave home without. He was also painfully aware there was little or no bird footage in the memory card.

The guard put the camera down and continued to shuffle through the articles spread on the floor. Everyone else looked on in silence.

Henry took a deep breath, scanning the surroundings. He was facing the long strip of short grass that made the compound's runway. No wonder it seemed so uniform from afar. It was still in use. To their left was a large pavilion covered by a camouflage tarp, housing an array of boxes, tools, and heavy equipment, including an excavator. He also saw a row of military tents and a wooden cabin farther up the clearing. The structures he had observed earlier were not abandoned after all.

The tarp, he thought, remembering the dark green and brown patch he had seen from the top of the pau mulato tree, angry at himself for trying to explain away the unfamiliar patterns. It had not occurred to him that the abandoned iron mine could still be in operation. That oversight could now cost his life and that of his two companions.

His thoughts were interrupted when the soldier found their identification documents and handed them to the man in the red T-shirt, who seemed to be the one in charge.

The compound boss took their documents and stopped the interrogation abruptly, ordering that the three captives be taken to a tent. Henry heard him tell one of the men in uniform that he would call in for instructions on how to handle the intruders. A chill traveled down Henry's spine; but he kept his head down, staring at the floor, afraid any one of the soldiers would notice he understood what was being said.

As the man in the red T-shirt made his way toward the cabin, the prisoners were escorted through the encampment, and the guards started talking to each other. Henry noticed they were speaking Spanish, not Portuguese. Being familiar with both, he knew the two languages were fairly similar, sharing some grammatical structure and words, but they *sounded* quite different, as he had realized when he first came to Brazil and started learning Portuguese. The men remarked how pretty the woman was, making Henry even more concerned for their fate, especially Clare's.

He forced himself to calm down and stay focused, looking around attentively, his mind racing, trying to observe as much as he could. They passed by the storage area under the camouflage tarp, and he had a better look at the equipment. In addition to the tractor and excavation machines, he saw shovels, wheel carts, and several boxes with different markings on them. Some had a distinctive yellow triangular sign that seemed to indicate they contained explosives.

A separate set of boxes stood apart from the rest. Henry couldn't distinguish the writings and markings on them, but from a distance they looked like a form of ancient script. *What is this?* he asked himself, wondering if the soldiers were digging for historical artifacts. Could this be the site of a lost civilization? That would certainly be worth a lot of money, but to his knowledge there were no archeological articles of much financial value to be found in the Amazon.

After they passed the equipment storage area and started to approach the tents, Henry saw an opening at the bottom of the hill, a man-made tunnel about six feet in diameter and supported by wood beams.

He quickly dismissed the idea of the lost civilization and concluded they were clearly at a mine. He briefly considered whether their captors could be some of the famous *garimpeiros* who illegally extract gold in the region. But those gold diggers were desperately poor men who were covered in dirt and wore ragged clothing. This was a sophisticated enterprise.

Arriving at the northwest corner of the compound, the three captives were forced inside a tent with cots lined in rows. He guessed it served as the sleeping quarters for the camp workers and soldiers. It was sparsely furnished, with unmade beds and olive-green backpacks leaning against them.

They were made to sit on the ground with their hands tied behind their backs, under the watchful eye of an armed guard.

"What is happening?" Clare cried out anxiously.

"I don't know," Henry responded. "But clearly the mine is not abandoned."

"You think?" she blurted out, followed immediately by an apologetic sigh. "Sorry, I didn't mean that the way it sounded."

"Easy, guys," Bill intervened, speaking firmly. "We are all scared. Let's calm down and start thinking how we can get out of this."

With a confused expression, the guard watching them took a step in their direction. Henry guessed he didn't understand English.

"No talk," the sentry barked.

"We need to find a way to escape," Bill finished.

"No talk!" The guard had yelled louder, approaching Bill and raising his assault rifle. It featured a curved magazine, similar to that of an AK-47, the automatic weapon of choice for criminal gangs the world over.

Bill bowed his head to the guard, nodding in submission and making eye contact with a humble look. Henry had read in detective novels that this helped create empathy with one's captors and guessed that Bill was applying his military training to their situation. That, combined with how quick Bill had been on his feet to back Henry's story about looking for birds, gave the biologist a dash of hope that they could figure their way out of this.

∽

The compound boss sat by the communications desk inside the cabin, waiting.

A few minutes elapsed before the voice on the radio gave him a coded message authorizing him to turn on the satellite phone for an encrypted call.

He punched in the number and exchanged pass phrases with the person at the other end of the line before giving a brief summary of the situation.

"We captured them just as they were approaching the camp. They are in our custody now."

The call had some background noise, but he could understand the other side clearly.

"Yes, two males and one female," he continued, reading their names out loud from the documents found in the confiscated backpacks. "One of our patrols found them nearby. It looks like they were coming here. I told the lieutenant to wait for further instructions. I can interrogate them myself to find out."

"We know who they are," said the voice on the other end.

The compound boss was impressed but not surprised. The operation he was running would not be so successful if his employers didn't have a far-reaching network.

"One of them is a researcher at the Pitiri Research Station. The others are filmmakers from abroad, supposedly doing a documentary about the cave."

"What are they doing here then?"

"That we don't know."

"What should we do with them?"

The voice across the line ignored the question.

"Are you sure there was no one else? There were two more people with them. We must assume they escaped before being captured and must be headed either to Pitiri or the Baniwa settlement."

"I see."

"You need to find them. As for the other three, try to learn exactly why they went there and who else knows about it. They can't be allowed to escape," the voice said.

The implication was clear.

"I'll take care of it," the compound boss stated confidently.

"Good. Keep me posted."

CHAPTER 8

HENRY WATCHED AS a soldier stood inside, guarding the detainees that sat on the bare ground with their hands tied behind their backs.

Through the flap door, he could see two other guards standing outside.

The beds in the tent were arranged in two rows of five, with some of their users' personal effects resting on top. The closest cot had a toothbrush, a comb, a worn-out soccer ball, and a magazine in Spanish with a voluptuous brunette on the cover. The backpacks were all standard issue and looked to be about three feet tall.

The soldiers in the compound wore fatigues, but there was no country flag on the sleeve of the combat jacket worn by the sentry standing guard inside the military tent.

The three prisoners must have been sitting there for no longer than fifteen minutes when they saw a soldier arrive at the entrance of the tent. He briefly said something to the two men standing outside, who nodded. One of them put his head through the opening and called out to his colleague.

"Me llamó el teniente. ¿Todo bajo control?" *The lieutenant wants to see me,* the soldier said to the man inside, asking if everything was under control.

"Positivo," responded the guard next to the captives.

Henry watched through the opening flap as two soldiers walked away. His heart accelerated. This could be their only chance.

"One of the guards outside left," he alerted Bill and Clare, assuming the soldier watching them didn't understand English. "Someone came by to ask him to go see a lieutenant."

Bill reacted quickly.

"That means we outnumber them three to two now," he said. "One man inside and one outside. I don't think we should wait to find out their orders."

"No talk!" the sentry cried.

Henry looked at their captor, intimidated. They outnumbered him, as Bill had noted, but the guard had a gun and they didn't. Not to mention that their hands were tied behind their backs.

Like a good scientist, Henry was the kind of person who studied all the variables and thought carefully about the different ways an event could unfold before deciding on a course of action. He had a good mind for it, but here, with his life at stake, he did not have the luxury of time to review all the options and identify the one most likely to yield a successful outcome.

Thankfully, Bill appeared to be of a different mindset, as he gave Henry an encouraging nod, barely noticeable. American taxpayers had spent a good amount of money to prepare the former US serviceman for this type of situation.

"This may be our best shot," Bill cried, taking charge. "Listen carefully."

He turned to Henry and Clare.

"Whatever happens, don't scream," he continued. "Follow my lead. When this guy attacks me, you take him down."

"What?" Clare asked.

Henry said nothing, paralyzed.

The watchman, not understanding a word they were saying, turned to Bill and yelled again, more forcefully this time.

"No talk!"

Henry understood what Bill was trying to do but was terrified to take on the guard. Afraid he couldn't contend with a trained soldier, he thought they would have a much higher chance of success if Bill made the attack.

That meant he would have to be the bait.

"You do it—you're stronger," he cried out, rocking his body back and forth and using the momentum to stand, not waiting for an acknowledgment.

The soldier was surprised by Henry's action.

"Sientate ya!" he yelled, pointing at the ground with his head.

"¡Quiero hablar con su jefe, pronto!" *I need to speak to your superior right away,* Henry demanded, improvising and baiting the man to attack him. Henry moved back and to the side, making the guard turn his back to the two filmmakers to engage. The soldier was taken by surprise that his prisoner spoke fluent Spanish, giving Bill and Clare an extra second to react.

Although he was braced for it, nothing could really prepare anyone for the blow of an assault rifle's heel coming down full force on their face. Henry suffered a violent strike to his right cheekbone that reverberated all the way to the back of his head, his brain shaking inside his skull. He fell on his knees, disoriented, not feeling any pain at first. Everything seemed to slow down. He was taking stock of the first strike when the second came on his shoulder. This one hurt right away, hitting just behind his collarbone, on the trapezius muscle. His body contorted and he fell into a fetal position, watching in a dazed state as the scene continued to unfold.

Bill had acted promptly, sliding his cuffed wrists under his feet, to the front of his body. Clare had followed his lead, doing the same. Just as Henry had felt the guard strike him the second time, Bill had jumped up and slid his tied hands over the head of the soldier, who was raising his rifle again in preparation for a third blow, this one aimed at Henry's temple. Natural reflex drove the soldier's hands straight toward his throat, trying to fight back the choke hold and dropping his rifle in the process.

The sentinel keeping watch outside had been lighting up a cigarette when the commotion inside the tent started. He put it down quickly and walked in, saw Bill choking his besieged colleague, and rushed to help. But Clare was waiting for him and wasted no time in grabbing the barrel of the rifle from the floor and whacking the sentinel with one swing from the ground straight up to his chin. The hit was not deadly but was strong enough to confound the soldier for a few seconds.

With his hands tied, Bill had only to pull both hands toward himself as hard as he could. The guard was strong, but Henry could see that the American had all the advantage, keeping his firm grip on the enemy's neck, compressing the man's trachea and blocking air from entering his lungs. It also stopped air from coming out, preventing him from screaming.

Still disoriented, the urgency and desperation of the situation brought a jolt of energy to Henry. Acting on pure instinct, he managed to slide his tied hands under his feet and got up, leaping clumsily toward the soldier struck in the chin by Clare and using his body to topple the man over. He jumped on top of their captor, straddling his stomach and pressing hard against the man's throat with the right forearm.

But looking in his foe's eyes and seeing the panic of someone who couldn't breathe, Henry hesitated, relieving the pressure on his opponent's neck. In wavering, and with his hands still tied together, he lost control of the fight when the well-trained soldier wrestled to turn Henry to the ground, reverting their positions.

After pinning Henry down, the man acted swiftly, pulling a knife from the sheath on his right leg. With no time to react, Henry watched as his assailant raised the knife that would take his life, closing his eyes in fear and resigning himself to his fate.

Then he heard a loud crack, and the man collapsed on top of him. When he opened his eyes, he saw Bill standing next to him, holding the rifle he had slammed against the guard's skull.

Bill extended his tied hands to Henry, who grabbed them and pulled himself up.

He felt dizzy but managed to keep his balance, his head starting to throb. He ignored it.

Two bodies lay still on the ground. Were they dead or just unconscious? Henry had no intention of sticking around long enough to find out, guessing the other two captives didn't either.

Bill walked to the tent's opening and peeked outside. The men around the camp were working near the pavilion and the tunnel, about a hundred yards away. It didn't look as though anyone had heard the fight inside the tent, but it would not be long before someone came around.

From the unconscious soldier's hand, Henry grabbed the knife that had almost killed him and cut the duct tape around his companions' wrists. Clare returned the favor while Bill checked the soldiers' pockets. They were empty. No wallet, cell phone, or ID on the men.

Henry and Clare turned to Bill, looking at the marine to lead them.

"How do we get out of here?" Henry wondered aloud.

Bill grabbed the machine guns and checked that they had the safety on before handing one to Clare and hanging the strap of the other on his shoulder. Then he took the knife from Clare and headed to the back of the tent, instead of to the front.

Henry did not understand what Bill was doing. By the look on her face, neither did Clare.

"What are you—" she started to ask.

Bill raised the knife above his head and sliced open the back wall of the tent. The structure backed to about 150 feet of open field before the edge of the forest. There was no one nearby. The tents were used as sleeping quarters, not detention facilities, and the rest of the soldiers had been occupied with their usual duties on the other side of the compound.

"Let's go!" he cried, walking through the opening he had just carved.

Henry gestured for Clare to go first. He instinctively looked around the room one more time, a habit he had acquired in the research camp to make sure he didn't forget anything before hiking for hours to a measuring station only to find he had forgotten something important.

He noted again the unmade cot beds with backpacks next to them.

"Come on. We have to move quickly," pressed Bill.

Henry ran to the closest bed and grabbed a backpack.

He put it on his back without opening it, feeling a sharp pain on his left shoulder where the soldier had hit him with the rifle. Then he went through the gap ripped open by Bill, stepping out the back of the tent and joining his fellow escapees as they raced across the open field as fast as they could until they reached the edge of the jungle.

CHAPTER 9

THE MOMENT HE was about to die kept playing in a loop through Henry's mind. He saw again and again the soldier holding the knife with a firm grip, a determined look in his eyes, showing none of the hesitation or mercy that had lost Henry control of the fight.

The pain on the right side of his throbbing face was brutal, but the disappointment of how he had reacted during the fight hurt considerably more. He was disturbed by how easily he had resigned himself to his death, lying passively, just waiting for his assailant to finish him off. Shuddering, he vowed never to give up like that again. He promised himself to keep fighting for his life until the last breath was *taken* from him, not a moment before, regardless of how dire his chances or improbable it might be to succeed.

"Henry!" Bill was whispering to him, trying to get his attention.

"Can you take us back to the research camp?" he asked when Henry finally tuned in.

He had been following Bill up till this point but now realized they were counting on him for their next move.

They were a few hundred feet from the edge of the compound. Their GPS, compass, and maps had been taken away along with all their other possessions. In turn, they had stolen two assault rifles, an army-issued knife, and a backpack, the contents of which were yet to be discovered.

The sun had set behind the hills. With night about to fall, having no navigation equipment would make it harder to find their way back to the camp. And yet they had to get out of there fast.

Henry paused. He felt the urge to run as far away as possible but knew how unforgiving the jungle could be to those lost in it.

"It will be dark soon, and we don't have a compass," he replied thoughtfully. "I can probably find our way back in daylight, but we could get seriously lost if we tried to navigate in the dark without any gear. I'm not sure that's a good option."

"It's the *only* option," Bill said forcefully. "We can't stay here!"

They were still close enough to the camp that they could hear some men shouting, no doubt organizing to come after them, if some were not in pursuit already.

"We have to get going," Clare insisted.

Henry was not as decisive as Bill, but now that he had a few moments, he forced himself to think. There were no good alternatives, but Henry identified the most logical one, if a bit counterintuitive.

"Follow me," he said, confident now, moving without waiting for a response.

He had a general idea of their position based on the direction they had started running from the tent and the shape of the valley. The camp had a rectangular contour, with the buildings on one end and a runway extending toward the other, to the east. By his calculations they were north of the compound, close to the western edge. Turning left would bring them roughly to the steep hillside at the west end of the valley.

The upheaval their escape had caused in the camp was inaudible now, but Henry expected a group of thugs to materialize from anywhere and grab them by surprise, just as had happened earlier. In absolute silence he guided the two filmmakers through the woods, walking slowly, looking every direction and stopping frequently to hear any hint of movement nearby.

As he had anticipated, the vegetation thickened when they got to the more sloped part of the hillside, making it difficult to walk but also hard to be seen. He pressed on, with no complaints from the others, finding his way to one of the steepest parts of the incline, where rocks emerged from the forest floor, vines dangling precariously from their edges.

It was a good hiding place, and the elevation afforded ample view of the camp.

Henry stopped there. Bill and Clare turned to him, waiting for an explanation.

"What are you doing?" Clare asked in a hushed voice.

"We can't outrun these guys," he responded in an equally low whisper. "They are going to comb the forest searching for us. And they know the surrounding territory better than we do. We stand a much better chance hiding in here and leaving at daybreak than trying to navigate the forest in the dark. They should already be out looking for us and are putting more search parties together. Look." Henry pointed toward the camp, where soldiers gathered in the space between the pavilion at the end of the runway and the row of military tents. They seemed to be receiving instructions. "They expect us to run, not to stay put."

It took Bill and Clare a brief moment to comprehend Henry's plan.

"And what if they don't?" Bill asked skeptically. "This is insane."

"Which is why it may work. Or at least give us a better chance than running away. I know our choices are not the most appealing right now." Henry's voice was very low. Clare and Bill came so close to him that he could hear their breathing.

"But this is the least bad one. It'll get dark soon, and we will not be able to keep a straight line in the dark, not on unfamiliar terrain. Moving now would make it more likely that they find us. I say we save our energy and make a break for the camp in the early morning, when we have a much better chance of not getting lost."

"It's a gamble," Bill pushed back.

"So is running away," Clare interjected, coming to Henry's side and inadvertently boosting his confidence.

Henry realized he was now responsible for the fate of these two people. The responsibility weighed on his shoulders but also encouraged him to advocate harder for what he thought was the best course of action.

"It's a calculated risk. The best of two bad options."

He saw the look of resignation on Bill's face and knew he had won the argument.

"For this to work we need to be absolutely quiet," he continued. "Try to stay still; and if you need to move, try to do it as slowly as possible to avoid disturbing the vegetation or making any noises."

Bill and Clare moved their heads in agreement.

It was as good a hiding place as one could hope under the circumstances. The vegetation was thick, providing good cover, and access was difficult. No one would see them unless looking at that exact place. And the dark made it harder for anyone to follow the fugitives' trail.

They sat on the ground in silence, and their bodies started to relax. Henry felt the right side of his face pounding, the pain getting worse. Finding it tender to the touch, he wondered how badly swollen and purple his face must be.

His shoulder hurt badly too, especially when he moved his arm. Carrying the heavy backpack had not helped. Luckily, the brunt of the blow had been on the muscle and not on his collarbone, which otherwise would have been broken from the impact.

Clare and Bill were in better shape, as far as he could tell. Bill was more composed than all of them, as he had been since the beginning of their ordeal, though Clare was also holding up admirably.

But there was no way around the fact that they were tired, scared, hungry, and thirsty.

As the ruckus at the mining compound subsided and night fell, Henry observed the camp below, looking for clues as to what they had stumbled upon.

The complex extended from west to east and was longer than he remembered from his first glance. He noticed the tent they had escaped from. It was the closest of five tents arranged in a row, in the northwest part of the valley. He trembled at the realization that he and his two fellow fugitives were so close to the place they had just been held captive and he had almost died. What had happened to the two guards? Had they been dead or just unconscious at the time of the escape?

There was little movement at the compound, and he guessed that most of the soldiers were out searching. Across from the tents there was an open space with tables where, he supposed, the soldiers would congregate and have meals together. Close to it was a field with two small goals for playing soccer, probably the only entertainment the soldiers had available during their downtime.

His focus shifted from the compound to the events of the day. While fighting the soldiers, Henry had almost died twice. He had been saved by Bill both times. He made a mental note to say thanks. It was not something Henry would ever forget.

The first search party came back shortly after dark, empty handed.

The young lieutenant kicked a loose tree branch in anger.

"How is it that you can't find a bunch of stupid gringos?"

Next to him, the compound boss summoned the two soldiers he thought most capable among the troops. He was not in charge of them, but the lieutenant deferred to him as he gave them instructions.

"I want each of you to lead a separate team. The fugitives are going back to the research camp. That's the only place they can go. I want you to head over there, trying to follow the most likely route they would take. My guess is that they must have come by way of the cave, so they'll try to go back through there. The other option is that they will cut straight to the river leading to the research station. I want you two to split up and pick a route. Javier, take some men with you and go to the cave, then to the research camp. Norbert, you follow the river to the camp."

"How long do we look for them?" asked Javier, the tallest of the two, regretting the question as soon as he finished his sentence.

"Until you find them."

After letting the moment linger to register how serious he was, the compound boss continued.

"For now, just follow the paths to the research station. It's possible they will get lost, and in that case we have no way of knowing where they will end up. If that happens, the other search parties have a better chance of finding them. But the fugitives' only chance out of this area is to get back to the research station. If you don't find them, wait at the research camp. There should be two other gringos there. They are all part of the same group. Stay as long as it takes for the other three to show up there. Then bring *all* of them back here."

CHAPTER 10

IN THE FIRST few hours, Clare would doze off and then wake up, alarmed by the crack of branches and leaves stepped on by the search parties passing close by. Bill and Henry lay still at her side on the steep incline; whether asleep or awake, she didn't know. At times, the flashlight beams were terrifyingly close to their hiding position. But as the three of them remained still and the night wore on, the noises gradually stopped.

Henry's gamble had paid off for now.

Reporting from remote corners of the world, she expected danger in her journeys. But she had never been through anything like this.

Her mind wandered to her family and friends back home in Australia. To her father, a tropical ecologist who had once wanted her to follow his career and the one who had actually helped secure the support of the Pitiri Research Station for their filming here. To her ex-boy-friend, who had seemed ready to settle down and start a life together. Looking back, she had turned away from a path where she no doubt would have found contentment and security.

But even now, with her life in jeopardy, the image of the safety and comfort of the road not taken brought her nothing but confirmation. She had no regrets. From a young age Clare had learned that her hunger for adventure could be satiated only by going to the places she ached to see and facing the risks that may come with it. She would have been far more miserable looking back and wondering what could have been.

She finally fell asleep.

᠙

Shortly before dawn, a cacophony of noise started to take over the forest. Birds chirping, monkeys vocalizing, insects buzzing. The rich variety of sounds announced a new sunrise. The forest was not for late sleepers.

Barely rested due to the pain in his jaw and shoulder, Henry decided it was time to start moving.

"Hey," he whispered gently, poking Bill on the arm. The former serviceman was in a light slumber and opened his eyes wide, tightening his grip on the assault rifle resting on his chest. He looked around, searching for his bearings.

"We should go," Henry continued. "The forest is waking up. The background noise will give us some cover when we move."

"Let's go," Bill answered lethargically, sitting up.

Clare opened her eyes, awakened by the two men moving around.

"We're leaving," Bill murmured.

She nodded, standing up slowly.

They gathered themselves, their bodies stiff and tired, and started to walk at a sluggish pace, careful not to make noise despite the background symphony of animal racket.

Henry calculated their position and charted in his mind the path they needed to follow. As long as they kept going uphill, he could stay on course. Once over the ridge, the sun would be up and navigation would get easier. When they started descending to the cave, toward more familiar terrain, he would be able to identify the features he had seen on the journey in and find their way back to the research camp.

They stopped frequently to pay attention to the sounds coming from the jungle, the first light starting to penetrate the canopy just enough to silhouette the different shapes of the vegetation.

The hours passed by in silence as they walked, fear and anxiety carrying them through hunger, thirst, and fatigue.

When they got close to the cave, Henry decided to bypass it, afraid it would be too obvious a stop, choosing instead to go north of the site.

He now had full command of the terrain, growing confident they were getting closer to their destination when they reached the flat ground he knew preceded the river.

He recognized an imposing amapa tree, with its large buttress that prevented the graceful shallow-rooted giant from being toppled over by the strong winds of tropical storms. He had seen a few other specimens along the way; but this was the largest, and it stood close to a young mahogany tree. Henry remembered thinking about the young tree on the way in, far enough into the jungle to survive illegal loggers.

As midmorning approached, he spotted an acai palm and decided it was a good place to rest. They had walked for hours, their bodies running on only adrenaline and internal reserves, without food or water for more than a day. He could feel the first signs of dehydration and knew the others would be in a similar condition.

"We should take a break," he said, stopping and turning to Bill and Clare. "This is a good place to get something to eat and drink." He spoke with a low voice.

"Eat what? We don't have any food or water," Clare said.

"We need to keep going, Henry." Bill looked tired but determined. "The sooner we get back to the research station the better."

Henry had been in the Amazon long enough, however, to learn to respect the rules of the land. Exhaustion could lead to mistakes, and the jungle showed no kindness to those who got ill.

"Sorry," he said a little hesitantly. "But we still have several more hours to go. The jungle can kill us if we don't take good care of our bodies. If one of us gets sick, there's nowhere to go and no one to help. Things can go bad fast in this heat and humidity, especially at the state of exhaustion we're in. There are tons of bugs and pests just waiting to strike at vulnerable targets. We need to hydrate and get some food. Staying healthy is the most important thing we can do right now."

"He's right; I need water," said Clare, agreeing with him again. "Besides," she noted, "there's a good chance we may not get a welcoming banquet back at the research camp. Whoever those guys are, they might be waiting for us there, and we may be without food even longer."

"Fair enough," Bill said. "It's a miracle we're still standing without any water or food. But where are we going to find it? We can get just as sick by drinking contaminated water or eating bad food."

"You are right. That's why I picked this place. There's our water source."

He was pointing at the treetops, where a bunch of thick vines dangled down toward the ground.

"Please keep an ear out for any unusual noise. There may still be search parties looking for us."

Henry reached for the group of vines, with their dark brown bark, wrinkly and tangled, grabbing the thickest specimen he could find and pulling it from the tree. As abundant as water was in the *rain* forest, finding some that was safe to drink wasn't so straightforward. Thankfully, the hollow branches of a few vines, such as the *cipó d'água* Henry had spotted, stored clean water for those who knew where to look.

With the same knife that had almost killed him the preceding afternoon, he cut the branches in two-foot-long pieces and handed them over to Bill and Clare.

"Here." He showed them. "Hold it above your head, and just wait for the water to come down. It's safe; I've had it before."

He did the same as he had instructed, holding the cut branch over his head with his mouth open, waiting for the water to trickle down. After a few seconds it came flowing down fast, as from a narrow hose, and he had to swallow it quickly to avoid spilling it.

"I didn't know these things held so much water," Bill said with a look of admiration.

Henry smiled and went for some food next. His shoulder still hurt badly, making it painful to climb an acai palm to harvest its nutritious, bitter-tasting berries. He employed the same technique he had used the day before when getting to the top of the pau mulato tree to observe the valley where the iron mine was.

Popular for its vitamins and antioxidants, acai was also rich in what the trio needed most at the time: calories from fat and sugars. And the berries contained a fair amount of protein, making just the right midmorning snack.

While at the top of the tree, Henry also harvested some of the top branches, extracting hearts of palm from the growing tree tips. The palm hearts were not as nutritious as the acai berries, but they were tender, moist, and remarkably tasty.

Not having the time or tools to puree the dark purple berries, they ate them straight up, careful not to bite too hard on the tough seeds that made up most of the small fruit. It did not taste as good as an acai bowl from the city, where the pulp was sweetened with sugar and served ice cold with granola on top. But it didn't matter one bit. They ate in silence, spitting out the seeds on the ground, unintentionally dispersing them just as nature intended.

Henry took advantage of the short break to finally open the military backpack he had stolen, turning it upside down and dropping all the contents on the ground. Squatting next to the pile, he sifted through it, a little uneasy about going through someone else's private possessions.

As he had hoped, it was a castaway's treasure chest. While digging past underwear, condoms, personal letters, and photographs, he found a flashlight, batteries, a fire starter, an emergency flare, and a first aid kit. He held the kit in his hands, realizing how lucky they were that they didn't need it at the moment, aware their luck could turn quickly. He also kept a few other items, including a whistle, tape, paper, and a pencil. He placed them back into the backpack, discarding the items he didn't think they would need and hiding them under a bush, feeling a dash of guilt for littering the forest.

Digging further through the remaining mound of clothes and personal effects, he saw a couple of tight-sealed black plastic bags labeled *Ración Individual de Combate*. He smiled broadly to Bill and Clare when he realized he'd found the real gold: ready-to-eat military ration packs.

"That oughta taste better than those berries," he said with a smile, throwing them over to Clare. "Save a little for me?"

She beamed when she saw what was in the package.

Clare tackled it like a kid opening a present on Christmas morning, finding individually wrapped meatball pasta and plantain chips, canned tuna, a cereal bar, orange juice, and a special treat: a tube of sweetened condensed milk. She had a bite of the cereal bar, then went straight for the condensed milk.

Henry turned back to the remaining items of the backpack and found a cell phone. He turned it on. It seemed to be working, but he knew there would be no signal in the jungle. Next, he opened the backpack owner's wallet. To his surprise, there were no reais, the Brazilian currency, but there were bills he did not recognize. The notes clearly stated their denomination and country of origin: bolivares from Venezuela.

Overtaken by an eerie feeling, Henry went on to check the documents in the wallet. Like the currency, the ID it contained was not from Brazil, but from Venezuela. To make things even stranger, it was not an ordinary document but a military one.

"What . . ." he wondered out loud.

Bill, having watched Henry sort through the contents of the backpack, seemed just as mystified. "What are these soldiers from Venezuela doing in Brazil?"

"I don't know," Henry answered. "But that explains why they were speaking Spanish and not Portuguese."

"What on earth did we run into out there?"

"Just when I thought this couldn't get any weirder," Clare added.

The peculiar finding filled Henry with trepidation. His spirits, lifted by the water and nourishing food, sank again. The sudden change in expression from both his companions indicated they had a similar reaction.

"We need to keep going, Henry," Bill said soberly, with the tone of someone who had just realized that what they were facing was even more serious than initially thought. "I was assuming we were dealing with an amateurish guerrilla group," he continued. "Especially after we managed to escape so easily . . ."

It had not seemed so easy to Henry, but he understood the point. A better-prepared force would never have allowed them to get away.

". . . but this is far worse. We are dealing with a unit with formal military training. We must get out of the jungle fast, before they catch us again."

"Yes, let's get going. Let me just get some more water for this." Henry raised a canteen taken from among the contents of the stolen bag and put on the backpack again. It felt lighter after getting rid of some of the items, but his left shoulder still hurt with the weight of the strap against it.

He paused before reaching to another vine on a different tree, noticing a branch on the ground. It seemed out of place. Examining it closely, he saw a clean cut. Henry knew how hard it was to slice one of those branches in that way. While the experienced caboclos could do it with a single machete swing, he had to hack it, making a jagged cut. This one looked smooth, sliced in one strong, precise movement by someone with enough practice. Either a local or a soldier trained to fight in the jungle.

"Someone has been here," he warned. "By the looks of the vine on the ground and the cut, it hasn't been long."

"We're pretty far from the mining compound. What are the odds that they made it all the way over here just to find some water?" Bill asked. "They came through here looking for us."

"They know we're going back to the research station," Clare noted, confirming her earlier suspicion.

Henry was starting to come to terms with the fact that they could take nothing for granted. "There aren't any other places around here we could have come from."

"My God!" Clare gasped.

Henry and Bill looked at her.

"Aidan and Liam!"

Henry's stomach dropped.

Bill looked worried, but his expression turned hopeful after a brief pause. "The men at the mine don't know we're together," he pondered. "If Aidan and Liam can stay cool, the militia guys won't find out."

He focused on Henry and continued.

"We must be careful getting to the camp, or we'll be caught just like we were when we arrived at the mine. Can you find a way for us to get there without anyone noticing?"

"I think so."

"I need you to be sure," Bill replied impatiently. "We were lucky to escape the first time. It won't happen again."

Henry was rattled, and Bill's expression softened, perhaps realizing he was not talking to a fellow soldier.

"Henry," he said, looking directly into the researcher's eyes, "you know this place better than those guys. And you're smarter too. You completely outmaneuvered everyone yesterday, including me, when you made us hide overnight while they looked for us. Don't sell yourself short. We may not beat those guys in a fight, but we can sure outsmart them."

Henry never saw himself as a leader. In his mind, leadership required a certainty that was incompatible with the character of an inquiring mind always open to new ideas. But if he had learned one thing in the past day, it was that when your life was at stake, you needed decisiveness and confidence, not an open mind. This was survival, not science, and he decided it was time to rise to the challenge.

"Can you teach me how to use these?" Henry pointed to the assault rifle hanging from Bill's right shoulder. "We were unprepared the first time. Like you said, we were lucky to escape. Let's leave no room for chance this time around."

A slow smile spread across Bill's face.

"I thought you'd never ask," he said, looking amused that the improvised pep talk had worked so effectively.

Clare stepped toward them.

"I never thought I'd sign up for shooting lessons, either, but there's a first time for everything."

Henry held the gun with both hands, as if he was scared of it. Which he wasn't afraid to admit he was. The rifle felt heavy in his hands. He examined it with interest and noticed the markings that identified it as a Russian-designed AK-103, a descendant of the infamous AK-47.

Bill went over it quickly.

"This is the magazine, where the bullets are," he explained, pulling it out. "The curved design is very characteristic of Russian rifles," he said as his fingers followed its contour.

"And here is the safety lock." He pointed to a latch on the right side of the rifle and locked and unlocked in front of Henry and Clare. "Now you try it," he said, looking at the two, who were still handling it a little tentatively.

"Be careful not to pull the trigger. Ideally, we should shoot a few rounds, but we don't want to give away our position."

He paused and let Henry and Clare hold the weapon, studying it as it weighted on their hands.

"There's not much to it," he continued as his students

locked and unlocked the safety. "You unlock, point, and pull the trigger. This is an automatic weapon, so holding the trigger will keep it firing. Be careful, though. We don't have a lot of ammo, so if we find ourselves in the middle of a shoot-out, we need to be smart about it.

"You also have to brace yourself for the recoil. It's a big kick."

"Got it." Clare nodded.

"And a final point: when you shoot, you shoot to kill. The guys on the other side surely will. This is not a game."

∽

Henry noticed more sharp machete cuts in the vegetation along the way. The soldiers were going for speed, not stealth, trying to reach the camp before the fugitives.

Henry, Clare, and Bill approached the research station in the middle of the afternoon, after the usual thunderstorm. The trio had remained dry under the canopy, but the air felt heavy and misty.

About a mile out, instead of finding the trail path used by the camp staff, Henry turned east, passing some of the scientific equipment he had placed in strategic places. The area had been mapped on a grid for the ongoing research, each imaginary square containing gear for regular measurements of humidity, pressure, and temperature, as well as camera traps to catalog the animals that dwelled in that section of the forest. Henry was so familiar with it that he could tell off of the top of his head the number of each square they passed through.

He led them around the main buildings of the research camp and advanced from the south, the least likely approach for someone coming from the iron mine or the cave, until arriving at a small subsistence farm near the main complex. It belonged to a local farmer named Chico, one of Henry's soccer buddies and the father of Ana Maria, the little girl who liked to follow Henry around.

They studied the manioc field for a couple of minutes before crossing, making sure it was deserted.

The farm was adjacent to the research camp but separated by a patch of jungle. Henry knew that wooded portion well. It was part of his ongoing investigation into how an isolated fragment of rain forest fared in comparison with the largest ones. He was trying to learn how to manage those remaining patches next to small farms all along the Amazon basin, in order to maintain or improve their ecological function.

A trail linking the crop field to the main complex cut the forest patch, but Henry avoided it, going through the thick of the trees. He knew one part of the area bordering the research camp was denser than the rest and silently walked there to survey the camp without being noticed.

They turned left inside the forest, approaching the camp's main building and stopping near the edge of the vegetation to observe. A large cabin stood on the northeast side, where some of the equipment was stored, while four other buildings surrounded a central square. The researchers and other camp staff usually congregated on the porch of the large cabin, facing the central square.

From the forest, the three of them could see part of the square through the gap between the buildings.

"This is unusually quiet," Henry whispered almost

inaudibly. The camp was normally full of people at this hour, when everyone was wrapping up their workday.

"We need a plan." Clare looked at Bill as she spoke, and Henry assumed that, like himself, she was counting on the marine's military experience to help them find a way to rescue their friends.

Bill turned to answer her, facing away from the buildings. He opened his mouth to say something when a series of loud bangs went off.

Pop, pop, pop.

Startled, Henry frantically moved from side to side, searching to understand what was going on. Something hit the tree next to him, producing a thud. The *pop* noises continued, like very loud firecrackers. Another thud emanated from the same tree. He looked up and saw the branch above move after something zipped over his head.

In the split second when he finally realized what was happening, Bill, standing in front of them, jerked forward with a loud grunt as Henry and Clare felt a warm spray on their faces.

Henry pushed Clare to the ground and threw himself down after her, facing the camp's main cabin, where he saw flashes coming out the window.

A man in green fatigues walked out of the building, carrying a machine gun, and started in their direction. Henry hesitated between running and checking on Bill, who lay facedown on the floor.

The soldier got closer, and the shooter at the window stopped firing, allowing his associate to pursue their target.

Henry seized the AK-103 strapped on Bill's shoulder. He took a deep breath and looked at the rifle in his hand.

It shook uncontrollably, along with the rest of his body. He closed his eyes, concentrating, trying to remember the short lesson from a few hours earlier.

It took maybe a second, but time seemed to slow down. He found the lock, switched it, and pointed the gun at the approaching soldier, taking another breath before pulling the trigger. Lying on the ground, the recoil didn't unsettle him. Luckily, the heel rested on his right shoulder, the one that was not hurt. The first shot appeared to have no effect, so he fired twice more. After the third shot, their pursuer went down, though Henry could not tell whether he was hit.

Henry got back on his feet and shot toward the window, this time holding the trigger and showering the back of the cabin with bullets, not minding how much ammo he was using, forgetting that Aidan Green, Liam Nguyen, or one of his colleagues from the station could be in there.

When he saw the other shooter move away from the window, Henry looked down. Bill was not moving. Clare sat with her back to a tree, paralyzed.

"Check him!" he cried, still looking at the window from the corners of his eyes, watching for signs of movement.

She crouched and turned Bill over.

"Are you okay, mate?" she shouted. Henry saw the desperation in her eyes.

But Bill's body was still and lifeless. His chest was crimson wet and covered in the dirt from the ground he had fallen onto. A puddle of bloody mud sat where he was lying before Clare had moved him. Henry helped her raise Bill to examine him. When he saw the orange-sized exit wound on Bill's chest, Henry had learned all he needed to know.

Bill Powers was dead.

"He's gone! He's gone!" she cried, covered in blood and holding Bill in her arms.

Henry took a last glance at the cabin window and fired again in anger.

He put the gun strap back on his shoulder and grabbed Clare's arm.

"Come on—we have to go! They will kill us too!"

She complied, looking shaken and disoriented.

They turned away from the cabin, and Henry threw the gun to his back, pulling Clare as they ran.

The shooter inside the cabin came back to the window, aiming his gun toward the two fugitives at the same time that the soldier outside the cabin raised his head from the ground, watching them run away. He had a bullet in his shoulder but was not fatally wounded.

Pop! Pop! Pop! They heard shots again, only this time the bangs were even louder. *How can they be so close?* Henry wondered, before realizing *why* the sound was so much nearer than before.

It had come out of his own weapon.

In throwing it over his shoulder to run away, he had forgotten to put the safety on. He stopped briefly, switched on the lock, and started running again.

His mistake had saved their lives. It had forced the two soldiers to go down for cover at the sound of the shots, allowing Henry and Clare to disappear from view.

CHAPTER 11

FROM THE MANIOC field south of the research camp's buildings, Henry glanced back at the forest with an anxious look, checking to see if anyone was coming on their trail.

He hesitated. They were blocked by the river on one side and surrounded by jungle on all others. Making a run for the forest seemed like the only viable alternative, but Henry knew that while it might buy them some time, there was nowhere to go.

"What now?" Clare cried out.

Before Henry could consider their situation further, a girl's voice called his name. When he turned to look, all he saw was a small figure being pulled inside the farmhouse. Henry guessed it was Ana Maria, her parents understandably afraid for her safety.

Chico, her father and owner of the field, stepped anxiously out of the wattle-and-daub structure and came running in their direction, shouting.

"A lancha! A lancha!" he yelled as he ran, gesticulating toward the river. "Pega a lancha!"

The farmer stopped a few feet from Henry and Clare, looking puzzled as to why the two of them were still standing there. Chico's body was slim and muscled, but the wrinkles on his forehead and the bags under his eyes gave away the hardships of frontier farming in the scorching heat and enduring humidity of the jungle.

"Of course, the powerboat!" Henry realized, his eyes lighting up with renewed hope.

"Thank you," he shouted, giving the farmer a quick nod as he grabbed Clare's hand and turned toward the river.

Henry looked again at the woods behind them. He didn't see any movement but knew they were pushing their luck by hanging around.

The crop field and the research camp were separated from the river—their only link to the outside world—by a forest buffer several hundred feet wide. It was a hassle to carry equipment from the boats; but when the water level rose above normal, the slightly higher elevation away from the bank helped protect the buildings and, more importantly, the expensive research and communications equipment.

Cutting down the forest next to a river was also illegal. Luckily for Henry and Clare, the research station was about the only property in a one-hundred-mile radius that followed the law, giving them the cover they needed. Provided, that is, the two soldiers—or were there more?—had not yet realized the boat was the only means of escape. There was a good chance they hadn't, Henry guessed, since their pursuers were not familiar with the camp and he had not thought of it himself.

A trail ran through the forest buffer to the small but well-constructed pier. Henry and Clare rushed to it without caution, arriving at the pontoon and, to their great relief, finding no one in sight.

The lone powerboat stood rocking gently on the water, fastened to the dock by a single rope. The tranquil scene contrasted sharply with Henry's sheer desperation.

They leaped on the launch, the same one that had brought them here just five days earlier. Henry shed the backpack and placed it under the bench, along with the rifle. He turned to Clare and pointed to her weapon.

"Do you remember how to use it?"

"Yes," she said firmly.

He moved to the stern and crouched in front of the outboard engine, his hands shaking, trying to block the image in his head of an armed soldier walking out of the jungle at any minute and starting to fire. If the shooters caught up with them now, they would be sitting ducks.

Henry looked up and saw Clare's eyes locked on the empty trailhead. She had tightened her grip on the machine gun and had her hand next to the lock switch.

"Hurry up!" she shouted.

He turned back to the engine and concentrated hard on the steps he needed to follow to turn it on. He lowered the propeller into the river and quickly checked the fuel level in the bright-orange tank next to the bench. It was about three-quarters full, enough to go pretty far if they followed the current. After making sure the hose from the tank to the engine was connected, Henry loosened the vent screw to allow oxygen in and put the throttle grip in the start position.

He raised his head and glanced at the forest once more. *So far, so good.* He stood up, keeping his left knee on the bench, and pulled the starter cord as hard as he could.

Nothing.

"Come on! Please start," he pleaded.

Henry tried again, to no avail.

"What's wrong?" Clare asked with urgency in her voice, stepping next to Henry and examining the engine setup.

Henry felt as though an eternity went by.

"What's that?" She pointed at a bulge in the fuel hose. "Did you pump the fuel?"

He shook his head in disbelief, cursing himself.

Immediately, he turned to the primer bulb, pumping fuel several times, and pulled the starter cord hard.

The motor stuttered noisily but still didn't start. He tried two more times, the engine stubbornly refusing to turn on. *What am I forgetting now?*

They could hear shouts in the distance, coming from inside the jungle. Henry grew more anxious.

"They are coming!" Clare warned.

Taking charge, she dropped the gun and jumped to Henry's position, pushing him aside. She held on to the throttle handle for leverage and reached for the cord, pulling it violently.

The engine roared to life.

As she clutched the handle for support, her hand inadvertently rolled the throttle, causing the boat to accelerate abruptly. The jolt caught Henry by surprise, and he lost his balance, falling partly out of the launch, his whole upper body on the water, rocking the boat hard.

It seemed certain they were about to capsize. Clare screamed; but instead of waiting to fall in the water, she reacted quickly, holding on to the throttle with her left hand and grabbing Henry's leg with her right.

The acceleration helped steady the boat, and Henry recovered, managing to pull himself back in.

"Sorry," she said, moving out of the way. "Here, you take it!"

Henry jumped to the back and seized the handle, asserting control of the engine.

"Hang tight," he warned, accelerating to full speed.

He turned the launch to the left, heading downstream toward the river bend.

His peripheral vision caught some movement at the trailhead.

"They are here!" Clare shouted. "They see us!"

Henry held tighter to the throttle and kept it at maximum speed, bracing for the sound of machine-gun fire. Steering the boat around the bend, he glanced anxiously over his shoulder just in time to see the soldiers on the pier disappear from sight, replaced by riparian forest as the launch left but a foamy wake behind.

CHAPTER 12

GOING ALONG WITH the current, Henry throttled down after a few miles to save gas, the noisy engine powering through the dark-water river as it gradually widened toward the Rio Negro.

A warm wind blew on their faces. Against the backdrop of a blue sky and a dense green jungle bathed by late-afternoon sun, the beauty of their surroundings remained undiminished by the tragedy.

Though earlier encouraged by the fact he had been able to muster the strength and wits to escape their pursuers, now he could not help but think he had led them straight to a death trap. In the time elapsed from escaping the mine to getting to the research camp, had he gone from insecure to overconfident? What had he missed?

Henry played the crossing of the forest patch over and over in his mind, trying to think of what he could have done differently. They had moved as carefully as possible, going through the densest part of the vegetation. Perhaps if he had gone alone, the shooters would not have detected any movement in the forest, even if they had been expecting their escaped prisoners. He would never know.

His mind could still see Bill Powers's body lying motionless on the ground. Those lifeless, wide-open eyes and the exit-wound gape on Bill's chest would remain burned in Henry's memory forever.

And to think that only a couple of days before, he had been just a research assistant disappointed with the way his career had turned out.

He had come to this position by happenstance. No one could last very long at the camp, an isolated post in an unforgiving place. PhD students and researchers would come for a few weeks at the most, collect their data, make their observations, and leave, returning to their climate-controlled offices to write papers.

That would have been Henry's fate, as well, but for one mistake, albeit a serious one. After being expelled by the university, Henry had been allowed to keep working at the site, managing the experiments on behalf of his former research team. The pay was bad, the conditions challenging, and others took credit for Henry's work and ideas. But he was thankful for the opportunity to stay involved in the study he loved.

Left to his own devices, he had learned everything on the go, with the help of the others who lived at the Pitiri Station year-round. Forced to speak only Portuguese, he was now completely fluent in Brazil's language. He had also learned to navigate the jungle as if it were his own backyard, discovering where to find food and water and mastering local survival techniques like climbing palm trees, and had forged a close bond with the caboclos, a culture many miles apart from his own.

Now, just as he was growing comfortable with the hard life in the tropics and was finding his groove again, it seemed he would have to add fighting a hostile army to his skill set.

⮬

Clare sat in the middle of the boat, directly on its aluminum shell, her back leaning against the bench, arms and legs crossed, watching the landscape go by.

The boat hit a dead log floating in the river, making a loud clank. She startled and looked back at Henry, but he seemed unfazed, concentrated on the river.

A couple of hours on, the waterway had widened further as it approached the confluence with another river. Henry turned off the engine, letting the current carry them. The sun had set behind the horizon.

"We need to find a place for the night before it gets dark," he explained. "They can't reach us now. Not without a powerboat."

"Okay" was all she could muster.

"That's the Rio Negro." He pointed ahead to a wide expanse of water. "If we keep following the river flow, we will eventually get to a small town where we could go to the police and look for help, but that's too far. We don't have enough gas to get there, and I worry that the guys who are after us expect we go that way. I was thinking we head in the opposite direction of where we *should* be going, at least for now."

"And where will that take us?"

Henry paused. He hadn't thought that far ahead.

The boat kept drifting down the river, but he was unconcerned. It could go only one way.

"Nowhere, really," he replied. "Eventually we would get to the border with Colombia or Venezuela, but we don't have enough gas for that either."

He paused again, remembering something.

"What?" she asked, following the change in his expression.

"One of my colleagues at the research station told me about a missionary camp that way. We could try to get to it. We could also wait here for one of the commercial boats that come down the river. They stop frequently to pick up the people who live on the riverbanks and in the surrounding small villages. I've seen them waiting in dugout canoes."

"You got us this far," she replied. "Let's go with your instinct. It worked well the last time."

"Upriver it is then. We'll go a few miles and then stop for the night before continuing tomorrow," he said, turning around and pulling the starter cord.

This time the engine turned over on the first try.

Turning right at the fork, they motored upstream until finding a small cove with a creek—the locals called it *igarapé*—cutting through the white sand of a river beach. The creek offered a good place to hide the boat, and the beach provided better access to the forest than did the dense riverine vegetation.

After paddling into the igarapé, Henry dragged the

boat out of the water. It was heavy, and bringing it inside the forest took considerable effort, especially with his shoulder still hurting. He then shuffled the sand with his hands and walked backward, erasing their footsteps and all signs they had disembarked at the small sandy shore.

Making a fire was out of the question. It would call attention, and he was determined not to take any more chances. For all intents and purposes, he assumed a whole army was in pursuit. He didn't even discount the absurd idea that they were being tracked by satellite, remembering the popular saying adapted from Joseph Heller's famous *Catch-22* novel: *Just because you're paranoid doesn't mean someone is not out to get you.*

Henry gazed at the sky, marveling at the heavy clouds lit crimson by the sun's afterglow. It looked like a painting. He closed his eyes and took a deep breath, filling his lungs with the warm, moist air of the early evening. The earthy scent of the jungle filled him with calmness. It reminded him of how much he loved the forest. Despite the horror they were going through, the moment made him realize there was still beauty all around them. He wasn't done just yet.

Clare did not look so well. She sat against a tree, her arms embracing her legs, rocking back and forth, shivering. Bill's blood, now dry, was still on her clothes. Henry had noticed her try to wash it with the water from the river, but it wouldn't come off.

He could see that the events of the day had affected her more than it had him. He was devastated to watch a good man die. But she had lost a *friend*.

Henry approached slowly and sat cross-legged in

front of her, facing Clare as her light-blue eyes stared catatonically at nothing in particular. He did not say a word, gently and tentatively putting his left hand on her knee. Her skin felt cold despite the hot temperature of the day, telling him she may be about to go into shock. It was bound to get worse as the night cooled the air.

He sat there for several minutes, thinking about what, if anything, he should say.

"I only knew Bill for a few days, but I liked him immediately." Henry purposefully avoided mentioning Aidan and Liam. "It seems silly, but I looked up to him even though I knew him so briefly. He had a kind of quiet confidence that makes you trust him right away." Henry wasn't sure this would help, but he felt compelled to say something. Besides, he meant it.

"I was really scared when we were taken into that tent. He was the one who kept it cool and got us out of there. Did you see how he took on those guys?"

He saw a faint hint of acknowledgment. She was biting her lips, looking as if she was trying not to cry. But she was listening.

"He saved my life twice on the same day. First when I was being clubbed with a machine gun and then when I was about to be stabbed. I will never forget that. I was waiting until the right moment to let him know how thankful I am. Now I won't get the chance."

He paused, thinking of the significance of Bill's actions. They were alive because of him. And his death would be in vain if they didn't manage to remain so.

He changed the subject, turning to more practical matters. "You have to eat something."

Henry took the food out of the backpack and waved it in front of them.

"How about some spaghetti and meatballs? Or . . ." He opened another bag, containing a different military ration. "Maybe some tuna?"

"I'm not hungry."

At least she was responding now.

He found some energy-drink mix in the ration pack and poured it in the canteen.

"Here, have some of this," Henry said after shaking it. "You need to get some water in you. You feel cold, probably because you have low blood pressure. This will help."

She drank it slowly. The sugary water seemed to make her feel better.

"Can you please eat something for me now? Just a bit. We can't get sick. Whatever you can handle is fine."

She nodded, reaching for the pasta. He saw a put-off expression as she tried the cold food. She sampled one of the energy bars and managed it a little better.

"That's it," she said after a couple of bites. "I can't eat it anymore."

"That's okay. At least you got something in you. Just keep drinking."

It was dark now. Henry ate some of the food and put the rest away in the backpack. He got up and walked in the direction of the river, stopping where the forest met the beach, watching and listening intently for any sign of human activity.

There was no indication of anything out of the ordinary. The night was eerily calm. He returned to Clare, kneeling next to her and touching her cheek with the back of his hand.

"You need to warm up," he told her.

He felt embarrassed by what he was about to say, terrified she may think he was trying to take advantage of her.

"Please don't take it the wrong way, but if it's all right with you, I'll use my body heat to warm you. Otherwise, I'm afraid you'll go into shock."

She looked at him with a deadpan expression.

"It's okay."

He gestured for her to move forward, getting between her and the tree. He used the backpack as a cushion and pulled her toward him, softly placing her body against his, her head lying on his chest.

She started to sob and he embraced her, tightening his arms around her, trying to offer some comfort.

"I'm so sorry," he whispered. "Crying is good, crying is good."

Her hands held his left arm tightly while he brushed her hair with the fingers of his right hand, letting her unload her grief. She cried for a long time before calming down, giving in to exhaustion and finally falling asleep. Henry noticed her breathing become slower and deeper, glad she was finally resting, and leaned his head back, trying to do the same.

CHAPTER 13

WHEN THEY LEFT the overnight camp, the water was flat, disturbed only by a gentle morning wind. A timber raft moved leisurely downstream in the opposite direction, accompanied by a small, rusty barge. Henry accelerated the boat, avoiding further contact with the haul of what consisted in all likelihood of illegally harvested logs. They had enough trouble as it was.

The terrain was level in this section of the river, making all the more dramatic the occasional bare rock formations surging abruptly in the distance. Impenetrable green leaped out of the margins, interrupted along the way only by scattered manioc fields with rustic plank houses, their glassless windows and doorless entrances strangely resembling a toothless face.

Sitting at the back of the boat with the warm morning wind blowing on his face, Henry imagined what it was like to spend one's entire life under zinc or thatched roofs, in near isolation and depending on the forest and river to survive. He had a taste of it at the research camp, but getting steady shipments of supplies in a well-funded facility was hardly similar to living at the mercy of the forest's waters.

Among the few threads linking all the different styles of the crazy American melting pot he came from were some common comforts sorely missing here: cars, roads, electricity, cell phones, schools, and the nearby strip mall. But as he was learning in his prolonged stay in the jungle, there was more to this way of life in the far reaches of the Amazon than met the eye.

The launch nearly out of fuel by late morning, Henry realized they would not make it to the missionary camp. So when they sighted a settlement of about five houses overlooking a deep cove, it looked like as good a place to stop as any.

With the jungle as a backdrop, the land was covered with crops and pasture save for a few scattered trees, while wood plank houses sat on stilts at the far end, where the elevation was higher.

Before turning in to the inlet, Henry disposed of the two assault weapons, throwing them overboard in the middle of the river and watching them sink in the black water. Two days ago, it would have been unthinkable for him to discard anything in this fragile ecosystem. But now, with their lives at stake, the guilt from the small environmental impact was a price he was willing to pay.

After tying the launch next to two dugout canoes

and an aluminum boat, Henry and Clare stepped on the muddy bank. They saw a woman in denim shorts and a burgundy tank top walk in their direction. Henry guessed she was in her late twenties. Two small, shirtless boys followed, half hiding behind her legs, studying the visitors with suspicion and curiosity.

A traveler unfamiliar with the region might have braced for an unwelcoming reception. Surely no one would react lightly to two unkempt strangers arriving unannounced at their isolated property. But the rules were different for the *ribeirinhos*, the river people, where remote communities and families helped one another along with the visitors that occasionally landed on their doorstep.

"Bom dia, tudo bem?" Henry greeted the woman politely. "Our boat capsized and we lost almost everything," he explained, making the story up on the go. "Luckily, we were able to roll the boat back over. We're okay aside from a few small injuries."

As he spoke, he pointed to the bruise on his face and the blood on Clare's shirt, suggesting they had been caused by the accident. Their sorry appearance corroborated the story, though as an inexperienced liar would, he worried the woman may not believe any of it.

His concerns proved unnecessary.

"I'm Marta," she said, extending her hand, unfazed by the surprise visit. Henry guessed they were not the first scruffy tourist-looking outsiders to arrive unexpectedly. "Is there anything I can get you to help with your injuries?"

"We're okay," he replied. "We just need a place to rest and wait for a boat to take us back to the nearest town."

Henry and Clare introduced themselves, and Marta

gestured toward a bench near the water, excusing herself and saying she would be right back. The two boys lingered for a moment, until she called them. Henry put the backpack down, and they sat facing the opening of the cove into the river.

The friendly reception was consistent with what Henry had experienced everywhere in his travels through the region. Without much happening around them, jungle dwellers craved contact with the outside world. And although Brazil was a violent country, acts of kindness were much more prevalent than were those of brutality, something Henry and Clare gratefully welcomed in their fragile condition.

After a few minutes a man who looked about the same age as Marta came to talk to them. His name was João, he said as he greeted them. He was an energetic man with smooth brown skin and a handsome rectangular face.

"I'm Marta's husband," he explained with a welcoming grin. "We have a spare house for visitors if you're interested. You can stay for a few days and see the area. We get people coming to stay with us a few times a year."

He offered to take the pair fishing, to guide them inside the surrounding jungle, and to even venture farther away to show them waterfalls, sandy beaches, and other sights nearby.

Clare nodded along as João talked, though Henry wasn't sure how much of the conversation she understood. The family would expect a fee for their hospitality and services, he knew, thinking the offer was born as much by the need for money as by the appeal of having some company and a connection to the outside world.

"We were supposed to be back several days ago," Henry declined. "Our families must be worried sick about us, and we need to contact them as soon as we can. I'm sorry."

He continued after a brief pause. "How can we reach you? I wouldn't mind coming back one day." He meant it, though he wasn't sure he would ever be able to.

João promised to share his email, and Henry, ever interested in knowing more about the people in the Amazon, asked how he liked living on the farm.

The family subsisted on farming and fishing, selling their surplus and occasionally profiting from tourists that came to stay with them. More than thirty years ago, the property had been settled by Marta's parents, Seu Pedro and Dona Madalena, who had raised their eight children in this very place. Five of them still lived at the cove, including Marta and two others who also had their own families.

Henry looked around at the site. Among the humble buildings on the property, the best kept was a small chapel, composed of just one room no more than fifteen by fifteen feet. It was the only one painted, with light-blue walls and a dark blue roof. He wondered if there was any connection to the missionary village upstream, though those settlements were commonly focused on converting the indigenous tribes, not the Portuguese descendants that settled the margins of the Amazon tributaries.

"People from all over the area come here to pray together," João explained while Henry gazed at the religious building.

As they continued to talk, Henry was pleased to learn

that despite the seclusion, a well-functioning community lived in the area. The farmers from different fields scattered around the margins didn't flock to this settlement just to occasionally pray at the modest chapel. They knew and helped one another, gave shelter to travelers up and down the river in times of need, and brought supplies to their neighbors when they could.

A man looking to be in his late fifties or early sixties emerged from the largest house in the settlement and walked in their direction, wearing a cowboy-style straw hat, shorts, and a worn-out, unbuttoned short-sleeve shirt that exposed his broad chest and flat belly. Tall and strong, he betrayed his age only by the wrinkles on his skin.

"This is Seu Pedro." João introduced him with a deferential voice.

Mr. Pedro greeted the visitors with a formal handshake and invited them to join the family for lunch, a display of generosity that Henry had grown accustomed to. It would have been rude to decline, so he and Clare welcomed the timely offer, hungry for the first real meal in days. It consisted, unsurprisingly, of stir-fried manioc flour, rice, beans, and fish, the staple of the region.

They entered the house and sat down at a handcrafted table inside. The walls were of unpainted wood, which made the interior a little dark. With no electricity, the only light came through the windows and the gaps in the planks. The inside was decorated with a large cross above the entrance as well as with worn images of Mary and Jesus.

Besides Marta, João, and the two boys, a son and a daughter of the elderly couple joined them along with their spouses and a small toddler introduced as Gema, the youngest grandchild of the land's original settlers.

Before they started to eat, Mr. Pedro asked the two visitors if one of them would like to say grace. Though Henry wasn't particularly religious and thought he lacked the eloquence to offer an inspiring prayer, it seemed only appropriate after all they'd been through.

He paused, thinking what to say.

"We thank you, Lord, for this meal and for the opportunity to meet new friends," he started, closing his eyes and thinking about the ordeal he and the film crew had been through, seeing the faces of Bill, Aidan, and Liam. Appealing to a higher power was as good an option as any, so he took the task to heart.

"Thank you for giving us the strength to fight and to survive our trials as well as for keeping us unharmed and in good health. Please take care of those who have left us, especially the ones that left us too soon, and protect our friends who are in harm's way, wherever they may be," he said with evident sincerity.

He was about to finish when he remembered they may have killed one of their captors.

"And please forgive us our sins. Amen."

Henry opened his eyes and looked around, worried that the family would be cringing at his improvised prayer.

But Mr. Pedro seemed moved. "Thank you for thinking of those who have left us," he said.

Henry smiled, nodding.

The family patriarch turned to Clare, asking, "How long have you been together?"

She smiled, not understanding the question, and looked to Henry for clarification.

He translated for her, then answered Mr. Pedro. "I'm sorry. She doesn't speak Portuguese. We're not a couple, though. Just friends."

Henry saw Mr. Pedro's expression turn puzzled and realized that a man and a woman traveling in the jungle as friends would seem strange to some. He guessed his answer raised suspicion around the table that they may not have been completely straightforward about their backgrounds. And once people's basic, obvious assumptions fell apart, they tended to question everything else too.

Henry tried to fix it. "We've known each other since we were kids. We're like brother and sister." But it was too late. An uncomfortable silence ensued, leaving Henry unsure what to say next.

Though she couldn't speak the language, Clare must have noted the awkwardness around the table.

"Place beautiful," she mustered in poor Portuguese, with a very strong accent.

The whole table turned to her, trying to understand what she meant. One of Marta's boys started giggling, repeating it as though it was the funniest thing he had heard all week.

"Place *booty*-ful!" he shouted, mocking her accent, with a loud, contagious laugh only a child could have. "Place *booty*-ful!"

She frowned and twisted her lips, pretending to be angry, making the boy giggle even harder. Then she laughed with him.

Mr. Pedro looked a little embarrassed at his grandson's behavior. But Clare's attempt at Portuguese and the boy's imitation of her were endearing, causing the rest of the table to crack up too.

"It's beautiful indeed," João said with a smirk.

"Tell us more about the places you take the tourists that stay at your property," Henry asked. "How far are the waterfalls? Are they big?"

That steered the conversation to less controversial topics. Everyone in the family was curious about the visitors; and Henry, in turn, was eager to learn more about the hosts. Even in distress, he could not help his desire to get to know the people who made a living in the middle of the Amazon jungle and who didn't think twice about sharing their table with total strangers.

The children seemed to like Clare, perhaps because she had the pale skin and blue eyes of many of the soap opera characters they watched, who looked more like the two foreigners than themselves. São Paulo and Rio de Janeiro, Brazil's largest urban and cultural centers, were in many ways more similar to Europe than to this corner of the country.

Though Clare couldn't understand a word of what the boys said, no one could resist being warmed by their affections as they showed off their toys and tried to talk to her. They elicited another big laugh when one of the boys, frustrated by the fact that she didn't understand what he was saying, screamed at her ear, thinking it would break the language barrier.

When the meal was over and they were preparing to leave, Henry insisted Seu Pedro take the launch.

"We lost all our money and have no way to repay

you," he explained, ignoring the Venezuelan currency in the stolen wallet.

It was a far-too-generous offer, especially considering the outboard engine, which went for an exorbitant price in these parts. Mr. Pedro seemed suspicious again. Noting the man's expression, Henry tried to explain himself.

"I don't know what else to do with it. We have no fuel left, and I can't return it before leaving the country. Please accept it. The owner has our deposit and will be fully compensated," he lied.

"It is very generous of you," Mr. Pedro said with clear hesitation in his voice, accepting the gift. "God bless you, Mr. Henry. My son will take you to the river now, to wait for a boat."

He turned to Clare, who was standing next to Henry, and wished her well. She thanked him with a bow and then squatted, extending her arms to embrace the kids.

"Place beautiful!" she cried, getting another set of giggles and smiling warmly in return.

Henry and Clare sat with one of Mr. Pedro's sons in a dugout canoe in the middle of the river, waiting for a boat.

Deep in the jungle, the riverside communities were served by a series of small boat operators hauling people, animals, and supplies—and whatever else was needed—up and down the river. The more distant areas, like this part of the Negro River, had irregular service. Sometimes it would take a couple of days for a commercial liner to pass, but there was always a cargo boat or another vessel passing through the river on other business.

There was no way of knowing what time one would come, however, so would-be passengers just waited, making sure they could be seen. A barge returning from delivering supplies to upstream communities, a tugboat towing log rafts, a private vessel, anyone who saw people waiting by the banks or in canoes knew to stop and offer transport.

Henry and Clare spent their time rocking in place, watching the river and listening to the forest, seeing the life of the region float by as people in dugout canoes and small boats moved around the area to fish, trade, or visit small settlements. For all the isolation, lack of infrastructure, and absence of institutions, things were predictable and worked remarkably well in this distant world, if one knew what to expect and learned to accept the slow pace of it.

After three hours of waiting, they got lucky and caught a regular liner, with proper accommodations for passengers. The wide, wood-built twenty-five-footer with an open deck was coming from the upstream village of Cucuí, on the border with Venezuela, picking up and dropping off ribeirinhos and cargo as it stopped and went at the will of its passengers.

They found a spot in one of the corners of the boat, next to an elderly couple carrying their belongings in a large, worn-out plastic bag. The wife scooched over along the bench attached to the railing to allow Clare to sit. With a military backpack and their ragged appearance, the fugitives looked just the part of adventurous tourists exploring the jungle.

Henry sat cross-legged on the floor in front of Clare,

facing forward and looking at the river as it went by. Night was falling, but the boat would press on in the dark while Henry anticipated his return to an urban area for the first time in many months.

CHAPTER 14

JUST UNDER TEN miles south of the equator, where the Negro River narrowed and widened again like an hourglass, the small town of São Gabriel da Cachoeira lay on the left bank. Surrounded by gentle green hills and indigenous reserves, the settlement sprang from a fort—now reduced to its foundations—erected by the Portuguese in the sixteenth century to defend from Spanish conquistadors invading from the northwest.

Henry had been to the city before, the gateway to all the settlements, research stations, religious missions, indigenous reserves, and military outposts in the northwestern Brazilian Amazon.

He had taken his time getting there, jumping at the chance to explore the beautiful country he was moving to. Rather than going by plane, he had boarded a four-story, seventy-foot boat from Manaus, the largest city in the eastern Amazon and the urban center serving the entire region, anticipating four days of calm and contemplation navigating up the largest tributary of the Amazon River.

He had gotten something else entirely.

The boat's top-deck bar had blasted popular Brazilian music with corny melodies, broken-heart lyrics, repetitive guitar riffs, and monotonous drum strokes, nothing like the exotic and ebullient samba beat or the smooth, laid-back bossa nova rhythm that reached beyond the country's borders.

At first he had found it charming that the boat had no seats, just hooks for passengers to set up their hammocks for the long trip—until he realized he would be crammed together literally butt to butt with hundreds of fellow travelers, since the hammocks all touched each other in the crowded decks, giving a firsthand lesson in the difference between American and Brazilian notions of personal space.

The chatter had been constant. Passengers spoke loudly so they could be heard over the music coming not just from the rooftop bar but also from competing personal boom boxes. The showers—with water from the river—got filthy very quickly. So did the bathrooms. Thankfully, all four decks were open, separated from the river only by waist-high railings, allowing foul smells to dissipate promptly.

He had known the trip could be dangerous too. Safety standards were lax, and it was not uncommon for a liner to flip due to the strong currents under the calm surface waters. The last stretch of the journey relied entirely on the captain's knowledge, no nautical charts being available for the last 150 miles before São Gabriel da Cachoeira.

And yet, the trip had exceeded all of his expectations. He was grateful to have heeded the advice to set up his hammock in the lower level, where the music from the bar was not so loud. The people had been kind, and he had enjoyed twice daily servings of—what else?—rice, beans, manioc flour, and either fish or chicken, all included in the price of the fare, though on the fourth day he had longed for some variety.

And then there had been the view.

Wide-open river with placid backwater, the jungle in the horizon with occasional lone trees standing taller than the canopy. The Negro River was dotted with islands, more than a thousand of them, and each new river bend had brought the sight of another one, covered in untouched tropical forest. Flocks of birds would fly close to the boat, and dense clouds, set against the light blue sky, constantly changed shape and color, from white to stormy gray to bright hues of yellow, orange, and red at sunset. To top it all off, a few of the region's legendary pink dolphins would follow the boat every now and again, eliciting squeals from the children—and from more than a few adults, captivating even the most jaded passengers.

The different characters on the boat had been another source of fascination. He had spent the first day observing families and business travelers, trying to guess their background story. Inhabiting a world apart from his own, they had seemed to have the same needs, quirks, and aspirations as travelers anywhere. The kids ran wild, adults were bored, families fought and made up. Only the setting was different. Much prettier, in fact.

On the morning of the second day, Henry had sat

cross-legged at the back of the rooftop, sipping strong, sugary coffee in a small, flimsy plastic cup. Facing backward, he had watched the bubbly wake left by the boat, marveling at the wide expanse of water and jungle left behind.

"Are you looking to explore the area?" He heard a voice with a heavy accent.

Henry turned and saw a young man standing next to him.

"My name is Marcos," the man said, extending his hand.

Henry stood up to shake it.

"I used to be in the army, so I've been to every part of the jungle. I could take you to any place you've heard of and a few more you haven't."

Henry didn't have to guess why he had been approached. He stood out as a foreigner like a polar bear in the desert. He explained he was there for work but took Marcos's contact information. Maybe someday he would take him up on the offer.

"Have you heard of the Pitiri Research Station?"

"No," Marcos responded. "Where is it?"

"I don't know the *exact* location. It's on the Içana River."

"In the Alto Rio Negro Reserve?"

"Yes."

"I've been to the area. But can't say I've heard of the name. There are a few research stations in the area. What will you be studying?"

Henry explained his research on tropical forest fragmentation. Marcos seemed curious about what would bring a gringo all the way down to the Amazon. Henry in turn was eager to learn what it was like to grow up in the area and live there. Aside from how central the river was to those communities, Marcos had gone to school, played, and got in trouble, like any kid, before going off to join the army. He had recently left the service and was now starting an adventure-tourism business in São Gabriel da Cachoeira.

Despite its remote location, the town attracted hardcore mountaineers who used it as a base for the long journey to Pico da Neblina, the tallest summit in Brazil. It was also close to a variety of waterfalls, river rapids, pristine rain forest, and arts and crafts from local indigenous communities. In the dry season Marcos took visitors to the white-sand beaches that revealed themselves when the water level receded.

With a shared passion for the Amazon forest and adventure, the conversation had lasted for the best part of the trip. But São Gabriel da Cachoeira had been the end of Henry's Brazilian explorations and the start of his research assignment. From there he had taken a small boat all the way to the research camp, where he would stay for months on end having little contact with the outside world save for the occasional satellite phone call to his parents.

It was fitting that his quest for answers should start here as well.

<svg>⚬</svg>

Because it was settled on the banks of river rapids that made navigation impossible, São Gabriel da Cachoeira had two ports, one linking the city to settlements in the north of the Rio Negro and another, about fourteen miles down a dirt road, serving downstream communities all the way to Manaus, the state capital.

Before sunrise Henry and Clare arrived at the north wharf—if one could refer as such to the muddy bank where passengers and cargo unloaded. Boats were docked on to one another for want of space, so the pair disembarked not on the bank but on another boat, walking through two more before stepping down a wooden gangway and getting their feet dirty on the mud littered with trash.

They scanned their surroundings carefully for signs that someone may be waiting for them. There wasn't much movement in the early hours of the day, save for one woman selling snacks to the new arrivals, a beggar, and a couple of dockworkers.

"We need to go straight to the police," Clare suggested as soon as they were on the ground.

Henry wasn't so sure. He didn't think the police would be of much help and harbored concerns that coming forward to the authorities could be risky. The operation they had seen seemed quite sophisticated. What if whoever was behind it had connections to law enforcement?

But there were people in danger at the research station, and he owed it to them to do everything in his power to help.

Arriving just a couple of blocks from the central business district, Henry and Clare were walking down Avenida Costa e Silva, the town's main thoroughfare, only minutes after getting off the boat.

Following the directions they got from a worker at the harbor, they found the *delegacia*, as police stations are called in Brazil, after a twenty-minute walk. The streets

were wide and deserted, filled with boxy two-story buildings, the dark roll-down gates of storefronts not opening
for another couple of hours.

The only officer on duty was wrapping up the night
shift. Henry wondered what a typical night was like, guessing it involved mostly domestic disputes and drunken
fights.

The station was a small and simple facility adapted
from a family home, a couple of old desks in the living
room serving as the office where police reports were filed.
The walls were washed-out green and peeling, filled with
posters warning against child prostitution and animal
trafficking.

They sat on blue plastic chairs, and the officer's
expression turned more and more incredulous as Henry
told their full ordeal, save for a few details. Because Henry
was afraid to share anything that could incriminate Clare
or himself, he omitted the part where the three of them
had attacked two soldiers to escape, and the fact that he
had shot at another with a machine gun a day later. In his
version of the story, they had been left alone in the tent
and had managed to escape through the back.

When Henry was finished, the officer tried to dismiss
them quickly, explaining that the local police were not
able to help.

"What do you mean 'outside your jurisdiction'?"
Henry asked, his voice growing louder.

"We are the Polícia Civil. We have authority only
over matters in our state. The indigenous reserve is federal
domain. You need to contact the Federal Police."

"Can't you call them? One person is dead and two others are in danger. You can't just ignore this."

The officer picked up the phone and called someone. Henry hoped it was the Federal Police; but listening to this end of the conversation, he guessed it was the officer's supervisor. After hanging up, the policeman stood, indicating the conversation was over.

Henry's face was red with frustration, and he gestured to Clare that they were leaving.

"What just happened?" she asked as they walked out to the door.

"He said this is outside their jurisdiction, which doesn't extend beyond the state. I told him it's a matter of life and death, but he insisted it's a case for the Federal Police. We need to take it directly to them."

"And that was it?"

"I just got a sense he didn't want to help. I don't think he believed a word of my story. He said he was sorry but kept repeating that this is a matter for the Federal Police, that there's nothing *he* can do about it."

"Do you think he is maybe covering up for someone?"

"Or afraid to look into it? Not really. He sounded more like he couldn't be bothered. But it's possible."

Henry paused, thinking what their next step would be before going to the Federal Police.

"We may get more out of the feds," he continued. "But at this point I think we stand a better chance going through our embassies and our contacts in Brazil. They may be more effective in getting the authorities to do something."

"And how are we going to do that?"

"Let's find a hotel. It's time to make some calls."

The sun was finally rising when they stepped out of the police station, the city waking up with it. A few businesses were starting to open, and the downtown area began to fill with people.

The visit had not been entirely fruitless. They had left with a copy of the police report, which would help explain the absence of their documents.

They found a small hotel on the town's main avenue, located at the top of a two-story building. The entrance was at the street level, opening on a stairwell to the second floor, where there was a small reception area and dining room facing the street. A hallway led to the few rooms in the back. Most seemed vacant.

The clerk asked for their passports and a cash deposit for the check-in.

"Sorry. We lost our passports in the river." He waved the police report at the woman behind the reception desk.

"And all I have left are Venezuelan bolivares," he continued. "I can pay you now if you'll take it. Or I can give you reais after I have a chance to exchange the money at the bank."

She looked slightly suspicious, choosing the foreign currency *now*.

The rooms were clean and simple, with air-conditioning, Wi-Fi, and a TV, but no phone or hot shower. Other visitors might find strange that a hotel would offer its guests air-conditioning before a hot shower. After living through the average temperatures of the region, Henry found the former far more essential.

With no devices to get online, Henry and Clare would

have to wait for the internet café nearby to open a little later. They spent the rest of the morning on the phone, placing collect calls from the handset at the reception desk. They decided against using the cell phone they had found in the stolen backpack. Depending on the resources their pursuers had at their disposal, the signal could be tracked to locate the two fugitives. Henry took out the battery, storing the device to use only in case of emergency.

He chose to not contact his family. He called California instead, waking up his best friend, Chris Ballard. After telling the full story, Henry asked Chris to contact Henry's former PhD advisor, the person who handled the relationship with the Brazilian nonprofit that managed the Pitiri Research Station.

Clare's first call was to her father, in Australia.

"I feel horrible making him worry," she told Henry after the call. "But this is not the type of information to withhold from family."

That was exactly what Henry had just done, but he preferred it that way. There was nothing his parents or sisters could do, so why cause them to worry? He felt he had disappointed them enough in being expelled from his graduate program. The latest events would just show them how low he had sunk.

"Dad wanted to come to Brazil immediately," she continued. "But I asked him not to. I said we are safe back in a city and planning to leave the country before he could arrive anyway."

Clare next called her show's producer, David Baignard, in London. Henry stood next to her, leaning his elbows against the reception counter.

She started to cry as she explained their decision to escape while Aidan Green and Liam Nguyen were likely being held captive, her tears turning to a sob when she told him about Bill Powers. The clerk lurking in the room looked away uncomfortably, pretending not to pay attention.

"David sounded so anxious," Clare reported after the conversation. Her voice trembled as she stared wide eyed at nothing in particular. "He promised to wire some money right away and to do whatever is in his power to get us out of the country safely. He will notify the families at least, so that's one thing we don't have to deal with. And contact some government authorities to ask for help. Oh, and he promised to arrange a plane to take us to Manaus as soon as possible."

Clare and Henry also called the consular services of Australia and the US, respectively. Despite the fact that each embassy had an emergency line, it took a while to reach a live person in both of them.

The American consulate seemed to take the case quite seriously, since Henry was reporting the death of a US citizen. The Americans were the only ones with a consular service in Manaus, and Henry agreed to appear in person once they arrived at the city. They also recommended that Henry contact the Federal Police immediately, providing the address of the local office. At least the officer at the local police station was right about that.

When they were done with all the calls, Henry and Clare went to the internet café two blocks from the hotel. They sent out detailed accounts of their story to several different people, including Fund-Ama's executive director,

Teresa Oliveira, since the foundation was responsible for the operation of the research station. Henry hoped his former advisor would reach out to her directly as well. Perhaps the head of the team he worked for would have more influence, given all the money the university paid for the privilege of using the Pitiri camp.

By the end of the morning, they felt more hopeful. Several people were now aware of what had happened and had promised to do whatever was necessary to help.

Even the Federal Police seemed helpful when Henry and Clare finally managed to visit the local office, before a late lunch. The agent was obviously skeptical of Henry's story, but he did say he would report it to the army, which had a large presence in the region. He also took note of the officers Henry and Clare had contacted at their respective embassies, so he could coordinate with the consulates and keep the pair informed about the investigation.

But despite all the sympathy from multiple corners of the world, Henry and Clare were no closer to finding out what they had run into.

CHAPTER 15

WHEN THEY FINISHED lunch, Henry and Clare walked north, away from the small downtown area. In a few blocks, the street pavement turned to red dirt, and assorted stores gave way to cinder block houses. The better ones were plastered and painted with light colors, mostly blue, yellow, or green, which the harsh climate had worn. The roofs were made with gray sheets of asbestos cement, not the best material for the blazing hot climate, but the cheapest.

Farther into the neighborhood, Henry found the house he was looking for. It had a simple facade, consisting of white metal windows and a front door framed by a light-blue stucco wall.

Finding no doorbell, Henry clapped his hands loudly to announce their presence, prompting a plump, curly-haired woman with small eyes to come to the door. She didn't act surprised at the sight of strangers at the door.

"Oi, só um minuto." *Just a minute,* she said, then

disappeared behind the door. A moment later, a short, muscular young man with the same small eyes came to greet the visitors.

He looked at the two people at his door for a few seconds before finally placing one of them.

"Henry, yes?"

"Right. We met on the boat from Manaus. It's been a while." He turned to his companion and introduced her. "This is my friend Clare."

"Yes, of course. I remember that trip. Nice to meet you, Clare. I'm Marcos. Please come in." He spoke with a strong accent, but his English was otherwise good, better than when Henry had met him, perhaps from practicing as an adventure-tourism guide with his foreign clients. Marcos let the pair into the small living room, leading them through an opened back door to the backyard and pointing to a handmade wooden bench.

"So, you finally decided to climb the Pico?" he asked with a grin, referring to Brazil's highest mountain. "I can help with all the arrangements, even the permits to enter the reserve."

The expression on Henry's and Clare's faces answered before they spoke.

"We would love to, but we're not here for pleasure," Henry said.

Marcos frowned, his friendly smile vanishing.

Henry paused, thinking how to say what he needed to. He decided to be direct.

"We're in trouble. I was hoping you could help us understand something that went down a couple of days ago near the research station where I was working. Do you remember that I told you I was going to join a project up the Içana River?"

Marcos nodded as he crossed his arms, waiting for Henry to continue.

Henry was brief and honest. He did not hide anything except for the same information he had omitted in his report to the police, mostly because he didn't think it was relevant.

Marcos listened without asking questions, staying silent when the account was finished. Henry was hoping the Brazilian would be more sympathetic, but the reaction was muted. He thought he likely would not have reacted any differently himself under the same circumstances.

He gave Marcos a few moments to process what he had just heard. Marcos looked puzzled, and Henry realized he had unloaded a lot on the man across from him.

"We have so many questions," Henry continued, breaking the silence. "I thought that with your experience in the army and knowing the region so well, you may be able to provide some answers. Someone killed our friend and tried to kill us."

"And kidnapped two others," Clare completed.

"I'm very sorry for what happened," Marcos finally said. "But I'm not sure how I can help you." Marcos's voice had a tone of sympathy and confusion.

"We think you can help us understand what's going on. You know the region. I realize it is still a lot to ask, but we have no one else to turn to," Henry pleaded.

"That was a big operation we saw out there," Clare jumped in. "Guys in military fatigues, automatic weapons . . . Clearly, it is something not only important but illegal, or they would not have gone through the trouble of trying to kill us. I can't imagine the people who live around here never heard about anything of this magnitude," she concluded, though in reality she probably had no idea what people in the area would and wouldn't know about.

"You guys have to understand something," Marcos started to answer. "This is one of the most isolated regions in the world. The jungle is a mystery and the perfect hideaway for all sorts of activities. Everyone here knows or thinks they know something odd is going on. There are lots of strange characters and suspicious activities all around.

"But whatever happens out in the jungle has nothing to do with the people who live there. Or here. We're just innocent bystanders. If you are asking if I know of anything specific happening up there, the answer is no. I doubt anyone here would, unless they are directly involved. But is there *something* going on? No doubt about it. We are near the border of three countries. Smuggling, drug trafficking, gold mining, logging, illegal extraction of minerals and other resources, I'm sure all of this happens on a regular basis. But no one here thinks it's any of their business. I certainly don't. Even if I wanted to inquire into every rumor I hear—and trust me, I don't—no one would know or say a thing.

"Every now and then the Federal Police will mount an operation and dismantle some illegal activity not too far from here. They arrest some people, it makes the national news, and a few months later it's all back to normal. And someone else takes the place of the people who were arrested, assuming they were in fact convicted and didn't return to it themselves in the first place."

"So you never heard of anything strange going on at the old iron mine?" Henry asked.

"I've heard of plenty of strange things going on everywhere. Drugs, illegal mining, UFO landings, the giant anaconda who ate a VW Beetle, the giant sloth . . . There are countless rumors and legends. No one can make sense of what's real and what's not. Did you know there's a widely accepted theory that the American government has mining operations in the Amazon, secretly stealing precious minerals right under our noses? One version I heard mentioned invisible planes hauling all the stuff out."

Marcos let out a nervous laugh at the absurdity of his last sentence before continuing.

"Some people believe Americans and Europeans kidnap our children to harvest body organs. Some other rumors are probably true, like drug operations and guerrilla incursions from Colombia. If you ask enough people, you'll hear any possible conspiracy theory you can imagine, from alien spaceports to secret military operations. It becomes background noise. And even if people believe some of this, no one is dumb enough to ask questions. The worse it sounds, the less you want to know about it."

The young guide's account was not inconsistent with what Henry knew about the region. "Could the Brazilian military be involved?" he asked.

Marcos looked surprised at the question. He stared at the sky, past Henry and Clare, taking a moment to reply.

"I don't think so. There may be corruption in the military, like anywhere else, but everyone I ever met there is very patriotic. I believe they would draw the line on having a foreign military operating in the country. I doubt that they would be actively involved in something like this."

Marcos looked thoughtful for a moment, and neither Henry nor Clare interjected.

"You know," he continued, "now that I've had some time to think about it, I wouldn't be surprised if you had bumped into a guerrilla group from Colombia hiding in the jungle."

Henry knew about the guerrillas. Colombian communist rebels were in a decades-old fight against the government. The Colombian military had managed to expel them from all but the most remote regions of the country. They were safer in Venezuela, where the local regime gave them refuge, but those groups sometimes made incursions into Brazil as well. He wondered whether they could be receiving support from the Venezuelan army, which would explain the military ID card they had found in the stolen backpack.

The theory seemed plausible.

"I'm sorry about all of it," Marcos repeated, trying to wrap up the conversation. "But there really isn't anything more I can tell you. It seems like you guys already contacted everyone you could. The only people that can help you are the Federal Police."

There it was again. All paths led to the Brazilian feds.

"Can we trust them?" Henry asked.

The answer was preceded by a discouraging wince.

"Maybe. If this is being done without their knowledge, they will probably intervene. But this is Brazil. They could have been paid off or told to look the other way.

Some people in the government are sympathetic to the Colombian rebels."

Henry's heart sank. He was hoping for a more positive endorsement. Everybody they had talked to, from the local police to their own embassies, had seemed to put his and Clare's fate in the hands of Brazil's federal agents.

He decided he had learned everything he could from Marcos. Perhaps they would have better luck looking for answers in Manaus, where Henry's colleagues at Fund-Ama were bound to have connections in the Brazilian government.

"Sorry to bother you with this, Marcos. Someone we know was murdered, and two others may be either missing or being held captive. My friends from the research station are in danger as well. We are desperate for help and don't have anyone else to go to."

"I understand," the guide said, reaching to shake Henry's hand and then stopping, as if trying to make up his mind about something.

"Perhaps there is one thing I can try to do for you."

Henry said nothing, waiting for Marcos to continue.

"We're not too far from the border, and the army monitors the area quite actively. Like I said, I don't think the military is involved, but it's possible they have detected the presence of the guerrillas and are waiting to act or are negotiating with them. If someone in the army is aware of the operation you mentioned, some people I know may be able to help you."

Henry's eyes lit up.

"Thank you, Marcos. I know this is sensitive. We

would really appreciate any help we can get. Could you put us in touch with them?"

"I have to ask first. But I think it's worth sharing this information with someone in the army, anyway. How long are you here for?"

"We hope to go to Manaus as soon as possible."

Marcos took another pause, seeming to search his brain.

"There is someone I know who used to be stationed here and is now based in Manaus. I can ask him if he would talk to you, but I can't make any promises. He might not know anything about it or feel comfortable talking to an outsider, especially a foreigner. And you have to absolutely promise to keep it a secret."

"No one will ever know about it."

"Give me your email," Marcos said, standing up and indicating the conversation was over. "Look for a message from me when you get to Manaus."

⁓

They waited at the hotel room for news from David Baignard, Clare's producer, who had promised to find a safe way to get them to Manaus.

Henry had blocked the door with a dresser, fitting the hotel Bible tightly under the handle to prevent it from being turned. It may not deter unwanted visitors for long, but it would give them a warning that someone was trying to come in. While they had not seen anything suspicious since arriving at this small town, Henry was determined to leave nothing to chance.

In the mirror, he finally examined his injuries. His jaw

and shoulder were swollen and bruised, but the pain was getting better. To his relief, nothing looked or felt broken.

Clare sat on the bed, playing with her wet hair, finally looking refreshed after the first shower in a week, while Henry peeked out the window again. It didn't provide a good view of the street, but it seemed to give him comfort to look and see no movement.

"Do you think they know we're here?"

"No idea," he replied. "But it's good to assume they do. We don't exactly blend in. The vast majority of people in this town are of indigenous descent. If whoever came after us has contacts here, they will learn we are around sooner or later. Besides, this is pretty much the only way out of the area; it's not hard to guess we would have to go through here."

His mind was still racing, trying to piece things together.

"I've been trying to figure this out," he said without taking his eyes off the street. "They were too organized for gold diggers, too militarized for a company digging precious ores, too quick to shoot for the army . . . I think Marcos's suggestion that they are a guerrilla unit makes sense. But these groups don't usually kill people straight away; they prefer to kidnap foreigners to make a political point and ask for a ransom."

"Maybe they can't afford to kidnap us because it would reveal they are operating in Brazil. Or maybe that's what they intended to do before we ran away," Clare argued.

"True. A rebel group from Colombia seems plausible. But why were they carrying Venezuelan money and ID?"

"Perhaps that's who's training them? We know one

soldier was from that country, because of his ID, but it doesn't mean most of the others were. That alone might be enough reason to try to kill us," Clare said.

"The Venezuelan army training Colombian rebels may be enough to bring the two countries to war. And that could be the very same reason why they are operating in Brazil. It gives the Venezuelan government plausible deniability. They can claim it's just a rogue faction of their military."

He paused. "But what about the iron mine? Is it just a coincidence they are there? I can't say for sure that they were actually mining anything based on what we saw, but it's strange they would pick that place," he concluded. "And all that equipment . . ."

Clare did not reply, and Henry let that thought hang in the air, starting to set up a hammock so he could lie down and rest. Many people in the region were not used to beds, preferring to sleep sunken in a hammock's soft fabric, rocking gently through the night. The hotel rooms in the region had hooks on the walls and provided a hammock free of charge, just like bedsheets, though most guests brought their own. Henry didn't mind sleeping this way, letting Clare have the bed.

He glanced at her before lying down to rest his eyes. She was leaning back on a pillow against the wall, her legs stretched, feet crossed, with her hands resting on the bedcover, alongside her body. She stared blankly at the wall.

"What do you think is going to happen to Aidan and Liam?" she blurted out. "Do you think they are okay?"

"I wish I knew," he replied as she pressed her lips together, holding her breath. "If by 'okay' you mean alive, then yes, I think they are. They're worth more alive than dead, especially when we are on the loose. There's a chance the soldiers did not connect them to us, but I doubt it.

"They must be scared, for sure. But the good news is that we set a lot of things in motion today. Three different governments, our research partners . . . Hopefully, the Federal Police will be on the case as well. We can also count on the director of Fund-Ama. From what I hear, she's quite well connected and influential.

"We'll do everything we can to help them, Clare." He looked her directly in the eye, hoping it would give her some comfort.

She grimaced and shut her eyelids tightly in what seemed an attempt to suppress tears. Then her face relaxed and she nodded, looking a little more hopeful.

He approached slowly and sat at the end of the bed, folding his left leg and resting his knee on the soft mattress so he could face her. He sunk more than he expected, slightly losing his balance and causing her to smile.

She watched him with curiosity and gave a short grin. They stared at each other for a few seconds while Henry thought of something to say.

"This mattress is really soft," he noted as he looked down, not able to hold her gaze and trying to lighten the mood. "I'm glad I let you take the bed."

"Aren't you the gentleman."

Henry could smell the cheap hotel shampoo coming from her hair. He wanted to comfort her but was lost for what to say next. He couldn't help noting, despite the circumstances, that she looked better without the makeup and all the production for the camera. Henry's lips moved, meaning to tell her she looked nice, but he held back, afraid of giving her the wrong idea.

"What?" she asked when he didn't say anything.

"Nothing. It's just good to see you smile a little."

"Thanks. And by the way, thank you."

He leaned his head to the side, confused.

"For all you did, Henry. I don't know what I would have done without you."

He had been improvising all that time, of course. They had managed to escape out of dumb luck more than anything else, but it felt good to know his efforts were appreciated.

"It takes two. I couldn't have done it alone. As I recall, I couldn't even turn the boat engine on."

"You seem to be so familiar with the forest. You walk through it like you have known it all your life. How long have you been in the Amazon?"

"Almost two years now."

"What made you so interested in it?"

"I've been in love with the rain forest ever since I was a kid," he answered, looking back to his childhood. "I don't know why, exactly. It was in the news a lot when I was growing up. Later on, in high school, my biology teacher saw my interest and encouraged me to pursue it. She showed me books, articles, documentaries . . . The more I learned about it, the more fascinated I was. How big it was, the isolation, the lost tribes, the exotic appeal— that's all I could think about. Everyone else wanted to be rich, a celebrity, or both. Me, I dreamed of becoming a jungle explorer."

"And you did."

He had never seen it like that, but Clare was right. With all the setbacks in his career, at the end of the day he was still exactly what he had sought to be. It made him feel better about how things had turned out for him.

"It's nice you found a teacher that took the time to help you with your passion."

He smiled, fondly remembering Mrs. Ruiz.

"Yes, she was a big influence on me."

He was about to ask how she had gotten into her line of work when he saw Clare's expression change. He had lost her. The small talk could only distract her from reality for so long.

"Do you think things will ever go back to normal?" she asked, her eyes breaking contact with his.

"I don't think we'll ever forget this. But yeah, we'll put our lives back together." He moved a little closer and continued. "Not that it'll be quick or easy. Or feel as if nothing ever happened. But we'll get through this. Eventually this craving that we have for exploration will overcome our fears and regrets, and we'll be back in our game, only wiser. We have to. We owe it to Bill to make our lives worthy of being spared the fate that could just as easily have been ours."

She was looking back at him now, leaning her head to the side with a sad smile. He could tell that his words resonated with her. The same purpose that drove her to this part of the planet in the first place would define her, not the bad experiences of the past few days. They seemed to be wired the same way.

Her left hand inched slightly toward him, hesitantly. He moved forward, seizing it with a comforting smile.

Then they heard a loud knock on the door. The hotel clerk announced there was a call for Clare.

A plane was waiting for them at the airport.

CHAPTER 16

ENRY'S BODY RELAXED after a warm shower, and he felt safe in the comfort of the hotel room where they had registered under fake names following the two-hour flight from São Gabriel. He was barely conscious when he let his body fall facedown on the mattress, stretched diagonally from one corner of the bed to the opposite.

But it was far from a soothing night.

As his breathing slowed and his mind started to wander, disengaging from the filters of his consciousness, random thoughts and images came in and out confusingly, blending reality and wishful fantasies.

He relived the moment when he and his two companions were surrounded by armed men, the time they were escorted into the tent, and the escape after attacking two soldiers. The faces on the soldiers that held them captive were familiar to him but did not match anyone he recognized from real life.

Powers was bleeding in Henry's arms, still alive. They had somehow managed to save him despite the gaping exit wound on his chest. Henry and Clare had personally brought Bill safely back to his parents' home, to recover from his injury, on a perfect summer day with no clouds in the sky.

It seemed so real, yet even in his sleep he knew that the scenes playing in his head were imagined, which made it all the more heartbreaking because he wanted so badly for them to be true.

The phone rang with their wake-up call at eight o'clock sharp. It took several rings for Henry to realize that the noise was not part of his dream. He felt more tired than before he had gone to bed about seven hours before.

Lying in the bed next to his, Clare struggled to get up, looking equally exhausted.

After they ordered room service, the strong coffee and the anticipation of the day slowly energized them.

Clare called her producer, David Baignard, the only person who knew where they were staying. He had consulted with lawyers and British authorities after hanging up with her the previous day and now passed on the advice to go straight to the American consulate and then the police.

But Henry disagreed. Their first experience with the police had not been exactly encouraging. And he wanted to talk to someone who knew the region and the lay of the land, not to a foreign official. That meant going to see Teresa Oliveira.

He had met her only briefly, a stocky woman with large, round eyes and short, curly hair. She came across as bright and straightforward, despite an air of arrogance. But she had a reputation for getting things done. Running an isolated research station in the jungle was matched in difficulty only by the challenges of overcoming the Brazilian bureaucracy. Henry knew her to be well connected and thought she would be in a much better position to help them than would some international bureaucrat who rotated from post to post every couple of years.

Clare didn't need much convincing to go see Oliveira that morning, so Henry set up an appointment with the consular service for after lunch. Since they had already filed two police reports, meeting with Brazilian law enforcement could wait until later in the afternoon, when they hoped to get an update on the progress of the investigation.

Hailing a cab on the street, Henry and Clare jumped into an old, white Gol, a compact model that had been a best-selling car in Brazil years before. The driver took them down a wide southbound avenue that linked the airport to the downtown area.

Henry recognized some of the sights from his previous visit, including the city's soccer stadium, where the demolition work had started for the construction of a brand-new arena for the upcoming FIFA World Cup.

A few minutes after the car turned left on a meandering four-lane road, they passed the Brazilian Institute of Amazon Studies, a prestigious government-funded local research center and graduate school commonly referred to by the acronym "IBEA."

Henry remembered the days he had spent there with one of their scientists.

Before embarking on the boat for his trip up the river to São Gabriel da Cachoeira, he had come to the institute to see Professor Egberto Rossi, one of his research team's frequent collaborators.

What was supposed to have been a short courtesy visit had turned into a budding friendship between the American PhD candidate and the old Brazilian scientist. They had hit it off immediately, engaging in an hours-long exchange on Amazonian culture, politics, and the nitty-gritty of the latest tropical ecology research.

They had ended up having dinner together the same day they met, and Henry had come back to see him almost every day until leaving for the research station. He had been not just elated by the IBEA researcher's insights but also stunned by his generosity. Many academic research-ers were so competitive that they were reluctant to share ideas, but the professor had been just the opposite. Henry had left Manaus thankful and full of new thoughts for his PhD dissertation.

Months later, when he was detained for trying to smuggle research samples out of Brazil and expelled from graduate school, the professor had been one of the few who stood by him. A close friend of Henry's advisor, Rossi had helped the disgraced student find an alternative career as a research assistant at the Pitiri Station. Henry would no longer be able to get his PhD degree; but thanks to the professor, he was able to continue doing the work he loved, even if the credit would go to his colleagues and former advisor at the university.

The ride was taking longer than anticipated, and Henry thought the driver was trying to take advantage of them until he learned they had to take a detour because some of the streets were blocked in anticipation of a student protest planned for later that day.

He knew they were close to the foundation's office when the taxi passed a small shopping mall and made a left into a middle-class residential neighborhood. The houses were fenced by tall brick walls covered with glass shards or electrified wires, the front gates all that were visible on most of the residences.

They approached a two-storied house, indistinguishable from the rest except for a large sign on the front gate in both Portuguese and English:

Fund-Ama

*Fundação Augusto Selbach Para o
Desenvolvimento Sustentável da Amazônia*

Augusto Selbach Foundation for the
Sustainable Development of the Amazon

The foundation was named after a Brazilian biologist who had been a pioneer of Amazon research and exploration in the nineteenth century. "Fund-Ama" was a clever play on words, "Fund" being a shortened form of the Portuguese for *foundation* and "Ama" representing both *Amazon* and a word meaning *he or she loves*.

They arrived unannounced, pressing the intercom

next to the front gate to gain access to the building. The foundation's boss was in an emergency staff meeting, and the young woman who sat at the reception desk said she could not interrupt it.

"Tell her Henry Foster from the Pitiri Station is here," Henry insisted. "Trust me, she'll want to see us."

The receptionist looked unsure but didn't have a response to Henry. She stood up and walked around her desk, toward the stairs that led to the second floor, with the reluctant look of someone who is afraid to irritate her boss.

She came back a minute later, her face a bit more relaxed.

"You can go up," the receptionist said. "You know where her office is?"

Henry nodded.

They saw four people filing out of Oliveira's office as they headed for it. She stood up from her desk as they entered.

"Please sit down," she said with a stern look, skipping the pleasantries.

They took the two chairs across her desk while Oliveira closed the door to the office so the three of them would be undisturbed.

"How are you two doing?" she asked as she sat, going on to say how relieved she was, after hearing of the attack, to see them unharmed and thanking Henry for his email with the account of their ordeal. Her accent was heavy, but her English was correct and confident.

"We are physically okay, thankfully, but quite shaken,"

Clare responded. "Do you have any news about Aidan and Liam?"

Oliveira inhaled deeply and took a moment to respond. Henry knew it was not good news.

"Your colleagues are missing," she replied. "Marcelo, our camp manager, radioed me yesterday, after the attackers left. Your two friends were unharmed, according to him, but they were taken."

Clare covered her mouth in alarm.

"Wait," Henry said as he did the math in his head. "The attackers stayed at Pitiri for two days?"

Oliveira paused, seemingly trying to set the timeline straight in her head.

"That sounds about right," she replied. "Perhaps they were waiting until yesterday for you to return."

Clare looked down, and Henry put his hand on her shoulder. Their faint hope that the soldiers would not connect Aidan and Liam to the trio captured at the mine had been crushed.

"Is everybody else okay?" Henry asked, thinking of his colleagues at the station.

"Yes, they are fine. They are a little—how did you put it?" she asked rhetorically, looking at Clare, "—physically okay but shaken."

"That's good news at least," Henry said. "How about Bill Powers? Did anyone find him?"

"Who?"

"The American, the one who was . . ." Henry paused, gathering the strength to finish his sentence.

". . . killed."

"Oh, of course," the Fund-Ama executive director replied, disconcerted.

"Did they find him?" Henry insisted.

"The Federal Police arrived at the site only last evening. I'm sure they will have some information on that soon."

Clare started to cry. "I'm sorry," she said. "He was a good friend . . . We saw him die right in front of us . . ." Her voice trailed off at the end of her sentence.

Henry moved his hand to hold her arm, saying nothing. Oliveira paused to give Clare a moment.

Henry looked around, letting Clare recover, and noticed the empty desk that belonged to Oliveira's deputy, with whom she shared the room filled with packed bookshelves and gray metal filing cabinets. The few wall spaces left were covered with dusty maps of the Amazon and posters illustrating the region's main mammal and bird species.

"Who *are* these people we met at the mine?" Clare blurted out, wiping tears with the back of her hand.

"I don't know. That's a very remote region, and the police have no regular presence there. *Some* criminal activity in the general area is to be expected, but certainly not at any of the sites you visited, and nothing of this magnitude. We have been operating there for several years without any incident."

The executive director looked pensive for a moment and then continued.

"Why don't we take a step back and you tell me what happened? I read Henry's email, but it would be good to hear you tell me."

Henry and Clare leaned back on their chairs and

alternated in retelling the whole story in detail, from the decision to visit the old iron-ore mine to their arrival in São Gabriel da Cachoeira. This time they left nothing out except for the conversation with Marcos, not because they didn't trust Oliveira, but to keep their promise to the young Brazilian to not tell anyone about their meeting.

They spent an hour going over the details. Oliveira had many questions, some uncomfortable, some that seemed unrelated, but Henry appreciated her thoroughness. Oliveira appeared to challenge them at times, and he was okay with that, thinking she had the right to be skeptical. It was what good scientists did.

When pressed for her theories about what was going on, Oliveira sounded remarkably like Marcos had on the day before. She had not talked to any authorities, she said, so she didn't know any details about what could be going on in that part of the jungle. There were far too many stories and conspiracy theories for anyone to care about them, and many people were reluctant to probe beyond the surface in case the rumors were true.

At the end of their account, they shared their idea that they may have run into a camp of Colombian rebels.

"That's possible." Oliveira nodded, though she didn't seem fully convinced. "They could have found some old structures and made camp there."

It was still the most plausible explanation, based on what they knew, though instinctively it didn't sit well with Henry.

"Back to your missing colleagues," she continued, changing the topic. "The Federal Police will be looking for them. I have some friends in the government, and

I'll talk to them. As bad as politicians are, they can be useful sometimes."

Henry noted a hint of satisfaction when she mentioned her connections, but he didn't mind. He was counting on that. It was the reason they had come to see her before the consulate or the police.

"This is a delicate question," Henry said with some reluctance in his voice. "But we came to you because we thought we could get an honest answer."

"Go on?" Oliveira replied with an intrigued look.

"Can we trust the police?" he asked tentatively. "I know this may sound obnoxious coming from a foreigner, but I'd be lying if I said we didn't have a few concerns on that front."

She smiled, seeming relieved.

"That's not so offensive, and it is a question we Brazilians ourselves ask often. I can tell you from experience that they can be quite competent when they want to, especially the Federal Police. And I will make sure this is the case. I'll share all you told me with the people I know in the government."

Henry felt more confident as the conversation wound down. As he hoped, Oliveira and her connections could help them get to the bottom of the story.

"Here's my cell phone," Oliveira said as they got ready to get up and leave, writing the number on the back of her business card. "Call me day or night if you need anything."

"Thanks again," Henry said sincerely.

"I'll make some calls this afternoon. How do I get in touch with you?"

"Email, I guess," Henry replied. "Or call the hotel."

They still had the cell phone from the stolen backpack but were reluctant to turn it on, afraid it could be used to trace their location.

"We left everything back at the camp. We will buy some prepaid cell phones after we get back to the hotel, when we find some time," Clare explained.

She grabbed a piece of paper and wrote down the hotel name and their room number for Oliveira.

"I'll send you an email if I hear anything. I don't expect to have any answers before tomorrow. Things move slowly with the government, and they are rightfully reluctant to share information about this sort of thing, but I'll try to find out exactly what they have learned so far."

She stood up and called the receptionist downstairs, telling her to have the foundation's driver take the pair back to the hotel.

❧

The trip back took twice as long as the drive to Fund-Ama had. Traffic was getting worse, the driver explained, as the students started to gather for their protest.

They entered the hotel lobby and were walking toward the elevator when they heard their names being called.

Two men approached at a hurried pace.

"Mr. Henry Foster and Ms. Clare Andersen?" one of them asked in Portuguese. "We are with the police. You need to come with us."

He showed his identification and badge, with the heading *Polícia Civil* in large capital letters above an elaborate emblem surrounded by a background of vertical blue, red, and white stripes. At a little over five feet, the officers were several inches shorter than Henry. The one talking looked older than his colleague, with a balding head and predominantly dark, but graying, hair. The other officer had a thickset frame and a square, weather-beaten face.

"Oh, hello," Henry replied, pleased to see that they were working on the case. "We have an appointment with the consulate in about one hour but are planning to come see you this afternoon to follow up on the report we filed in São Gabriel da Cachoeira. Is there any news on the case?"

"Mr. Foster, you need to come with us," the man repeated.

"Look, I appreciate that, but they will be waiting for us at the—"

"If you don't come willingly, we will make you come by force," the second officer interrupted aggressively, raising his voice and drawing the attention of the people around.

"Are we under arrest?" Henry asked, incredulous.

CHAPTER 17

THEY SAT IN what appeared to be an interrogation room at the police station. The walls were covered by white ceramic tiles and the floor by those of garnet red. It reminded Henry of a butcher's shop. Not an encouraging thought.

Their only connection to the outside was an awning window at the top of the wall behind them, wide but with a height that made the opening too narrow for a person to go through.

"What do they want?" Clare asked.

"I don't know," Henry replied. "I'm hoping this is part of their investigation into what happened at the reserve. Maybe it's a sign they are taking it seriously."

"It doesn't feel like it."

She was right. It seemed too optimistic to look at it that way, seeing how they had been brought in.

The way the two of them had been approached at the hotel was odd, but they had not been handcuffed or separated. Nor had they been informed of their right to a lawyer. But then, who knew what the law in Brazil was in that regard?

The two police officers who had picked them up came into the room.

They were followed by a tall man with short, curly hair. He had a large build, looking even more substantial next to the two short law-enforcement officers. His eyes were wide, and his lips seemed disproportionately big, but what drew Henry's attention was the red and wrinkling skin of someone who did not have the right complexion for the tropics.

The officers stopped and stood by the door while the tall man approached, addressing Henry and Clare in English.

"My name is Angelo Knowles. I'm with the US Consulate."

"Oh, thank God. You have no idea—"

Knowles continued, not letting Clare finish.

"I presume you are Henry Foster and Clare Andersen?"

They both nodded, feeling buoyed by the visit of the American official. But when he spoke, the floor vanished from underneath them.

"I am here because the Brazilian government is conducting an investigation involving the two of you. You are suspects in a murder case."

His abrupt and cold delivery hit them like a brick. Henry held tight to the table, afraid of losing his balance even though he was sitting down. *Murder?* He couldn't wrap his mind around it, like a bizarre dream where nothing made sense.

"What?" Clare cried in outrage.

As if having been chased down by thugs and almost killed was not bad enough, they were now being confronted by the very people who were responsible for protecting them.

"Is this a joke? We have been—"

"Ma'am," Knowles interrupted calmly, "I'm just relaying the news the local authorities gave me."

She didn't hear him. They spoke at the same time, past each other.

"—going through hell, and instead of coming here to *help* us, all you can do is stand there and say we are accused of murder? Did you even stop to think how ridiculous this sounds?"

She was shouting, her frustration palpable. Henry was grateful one of the two of them had the wits to fight back, but the diplomat remained unmoved. Henry guessed he had dealt with many Americans in trouble with the law in a foreign country. Most protested their innocence. Most were invariably guilty.

"I *am* trying to help, ma'am," Knowles answered, unable to hide his condescension or perhaps deliberately showing it.

She shot Henry a *can-you-believe-this-guy* kind of look and threw her hands in the air, giving up protest.

"I'm not here to represent you or provide legal advice. The police contacted the American consulate as a courtesy. My role is to check if you are being treated fairly and to explain how the judicial process works in this country. I can also provide you a list of lawyers. I recommend that you hire one."

"Are we under arrest?" Henry asked, finally able to speak after recovering from the news.

"No. Not yet, anyway. They are officially investigating you in connection with a homicide and smaller charges."

"What homicide?" he asked, terrified he knew the answer.

"I'll explain in a moment." Knowles turned again to Clare. "The police also contacted the Australian consulate, and they can provide support to you along the same lines that I described. In the meantime, I was asked to explain the charges and the process to you, since the Australian consulate has no representation in Manaus."

"Sir," she said tersely, "thank you for being here." There was more than a hint of derision in her voice. "But it's hard to believe you are not aware of how preposterous this accusation is. Henry called the consular service yesterday and talked to one of your colleagues. They have our whole story. I'll be glad to repeat it all to you."

"There is no need for that," he responded. "Like I said, I'm not in a position to help beyond explaining the potential charges against you and seeing that you are being treated according to the law. It's the police you need to talk to. You are currently in the custody of the local police. They detained you on behalf of the Federal Police, who have the lead in the investigation. The local officers are waiting for the federal agents to arrive with a translator so they can interview you."

Americans who were arrested in the Amazon were usually involved in drug charges, some minor, like possession, others more serious, involving trafficking. But murder charges were rare.

The backgrounds of suspects varied. Most often they were career criminals or middle-class youngsters seeking adventure. The reactions of the latter were not unlike Clare's outrage and protests of innocence and were followed by their claims of being set up, then by acceptance and a realization that the situation they were in was deadly serious.

Then they got scared, pleaded for mercy or help, and demanded special treatment for being an American citizen. That always backfired. The police did not like to be seen as soft on foreigners, and prejudice against Americans ran deep in Brazil.

Career criminals dealt with the arrest a lot better. The country's judicial system being messy and prone to bribery, many escaped or managed to be cleared after a long process.

Knowles opened a manila folder he carried with him and checked something before addressing Henry.

"You said on the phone that Mr. William Powers was shot while you two were approaching a building at a research camp at the Alto Rio Negro Indigenous Reserve, is that correct?"

"Yes," Henry confirmed.

"According to the police, earlier this morning they received some communication claiming that the two of you . . ." He paused, probably thinking about the best way to put it without generating another outburst from Clare.

". . . are responsible for his death."

"What?" she cried out again, standing up. She turned to Henry with another look of disbelief in her eyes, as if the only logical explanation was that they were the victims of an elaborate prank.

"That's what the police have told me."

She took a deep breath and sat down, throwing her hands up in the air again. She must have decided, like Henry, that Knowles wasn't going to be of much help.

Following the accusation, Henry had been numb, in a state of utter disbelief, but Clare's outburst helped him snap out of it. He put his hand on her shoulder, pulling her gently toward him and placing his left arm around her back.

He then faced Knowles, letting out a nervous chuckle as he spoke.

"Does any of this make sense to you?" he asked with disarming sincerity. "Don't any of these accusations strike you as odd?"

"Mr. Foster," Knowles said more sympathetically, "I know it is frustrating for you, but this is a local police matter. I don't know the answer to any of your questions. Neither I nor anyone at the consulate or the American embassy has the authority to intervene. All I can do for you is recommend a good lawyer and contact family members on your behalf. I will of course follow your case. If at any time we believe due process is not being followed, we will communicate that to the proper authorities."

None of it was reassuring. Henry realized that the US government would be useless.

"Leaving this aside for a moment, what are you doing about Aidan Green and Liam Nguyen? Do you have any news about them?"

Clare sat up straight at the mention of their names.

"No. The police did not mention anything about them. Since they are not American citizens, upon receiving your call we passed the information to their respective embassies and will collaborate with them in trying to locate their whereabouts."

"What happens now?" Henry asked with resignation.

"They can detain you for up to five days, with an additional five-day extension possible. Seeing as you are suspected of a serious crime and can be considered a flight risk, they are likely to request preventive detention, and I believe a judge would grant it."

"I take it we are not going back to the hotel today then?"

Knowles opened his mouth to respond, probably another inane line about being there only to check whether they were being well treated, when a woman came through the door, interrupting before he could speak.

She looked to be in her forties and was heavyset, but strong, not fat. Henry watched as the two police officers by the door deferred to her, concluding that she was in charge. A woman leading a police precinct was unusual but by no means unheard of in Brazil.

She approached the consular officer and the two policemen and said something outside Henry's earshot. Knowles raised his eyebrows as he listened, but Henry couldn't read his expression to determine if it was good or bad news. The boss then left with the two officers, and Knowles turned to Henry and Clare, who were staring at him, waiting to hear about what had just happened.

"Mr. Foster and Ms. Andersen, the officer in charge has just informed me that they are taking you to the Federal Police building. They can't get a translator here today, so they are transferring you there, where they have people who are fluent in English."

Henry's stomach sank further, and he got shaky again. The first thought he had was that if the cops were connected to the conspiracy he and Clare had discovered, the police building may not be their destination.

"How can you be sure they are not taking us somewhere else?" he asked with tangible fear in his voice.

"Mr. Foster, this is routine. You are just going from one police station to another. If anything, the Federal Police are more professional and can handle the investigation better."

Henry insisted: "Isn't the US government at least responsible for making sure we are safe? Given everything that's happening to us, I wouldn't be surprised if they take us back to the jungle to kill us. Can you at least come with us to make sure they are actually taking us to where they say they are?"

Knowles's condescending demeanor returned in full display.

"It was the police who contacted the US Consulate. If they want to take you anywhere other than to the Federal Police building, they would not have brought you here in the first place, giving you a chance to talk to me and alerting the US authorities that you two are under police custody. Brazil is hardly a perfect country, but it's not entirely devoid of due process and accountability."

The foreign service officer had a point. It seemed more likely that the policemen were pawns in a bigger game. Whoever was behind the operation in the jungle may be feeding false information to the police in order to find them.

"Just one last question," Henry said to Knowles.

"Everyone we've asked has told us that the Polícia Civil has no authority over this case. So why were we picked up by the civil police instead of the federal?"

"That I don't know," Knowles stated matter-of-factly. "But the two forces can work together on a case."

The answer was far from satisfactory. When they went to the local police in São Gabriel da Cachoeira, the officer had wanted nothing to do with them, saying it was outside their jurisdiction. What had prompted the civil police to actively help with the case? He granted that the circumstances were now different, but something smelled fishy.

Knowles walked to the door. Before leaving, he turned to them and provided the last piece of advice.

"You two should get a lawyer. I will send one to you at the Federal Police building."

The thought that they were not about to be executed and buried in the jungle brought Henry a measure of reassurance. All they had to do now was beat murder charges with the deck stacked against them.

CHAPTER 18

THEY WERE HANDCUFFED to each other, Henry's right hand tied to Clare's left.

"Is this really necessary?" Henry had asked in Portuguese. The officer had responded with an almost imperceptible nod, barely acknowledging the question and not meeting Henry's eyes.

A uniformed policeman guided them to the parking lot and into the back of an old Fiat Palio Weekend, a compact station wagon with large red, white, and blue diagonal stripes stretching from the lower front to the back of the car. Those were the colors of the flag of the state of Amazonas, of which Manaus was the capital. The front doors had large blue letters with *Polícia Civil* printed on them.

Steel-mesh barriers separated the back seats from the front of the car and the station wagon's trunk. Henry noticed that the door handles were absent. The doors could be opened only from the outside.

They waited in the back seat while the officers got ready, allowing them an opportunity to talk freely.

"That's just perfect. We are accused of murder now?" Clare asked, looking perplexed.

"It makes sense when you think about it," Henry answered.

"How so? Is this how they, whoever *they* are, cover up what happened?"

"That's what I'm thinking."

She raised her eyebrows and nodded.

"Whoever is behind this, whatever operation they have going on, they can't afford having us expose it. But they know the story will come out. We've already told everything we know to the police, the governments of three countries, and a lot of other people. There's only one thing they can do."

"Take away our credibility," she finished his thought. "Who is going to believe two people who killed their own friend?"

"Exactly. And by contacting the American consulate, they are signaling that their investigation is completely legitimate. Being pursued by a secret military contingent in the middle of the Amazon sounds improbable. It can be easily dismissed as a desperate and far-fetched excuse by two people trying to escape murder charges."

"Oh no," she cried. "They are going to frame us as the psychopath lovers who went on a killing spree!"

Something stirred inside him. He wasn't prepared for being referred to as her lover. Especially not by her.

"How do we fight this?" she asked, not noticing him blush.

"I guess we get the best lawyer we can afford," he replied. "As bad as this looks, we are innocent, after all. We hope the truth prevails at the end."

It wasn't a great answer, but it was the only one they had for now.

"I can see the news flashes already. We're going to be called the Bonnie and Clyde of the Amazon," she said with an air of amused dread.

He smiled.

"So that's how the brain of a journalist works. You are already writing the headlines of our own arrest."

"I suppose." She smiled back. "I hope I'm wrong. But I can see the media being all over a story like this."

Henry knew she was right. And when that story was combined with his previous smuggling charges, their credibility would be in tatters.

◈

A few minutes later they were riding down a busy avenue with two lanes on each side, divided by a concrete median strip. The day was already hot, and the car either did not have air conditioning or the officers chose not to use it. Henry guessed it was the former, seeing how old the car was. The only relief from the heat came from the wind blowing through the front windows.

The same two cops who had picked them up at the hotel were in charge, the one with the balding head and graying dark hair at the wheel. His thickset, square-faced colleague sat in the passenger seat, looking restless.

Henry did not like the nervous demeanor of the younger officer and wondered once again whether the officers could be taking them somewhere other than the police station.

But that would not be a very smart move on their part, he reflected. If someone was really framing him and Clare for murder, killing them in police custody would be a terrible idea. It would give credence to their story, which was already out but could be easily disputed. He was glad they had told what happened to as many people as they could.

The car came to a complete stop. Henry thought nothing of it, assuming it was just a normal traffic light. But the driver smashed his right fist on the dashboard, turning to his colleague and yelling.

"Caramba, é a greve!"

The other officer sighed heavily.

"Esses estudantes de m . . ."

Henry put it together promptly, realizing why the officer had been nervous.

"We seem to have hit a roadblock. There is a student strike ahead of us," he told Clare.

They were in the right lane, hemmed in by cars on all sides except toward the busy sidewalk, where students moved toward the protest while others walked away from it.

Some drivers went crazy with their horns, but the cacophony died down after a couple of minutes, once they resigned themselves to the situation. With no vehicles moving, there was nothing to do but wait.

A few people stepped out of their cars to stretch their legs or to get a glimpse of the protest. The officer turned off the engine to wait it out.

Henry looked anxiously at Clare, seeing an opportunity.

She must have understood he was up to something, because she shook her head quickly from side to side, silently telling him it was a bad idea, whatever he was thinking.

In the front of the car, the two officers looked focused on what was taking place ahead of them.

Having evaded thugs twice in the past few days, Henry's confidence was starting to grow. He had been paying attention to the cops and thought they seemed sloppy, like they were sure the two foreigners would not dare to try to escape.

It was incredibly careless that no one had bothered to consider the protest along the route and that they were being moved without an escort, which confirmed Henry's assessment that these policemen were not the best at their jobs. It seemed hard to believe the police could be so inept, but there was a reason why only one in every twenty homicides in Brazil was ever solved.

He hadn't yet put together a plan but decided they stood a fighting chance if the right opportunity presented itself.

Even if they tried and failed to escape, what did they have to lose? If they were not shot, which seemed like a good assumption with so many people around them, they would be left exactly where they were now. An added charge of attempting to escape might make their situation a little worse, but not by much compared to what they were already facing.

The driver picked up the radio and let the dispatcher know they were stuck in traffic.

Well, at least they did that, he thought. Was he becoming overconfident again, the same hubris that had gotten him in trouble with the Brazilian authorities and the university? It had caused him to be expelled before; maybe it would get him killed this time.

He would find out. Better than spending the rest of his days in a Brazilian jail for a crime he didn't commit.

But first he needed to get Clare on board.

"Hey, it's really hot in here. Can you please open the window?" he asked the officers, in Portuguese. With the car stopped, the heat was, in fact, making it uncomfortable for the two prisoners. It was a reasonable request.

"Be quiet," he heard back.

Clare fired a dirty look at him.

"This is our only chance," he said casually, as if talking about the hot weather, counting on the fact that the officers didn't understand English. The whole reason they were being moved was to get a translator, after all.

"Do you really want to find out how bad the Brazilian jail is? Maybe it's better for women, but the men have to take turns sleeping, because there's not enough room in the cell for everyone to lie down at the same time."

He gave her a moment to think about it, then continued.

"After we get there, they'll separate us. This is our last chance. Who's going to help Aidan and Liam if we are in prison? Time is not on their side."

The officers glanced back impatiently. Henry knew he was making them suspicious.

He studied Clare's reaction and saw her coming around. She looked as he felt, terrified.

"Senhor, please. The woman is not feeling well. At least open *her* window. It's baking hot back here."

Henry was talking to the officer in the passenger seat. The man looked at his partner and shrugged, raising the palms of his hands. The older officer regarded Clare, who did her best impression of a lady in distress, muttering a sad "Por favor."

The officer rolled his eyes, turning the key to activate the battery and opening Clare's window, keeping Henry's shut. It was a small victory, though still not much to go on. Henry decided they needed to bide their time and wait for the officers to be distracted before trying the next move.

He wasn't sure how many minutes had passed as they continued to wait. He could now hear some faint chanting in the distance and guessed the student demonstration was starting.

Inside the car, with the vehicle stopped in the street, the heat was becoming unbearable for the two out-of-towners, though he guessed the officers were used to it. Although they were in a city, this was still the tropical jungle, and the sun felt blazing hot even as the afternoon was coming to an end. He was also thirsty, and that gave him an idea.

"We need water, please. She will faint; it's too hot back here," Henry protested, hoping one of them would leave to fetch a water bottle.

The officers looked at each other again. They were probably thirsty as well.

"You'll have to wait," the driver said firmly.

Henry tried to contain his frustration and judged it

was best not to push his luck. It would be wiser to take a step back and be patient.

As more time elapsed, the traffic did not move an inch. The drivers around them were chatting now. Some had noticed the two prisoners in the back of the police car and stared curiously.

The chanting of a crowd was getting progressively louder, which meant the protesters were marching in their direction.

The officer in charge got the dispatcher on the radio again and this time asked for reinforcements.

There goes our chance, Henry lamented. He needed to do something quickly.

As they heard the protesters get closer, he saw a concerned expression on the officer in the passenger seat. The driver opened his door and stood up outside the car, trying to estimate where the crowd was. His partner did the same, curiosity getting the better of him.

Henry quickly turned to Clare while the officers had their attention on what was happening ahead of them.

"Grab the handle outside the door," he whispered. "Be ready to open the door at my signal."

Clare slowly moved her head in agreement. Her hand trembled as she reached outside the window and felt her way around the surface of the door. She gave Henry a short nod, indicating she had grabbed the handle, then nervously glanced at the cops, who had their backs to the car. She let go of the handle and casually rested her forearm on the window opening, waiting for Henry to give her the go-ahead.

The chanting continued to grow louder. They could

now see the mob approaching. As the protesters came into sight, the officers got back in their seats, causing Henry to wonder whether he and Clare had missed their chance.

She looked at him anxiously. As the two men in the front seats started to close their doors, Henry articulated the word *Now* without voicing it. Clare read his lips and lowered her right hand, finding the handle and pulling it with one motion.

The officers turned as soon as they heard the click of the opening door, noticing the action behind them. Henry pushed Clare out of the car with his right hand, the one attached to her by the handcuffs. They crawled out of the vehicle and fell over on the ground.

Both officers immediately got out of the car. The rear right door gave the two prisoners cover for just enough time to allow Henry to stand up, hastily pulling Clare by the handcuffs to get her off the ground. She groaned in agony as her wrist was jerked around and bore her weight against the steel.

Henry had timed it well. The crowd was just upon them now, moving through the spaces between the cars and the sidewalk. He and Clare would have quickly merged into the sea of people but for the officer in the passenger seat reaching out over the rear door to seize Henry's neck, choking him while the other policeman ran around the front of the car toward the couple. With his stronger arm attached to Clare, Henry couldn't get rid of his attacker. His airway was blocked, and his Adam's apple hurt badly, paralyzing him with pain.

Clare punched the officer hard in the face, causing him to loosen his grip on Henry. Without thinking,

Henry managed to lower his head enough to sink his teeth into his assailant's forearm. Despite being oxygen deprived, he found the strength to bite hard enough to draw blood. The cop screamed in pain, letting Henry go.

Freed from the officer's grip and tasting blood in his mouth, Henry saw the other officer approaching with his revolver in hand.

Clare reacted quickly by pulling Henry away and putting a couple of people between them and the officers.

"Gun!" someone yelled.

One brave protester pushed the officer's arm down, afraid the cop was aiming at the students in the crowd. Another young man joined in, putting both arms around the policeman and immobilizing him.

The attack made the officer accidentally fire his weapon into the ground.

No one was hit, but the sound of the shot turned the panic into mass hysteria. People ran for cover, some hiding behind the cars, a few diving to the ground, others running on top of them. Many were screaming in fear.

The officer with the bleeding arm turned around to help his colleague, waving his badge.

"Polícia, Polícia!" he screamed.

Henry saw him approach the two men holding his partner, but the protesters thought the police were there to arrest them. The officer pleaded with them and loudly tried to explain the situation, pointing to the car and back in the direction of the two fugitives.

When the two officers finally managed to extricate themselves from the mass of angry protesters, Clare and Henry had already disappeared into the crowd.

CHAPTER 19

EVERY TRANSIT BUS in Brazil has a fare collector. The *cobrador* sits in the middle of the vehicle, next to a turnstile. Passengers are required to get on through a rear door, paying for their ride when they move to the front to exit. At the end of each run, a supervisor checks the number of riders that went through the turnstile and matches it to the amount of money collected from the fares.

Henry had taken the bus regularly when he was in the city and had seen a few people just jump over the turnstile, under the indifferent eyes of the cobrador, to avoid the fare. As long as the number of passengers matched the cash in the drawer at the end of a trip, the fare collectors didn't really care.

Their possessions confiscated by the police, with no money and on the run, Henry and Clare were forced to resort to this trick, not without a fair amount of guilt and embarrassment.

"We got robbed," Henry muttered apologetically as they leaped over the turnstile. The fare collector stared humorlessly, noted the handcuffs, and didn't say a word. Folks in this line of work knew better than to raise trouble over money that wasn't theirs. Especially with criminals. The other passengers didn't seem to mind. Most of them had probably seen worse.

Henry and Clare had caught the bus as soon as they saw it coming on a wide avenue, several blocks from the massive confusion they had set off. Traffic was light away from the protest. After riding for about thirty minutes, Henry figured they had gone far enough.

He had no idea what part of town they were in. It was a busy neighborhood, with a mix of small storefronts, businesses, and tall residential buildings. The afternoon was coming to an end, the sun still out but low on the horizon.

Henry took off his shirt and rolled it over his right arm, wrapping it around the handcuffs. Walking around town bare chested wasn't exactly customary, but it wasn't out of line, either, in this balmy city smack in the middle of the tropical rain forest. A little eccentric perhaps, but a shirtless gringo holding hands with a woman would draw far less attention than would a couple in handcuffs.

Clare glanced at Henry's torso. His arms and neck were tanned while his chest and back were not.

"I don't think anyone will notice you don't have a shirt on," she teased him.

He seemed confused for a moment and then smiled, after looking down and seeing the tan lines.

"If anyone does, I'll just say I'm trying to even things out," he replied.

They walked for over a mile, getting some distance from the bus stop, where someone may have called the police after seeing a couple in handcuffs. The sun had now dipped below the horizon. The natural light would soon be gone also.

Henry spotted a small shopping center on the ground level of a commercial building. The stores were modest but inviting—a neighborhood barber shop, a couple of clothing outfitters, and a cell phone retailer. But what drew him in was the unassuming bar and restaurant next to the entrance.

He took Clare with him into the establishment, desperate for some water. Though he no longer tasted the blood in his mouth, he couldn't wait to wash it off. He felt self-conscious without his shirt on but tried to sound nonchalant as he asked for a glass of tap water.

A short man behind the counter obliged.

Henry washed his mouth with the water and spit it out discreetly in his glass.

The place was not busy, with patrons scattered at folding aluminum tables and chairs surrounded by bare ceramic-tiled walls. They were mostly college age, and Henry guessed they must be near a university.

"I don't think coming here was such a great idea," he noted to Clare. "I'm hungry and we have no money. And it doesn't bring us any closer to finding a way out of these," he pointed, dejected, to the handcuffs wrapped in his shirt.

"I'm not so sure about that," she said with a look of amusement, perhaps thinking of the irony of seeing the defeated demeanor of someone who had engineered escapes from armed bandits in the jungle and from the local police.

He detected confidence in her voice too. She scanned the restaurant, watching the young crowd of college students patronizing the place.

A group of four students, three guys and a girl, sat in the corner, drinking beer and smoking, so lost in conversation that they seemed to be the only people who hadn't noticed the two gringos enter.

"Come with me," she commanded, pulling him away without waiting for an answer.

They walked up to the group of friends, who were still oblivious to the tourist-looking pair approaching. The students' playful expressions and laughter hinted at an exciting conversation, similar to those Henry himself would have enjoyed back in his college days, when his whole future and full potential were ahead of him.

"Hey, guys," Clare said with an impish smile.

The conversation at the table stopped suddenly, and the group turned to her.

"Do you speak English?" she asked. Like Henry, she must have experienced that young people were always eager to practice with a native speaker. As ragged and bruised as their appearance was, the two of them still looked more like scruffy tourists than fugitives of the law.

"Yes!" answered one of the boys enthusiastically. One side of his head was clipped short, and the other had long, dark hair. His right eyebrow was pierced by a pin.

"What's *up*?" he asked flirtatiously, prolonging the vowel in the last word.

"Well, we are in a little bit of trouble."

She raised her left hand, lifting Henry's entire arm with it, unwrapping the shirt just enough to show the handcuffs. Her left wrist was bruised from being pulled by Henry just about an hour before.

She had the full attention of the foursome at the table.

"We were, um . . . *studying* in my hotel room . . ."

They all chuckled. Henry hadn't seen her speak like that before. She was entirely charming, and he imagined that, unlike him, she made friends easily.

". . . and we had these on, you know, just as a *joke*. But then my dad showed up earlier than I expected, and we didn't want to . . . give the wrong idea, you know? My dad *really* doesn't like him." She pointed at Henry with her head. "So we had to sneak out before he would see us like this. But I forgot to take the key!"

The four friends looked amusedly at Henry, who had no idea where Clare was going with this but nodded along, reflecting a genuine embarrassment that made their story seem more believable.

"So, you see, now we need to find a way to get these off," she finished, with a pleading, seducing look.

The girl in the group spoke first.

"*Studying*, of course!" She looked at her friends, who were laughing.

"We all use handcuffs for that," said the one with the half-shaved head, in a strong accent.

"I prefer a leash—it's way more fun. I mean, better for *studying*," teased one of the others.

"I'm so glad you guys understand," she joked along. "So . . . do you think you could help us out? Maybe you know someone nearby with some tools that can help us get out of these?"

❧

They walked a few blocks to an apartment building where Rodrigo, one of their four new friends, lived with his parents in a three-bedroom condo on the sixth floor. Unlike in America, unless they went to a school at a different city, young people in Brazil typically stayed with their families until they married or had an established career and could afford a place of their own.

Both parents were at work. The place was empty but for a high-school-age girl so immersed on her smartphone that she didn't acknowledge the arrival of her older brother and his friends beyond a short mumble.

It didn't take long to cut through the metal with the hacksaw Rodrigo took from his father's toolbox, though Henry and Clare did it carefully to avoid cutting their wrists in the process.

Henry was glad to have his hand free and his shirt back on. He was amazed how easy it had been to get help from a handful of kids they had just met at a college hangout. But then he remembered how welcoming and laid back Brazilians were, including those who had helped them a couple of days before, when they had been stranded on the Rio Negro.

He wasn't sure the college students had bought their story, even the one implied behind Clare's original tale. But the four friends didn't seem to care. Henry and Clare weren't exactly threatening, even if they looked disheveled. At worse, their helpers must have assumed the pair had been busted for some minor infraction.

What the college kids lacked in suspicion, they more

than made up for in curiosity. After getting rid of the handcuffs, the two foreigners were bombarded with a succession of questions.

"So where are you from?"

"What brings you to Manaus?"

And it didn't take long for the obvious inquiry about why they were *really* in handcuffs.

Clare did most of the explaining, looking comfortable at small talk and connecting with some of the local people. She said they got caught up in the protest and were handcuffed by the police before running away when some shots were fired. It was all true and yet still a lie. No one could guess what had really happened or had reason to believe they were up to anything worse than what she was telling them.

"Ah yes, the protest near the federal university today," mentioned one of the students. "Traffic must be awful. My parents will probably be late."

"Are you guys hungry?" asked Rodrigo, the young man who lived in the apartment.

He might have offered a million dollars and a ticket home, and Henry still would have preferred the food. He and Clare eagerly feasted on ham and cheese sandwiches with milk, to the amusement of all.

"We were in custody for a while," Clare noted. "The last meal we had was at breakfast."

After the questions died down a bit, Clare asked to use a computer.

"We need to contact some friends before we can sort this mess out," she explained. "The police are holding on to our documents and money."

༅

In his inbox, Henry found several messages but went straight for the one from Marcos, his friend in São Gabriel da Cachoeira.

> Hello Henry,
>
> I was able to connect to my friend. His name is Mauricio and he'll meet you today at 20:00 at the Boi da Floresta. It's a famous tourist hangout spot, it should be easy to find. I hope he has answers for you. Please be careful and discreet. If anything you say is true, his career could be in danger just for meeting with you. Get a table near the bar and he'll recognize you and your friend. Good luck.

Marcos had been careful not to put any details in writing. Henry looked at the watch on the lower right corner of the computer monitor. It showed 19:06.

He quickly scanned his other messages. Things seemed to be escalating quickly, with people from the university and the US government getting involved. He saw a message from his friend Chris Ballard, saying there was some money waiting for him at a local bank and asking Henry to call him. He wanted to read further, but they needed to leave right away if they were to make it to the meeting on time.

Logging out of his email account, Henry got up and walked to the kitchen, where Clare was chatting with their hosts while waiting for her turn to check her messages. She was keeping up the appearance of casual tourists in trouble with the law. Henry imagined that must be exhausting, but she was more of a social animal than he was and seemed at ease conversing with them, perhaps even enjoying herself.

"I'm sorry, but we have to go," he interrupted. "There's somewhere we need to be in less than one hour."

"Where do you have to go?" one of them asked, sounding as though he was trying to help. "Do you have an address?"

Henry froze, not knowing how to answer. He couldn't say where he was going. It could endanger the college students that had been so kind to them, as well as the army officer who may be risking his life and career.

Henry needed to answer promptly to avoid suspicion. Instead, he blanked.

"Is it the consulate, honey?" Clare stared at him, prompting Henry to confirm and finding him a way out before it got too awkward.

"Uh, yes," he said. "We need to go right away. They are closed, but the email said they can still see us if we get there by eight o'clock."

He didn't notice any suspicion about their story. The students even pulled together some cash to cover cab fare and other minor expenses. Amazed by their generosity and Clare's sharpness, Henry thought that he and Clare may well find a way out of this mess after all.

CHAPTER 20

"THANKS FOR RESCUING me earlier," Henry said while they rode in the beat-up compact car ferrying them around the city. "That was impressive today, the way you talked our way out of the cuffs," he continued with admiration.

"We are a good pair," she answered with a broad smile. "You handle the jungle; I handle the talking."

"And we both take on the bad guys. I liked how you punched that cop."

"Did you really bite him?" she asked with a grimace.

"I'm afraid so." He gave her an embarrassed grin.

"I still can't believe how nice and generous those kids were to us," Henry said, changing the subject. "Do you think they were suspicious that we didn't tell the whole story?"

"Maybe. But I don't think they care. I learned never to underestimate the potential for human kindness, especially when it comes to helping someone in need. Besides, they seemed to enjoy the *adventure*." She raised her hands, making air quotes with her fingers as she emphasized the last word. "They will have a great story to tell their friends, which I imagine will be a tad more dramatic than what really happened."

They arrived at the Boi da Floresta with a few minutes to spare. The name meant *forest bull* in Portuguese, a reference to the local festival celebrating a traditional folktale of a slave who, to satisfy his pregnant wife's craving for beef, killed one of his master's bulls. After the slave was arrested, local shamans worked to resuscitate the animal. No one knew exactly how the story had become so ingrained in the Brazilian culture, but there were dozens of versions told all over the country, with matching festivals to commemorate the legend.

The nightclub took up an entire block and was surrounded by eight-foot-tall cinder block walls littered with graffiti. The entrance gate was made of logs, giving it a fake rustic feel. It stood under a giant banner with the place's name and some drawings of a man playing the drums next to two bulls, one red, one blue, plus three women dancing in small bikinis, a reference to the local version of the bull festival.

The banner said Live Music, in English. The place catered to tourists in an obvious way, but the clientele went there for fun, not authenticity, and that they got in spades.

Henry and Clare paid the cover charge and went in. To the left of the entrance was a large stage, with several workers busily setting it up for the coming band and the dancers who would entertain the crowd later on. A long bar counter stood at the opposite side, with tables and a dance floor between the bar and the stage.

It was an outdoor venue, though the stage and the bar were covered by a zinc roof to protect patrons from tropical downpours. Some of the seating areas were sheltered by thatched roofs, adding to the tropical theme, though they did little against the high temperature, which was particularly punishing this evening.

The show wouldn't start until later, but there were already plenty of tourists eating at the tables, trying some of the traditional local food. It included a lot of different fish fresh from the Amazon River, manioc-based dishes, and a variety of fruit from the rain forest.

The pair walked to the bar and ordered a couple of cold sodas to alleviate the heat. Henry got his drink and turned around, leaning with both elbows against the counter and facing the dance floor. The place radiated excitement in anticipation for the show, and Henry thought he would have liked to be here under other circumstances, just to enjoy the party.

He surveyed the area, searching for a young man sitting alone.

"See anything?" asked Clare.

"No," he replied. "Maybe it's best to have a seat and let him find us."

It did not take long. A young man approached their table about twenty minutes after they sat down.

"Are you Henry and Clare?" he asked.

"Yes," Henry replied. "And you are?"

"My name is Mauricio." Brazilians usually did not give their last names except on formal occasions. It mattered even less in this case, since Henry suspected their new acquaintance was using a fake name. "I'm a friend of Marcos."

Mauricio spoke in Portuguese, which meant Clare would not be able to participate in the exchange. The table was square shaped and accommodated four people on white aluminum folding chairs. He sat to her right, facing Henry.

"Thank you for coming." Henry treaded carefully, unsure how to approach the conversation. "I can't tell you how much we appreciate it."

The young man nodded but did not say anything. He looked nervous and hesitant.

"I understand you are with the army?" Henry tried to make some small talk.

"Yes. I'm a captain with the Jungle Infantry Brigade."

"What's that?"

"A unit specialized in jungle warfare. You know, in case the *gringos* decide to invade."

Henry couldn't tell if Mauricio was being sarcastic or confrontational. Maybe both. *So much for trying to break the ice.* He decided to cut to the chase.

"Did Marcos tell you why we want to talk to you?"

"Only that you ran into some paramilitary operation up in the Alto Rio Negro and that I may be interested to hear about it. He said you'd give me the details."

"They were dressed in fatigues and carried machine guns. I guess 'paramilitary' is a good description. I heard them speaking Spanish, though the guy in charge spoke Portuguese without an accent. It was a sophisticated operation, with a landing strip, military tents, lots of gear, and heavy equipment."

Henry went on to tell the relevant parts of the story, keeping it short so he would not lose the captain's attention.

"Why did you go see this abandoned mine?" Mauricio asked after listening patiently.

"She and her colleagues are journalists and wanted to film the place for their documentary," he replied.

"What kind of documentary?"

"It's a TV show about remote places. It helps protect endangered areas and promotes tourism in the countries they visit." Henry thought it was important to mention the last part to show their good intentions, trying to placate Mauricio's obvious suspicion.

"How was the mine relevant for this?"

Henry disregarded the mistrust in the captain's tone, thinking the Brazilian was entitled to it. He suspected, by the nature of the questioning, that Mauricio may be collecting information to report back to his superiors. He was fine with that too. The more people who knew their story, the better.

"Curiosity and the mystique around the large abandoned projects in the Amazon. You know there is a lot of fascination around the Jari, the Trans-Amazonian, and other failed megaprojects in the jungle."

"Are you sure that they are journalists?"

Despite the skeptical direction of the questions, this one took Henry by surprise. He thought for a moment. He had never considered that Clare and her colleagues could be anything other than what he was told they were. It seemed absurd, but so was the entire incident. As a scientist, he had to think of all the angles, and he had completely missed that one. Could they be something besides filmmakers?

He answered the captain after a brief pause. "If they are spies or whatever, they wouldn't have been that careless and let us be captured so easily. And there would be no need to reach out to you or Marcos." He wondered if Mauricio was questioning Henry's own identity as a researcher but ignored it, since he wasn't asked about it.

"Besides," he continued, "there's an American, an Australian, and an Englishman. They are all from different countries. If they were spies, wouldn't they at least be from the same country? And if you search the internet for the name of their TV show, you can confirm it."

Clare was sitting across from Mauricio, looking confused. She could probably tell they were talking about her and her colleagues, but Henry guessed she would never imagine they were speculating whether she was a spy.

"What kind of equipment?"

"Excuse me?" Henry asked, thrown off by the abrupt change in the line of inquiry.

"You mentioned some heavy equipment. What kind?"

Henry looked up, trying to remember everything he saw.

"Lots of boxes. They were in a large yard, under a camouflage cover. I'm guessing the tarp was there to fool the satellites. Oh, and a big excavator. I remember wondering how it got there."

"An excavator? That's a heavy piece of equipment," Mauricio noted.

"Yes, I thought so too. And it was in fairly decent shape, definitely not abandoned."

"The paramilitary could be guerrillas from Colombia," Mauricio speculated. "They sometimes enter Brazilian territory to escape the Colombian army."

That seemed to be the prevailing theory.

"But it doesn't add up," the army officer kept going, wondering out loud. "The Colombian rebels are constantly on the move. They pack light. No way they would have an excavator or other heavy equipment. And the army would not allow them to move around the area. Not unless they are ordered to."

Henry picked up on the last sentence. It was the confirmation that an operation of that size would not go unnoticed.

"They were not Colombians," Henry interjected. "I mean, there may have been some, but the ID we found was from the Venezuelan army. Which raises the question, What is the Venezuelan military doing in Brazilian territory? And why is the Brazilian government allowing them to operate freely?" He pressed a little to see how the captain would react, but Mauricio didn't take the bait.

"How did you find this ID?" Mauricio asked suspiciously.

Henry was flustered but decided to tell the truth.

"We took a backpack from one of the tents when we escaped. It was among the personal effects of one of the soldiers," he answered without elaborating on how they had escaped. "Is the Brazilian military allowing the Venezuelan army to operate in your country?" Henry pushed again.

He knew he was taking chances by being blunt, but it didn't seem he was going to get anything out of the conversation otherwise.

Mauricio leaned back silently, looking thoughtful.

Henry let him take his time to decide how much he could share.

"You have to promise that you'll never connect me to this story," he said after a long pause.

Henry nodded reassuringly.

"Yes. If what you are saying is true, it's hard to believe that the army wouldn't know about it. We all hear rumors about gringos operating illegally in the Amazon, but the reality is that an operation of this magnitude wouldn't go unnoticed by our military."

Henry realized that *gringos* meant any foreigner, not just Americans. But the part that really got his attention was the mention that the army must know about the activity at the mine.

"I've been in the armed forces long enough to know that the Brazilian military would not willingly allow a paramilitary force or foreign soldiers to operate in our territory," Mauricio continued proudly. "If they are, the order is coming from the highest levels of the government."

Henry felt his blood chill at the confirmation of his suspicion. If top Brazilian officials must be complicit with whatever was going on in the jungle, he and Clare would never get out of the country alive.

"How high?" Henry asked, his dread palpable.

"I don't know. High. It could go all the way to the president. Or pretty close."

Henry saw the captain's expression change as soon as the words came out of his mouth. He could tell that Mauricio thought he had said too much.

"I have to go now," the Brazilian said hastily. "That's all I know."

"Who is protecting these people? And what do you think is going on over there that's worth killing for?"

"I already said more than I should," the Brazilian soldier responded.

He stood up, and Henry could tell he wasn't going to get anything else from him.

"Who does know? How do we find out more?" he insisted anyway.

"Please don't follow me," Mauricio said, starting to walk away.

"Wait! Just one more thing," Henry shouted.

The army officer stopped and turned back to them with an air of profound discomfort.

"Thank you," Henry said with a sincere look. "And don't worry. No one will ever know we had this conversation."

Mauricio nodded courteously. His face relaxed, and he stood still for a moment as he appeared to consider something.

"Just a final thought," the young army officer said in a low voice. "This is not guerrillas on the move. Whatever they are doing, with all the equipment you've seen, it must be related to the mine."

Without waiting for a reaction, the captain turned around and left.

CHAPTER 21

A BAND CAME ON stage and started to play a buoyant and intoxicating beat that made it nearly impossible *not* to get up and dance. Most patrons did, many not gracefully.

Henry and Clare stayed at their table.

The air was hot and thick with humidity, almost like a sauna. After the tense conversation had ended, Henry's body had finally relaxed, and the cumulative impact of the events of the day started to take a toll. The night had fallen, but the heat had not dissipated. He felt sticky and tired.

Henry stood up and walked to the bar, coming back with two bright-red cans of cola.

"Here." He put them on the table and slid one over to her.

The shiny red can was engulfed by the droplets produced as the ice-cold aluminum touched the thick, warm air. Henry had quickly learned to appreciate the Brazilian habit of serving nearly frozen beverages, which they liked to call *estupidamente gelada.* Stupidly cold.

He saw Clare use a napkin to wipe the top of the can before touching it with her lips, the habit of having traveled to too many countries with unsanitary conditions. Henry brought it straight to his mouth. Before drinking, he looked at Clare with a light smile and raised the can in a toast. Not waiting for her to reciprocate, he took several big gulps, leaning on the back of his chair and savoring the crisp and sugary syrup as it cooled his body.

"What now?" she asked after he translated for her the entire conversation with Mauricio. "Should we find a hotel?" They were sitting far from the stage and could carry on a conversation despite the music. She looked tired, but the caffeine-and-sugar boost seemed to have given her a second wind.

"We can't go back to a hotel," he replied, also feeling a little rejuvenated. "If the police found us the first time, they'll find us again. Even with a fake name. Besides, we don't have enough money."

"Then where do we go?"

He gave her a look that said *good question.* He gazed up in thought, noticing the rustic round wood beams framing the thatched roof sheltering their table.

"Before we decide anything," he looked back at Clare, "let's try to put together what we have so far. I think it will help us figure out our next move."

They sat in silence for a brief moment. The small pleasure of a cold drink on a hot night was probably the most enjoyable moment they had experienced together.

Henry broke the silence.

"We made progress today."

She nodded but didn't seem so convinced. "What *did* we learn?"

"First, this is big. According to Mauricio, none of this would be possible without the Brazilian government being complicit. Someone very high up must be telling the army to look the other way and allow this to go on."

"But *what* did we run into?" she asked.

"That's where it gets confusing. I think Mauricio was wondering about it himself. He seems to believe whatever this is, it's related to the mine."

"It could be a coincidence. The equipment may have been there when they arrived," she said, raising another possibility.

"Too big a coincidence, though, don't you think? Besides, the equipment didn't look old. Things decay remarkably fast in the jungle, with all the humidity and heat."

"The key to our mystery is the iron mine then."

"Why is Brazil allowing the Venezuelan military in their territory?" Henry asked.

"Oil prices crashed. The Venezuelan government needs money. Could be as simple as that," she answered.

Henry hadn't been following the news since he had arrived in Brazil. But he knew Venezuela's economy was heavily dependent on oil exports.

"So the Brazilian government lets them explore the mine to allow Venezuela to pay the bills. Why wouldn't Brazil do it themselves and give the money to Venezuela? Or set up a legitimate company to do it?"

"It wouldn't sit well with Brazilians," she replied.

"This is not a rich country. The opposition would go ballistic. Voters would not take well to their government giving money to their neighbors while so many in their own country lack basic services."

"And Colombia and Venezuela don't get along very well," Henry continued her thought, trying to show he wasn't entirely ignorant of geopolitics. "Maybe it's also a way for the Brazilian government to curry favor with one country without antagonizing the other."

It was a good theory, and they were encouraged to finally start making some sense of what was going on. Except that the more progress they made, the worse their predicament looked.

"What is it?" Clare asked as Henry's expression changed at another discouraging realization.

"Their leader was a Brazilian!" he cried. "The first guy who came to talk to us, the one wearing the red shirt. He was in charge. And he spoke *Portuguese*."

He paused before continuing, putting his thoughts together as he spoke.

"It's not just that the Brazilian government is looking the other way while some foreign army operates in their territory. They may be actively collaborating."

"We don't know that for sure. Maybe he's with the Venezuelan army but spoke Portuguese?" Clare questioned. "Like a liaison."

"It's possible. But he had no accent. It's hard for native Spanish speakers to talk without an accent, because Portuguese has some very unique sounds." Henry spoke from experience, having struggled with the language's pronunciation. "And do you remember that he was not in uniform?"

She nodded. "It means he is not part of the military detachment," she concluded. "But that still doesn't mean he is connected to the Brazilian government."

"True. But how else would the local police be after us so quickly?" Henry asked. "There has to be some connection. Which means we're up against someone—or something—very, very powerful."

CHAPTER 22

ENRY CALLED OLIVEIRA after they left the nightclub. It was a desperate move, but he couldn't think of any other option. She agreed to meet them for the second time that day, telling Henry to go to Fund-Ama.

Oliveira sat diagonally across from him and Clare, on a couch in the reception area. She started the conversation by asking if they were okay, though her tone did not convey the concern implied by the question.

Henry reckoned that their detention by the police and ensuing escape had put her in a delicate position. When they had seen Oliveira that morning, they were innocent targets of a paramilitary group. Now, late at night, they were fugitives wanted for murder. He tried to put himself in her position, wondering if she perceived them as victims or perpetrators.

The reception area of the Fund-Ama offices was the living room of a three-bedroom house originally intended as a residence. It felt eerie in the quiet of the night, with no natural light coming from the large front window and none of the lively agitation of people coming and going during office hours.

"Why did you run from the police?" Oliveira asked coolly, looking Henry directly in the eye.

Intimidated, he looked at Clare, trying to come up with an answer. But Oliveira didn't wait for one.

"I thought you told me everything this morning." She sounded more disappointed than angry. "I can't help you if you are hiding something from me."

"We told you everything we know. And all of it is true," Clare answered defensively.

Henry also resented the tone of the foundation's boss. He needed a time-out to recover, both mentally and physically, just as he knew Clare did. Could Oliveira really think they were guilty? Was that how everyone else saw them now?

"I can't help you hide from the police. It would be a crime and could jeopardize Fund-Ama and all the work we are doing. As a courtesy to you and our partners from your university, I'm willing to listen to you and will try and assist you as best as I can."

Her tone was friendlier now, but her expression was still deadly serious.

"Thank you," he replied as he composed his thoughts. Oliveira's concern for the reputation and well-being of her organization resonated with him. Everyone who worked there was just as passionate about the rain forest as he was.

"We went willingly to the police station," he started, his tone a little harsher than he meant to sound. Much as he understood her suspicion, he couldn't hide his frustration. It was one thing to be doubted by the police, but another altogether to be seen as a potential murderer by the one person he thought could help them the most. "We thought they wanted to learn what was going on, *help* us, help find Aidan and Liam. So you can imagine our shock when we learned that we were there as suspects, not witnesses.

"They were transferring us, and no one seemed the least interested in listening to our story. It would have taken days to sort everything out. We don't have days. Aidan and Liam are in danger. We thought that the two of them had a better chance if we were out trying to help them instead of working to prove our own innocence from a jail cell. We panicked. When the opportunity presented itself, we took it."

He paused, trying to gauge her reaction. She looked impassive.

"Listen," he continued. "We told you everything. I know the police have us as suspects right now, but surely you realize how absurd these accusations are? You heard from Marcelo. Didn't he tell you what happened at the camp?"

The director gave a sympathetic nod. "This is not about what I think. I have to consider what's best for this foundation. We can't just ignore what the police are saying."

Clare and Henry remained silent.

"Even if the police are wrong," she went on, "your best alternative is to turn yourselves in and confront the situation head-on. Running away will make you look guilty at best—and at worst, it will get you killed."

They nodded.

"Have you discussed this with anyone else since we met?" she asked, looking as though she was warming up to their predicament.

"Not since then," Henry replied. "Except, of course, for the police and the guy from the American consulate."

Although he didn't feel comfortable lying, he omitted the meeting with Mauricio. Just as they had promised Marcos to keep their discussion a secret, they would not expose the Brazilian army captain, even to those they thought they could trust. At any rate, those meetings did not seem to have any relevance to the issue at hand.

"I'm sorry, but I need to ask you again. Is there anything else you haven't told me?"

"We've told you everything we know," Henry confirmed firmly.

"And where have you been since you escaped from the police?"

Clare stepped in before Henry could respond. A good thing too, since he wasn't as quick on the feet as she was.

"We met some college students," she replied, going on to tell Oliveira about their encounter with the four young friends after taking a random city bus, and explaining how their new acquaintances had helped remove the handcuffs. In her version of the story, she and Henry had come to Fund-Ama straight from the apartment.

"The parents were arriving soon, and the young man asked us to leave. We didn't have much time to talk to anyone," Clare completed. "That's when we placed a collect call to you."

Oliveira nodded.

"We know how this looks from your perspective," Henry spoke. "And you are probably right that our best option is to go back to the police and try to show that we are innocent. But for now, all we need is a place to spend the night and put ourselves together. And someone to listen to our side of the story."

"I can't harbor fugitives," Oliveira responded. "That would make me an accomplice, and Fund-Ama could lose our nonprofit status and our funding." She paused and then became more decisive as she continued, as though she had made up her mind about something. "The best I can do is help you find a lawyer before you go back to the police."

Henry was taken aback by her bluntness and terrified at the prospect of spending the night in jail. But Oliveira was their last hope. It seemed they had finally hit the end of the road.

"I would be taking a big chance by letting you stay here. If I'm found to be helping you, it could destroy everything we've built, all the research we support. I don't take that lightly. It's my life's work."

Henry's heart sank, though he could sympathize. He had hoped this would be his life's work too, until just a few days ago. Now all he cared about was staying alive and getting out of this mess.

"Now," she continued after a few moments, "did you tell anyone you were coming here? Does anybody know that you called me tonight?"

"No," Henry said truthfully.

"Not even your friends abroad?"

They shook their heads. Henry's eyes filled with hope, guessing where she was going.

"If word gets out that I'm letting you stay here, do you realize the foundation will be in serious trouble? But I understand that you need some rest and time to think this through. So as long as no one knows you are here and you promise to never, ever tell anyone, you can spend the night."

Henry felt a gigantic sense of relief.

"Thank you," Clare said sincerely. "Really, thank you."

"There is one condition. Tomorrow morning you are going to see a lawyer and then turn yourselves in."

Oliveira's tone left no room for argument.

"I know you may think Brazil is a country of poorly enforced laws and that we have an unreliable judicial system. And you are not wrong. But we are far from a banana republic that sends innocent people to jail without due process. The best advice I can give you is to make your case in the courts.

"I will help you as long as I don't have to do anything illegal or that hurts this organization. Do I have your word you will turn yourselves in tomorrow?"

They looked at each other and nodded affirmatively. Henry realized they couldn't run forever. Going back to the police wasn't appealing, but they were out of alternatives. At least they'd have a chance to see a lawyer first.

"Yes," Henry answered firmly for both of them.

"We have an agreement then," Oliveira said decisively as she stood up. "I'll make some calls. I know some people who can help you."

"Thank you," Henry said.

"There's a shower in the bathroom upstairs." She pointed upward. "There's also some food in the kitchen.

Take whatever you need. I'm sure whoever the food belongs to will understand."

Oliveira approached the door and opened it. Henry and Clare followed to see the Fund-Ama director off as she stepped out onto the front patio, which also served as the garage. It was covered and surrounded by walls, with a large iron gate in the front, separating the house from the sidewalk.

"We have a big day ahead of us tomorrow," Oliveira said as she raised her hand and waved.

Can't be worse than today, Henry thought.

"Thank you again," he repeated. "I know we put you in a tough spot. We promise you we won't get you in trouble."

"Get some rest," she said with a motherly look. "No one knows you are here but me. You'll be safe until tomorrow."

The only way in was with a key or a metal saw. An intruder would still have to go through the thick front door into the reception area or through an iron door into the kitchen. All windows had bars, including those on the second floor. Most houses were like that in Brazil. This one, with expensive equipment, computers, and valuable scientific data, was no exception.

Henry saw the executive director shut the door and lock them inside. That's when he realized that as hard as it was for anyone to get in, they couldn't get out either.

CHAPTER 23

ENRY WASHED HIS face in the bathroom sink and looked at himself in the mirror. He was thinner and more tanned than the first time he'd been at the Fund-Ama offices, back when his assignment was starting. The purple on his jaw seemed to be receding, and his shoulder was still sore but improving.

Despite the hectic few days since his injuries, his body was healing. He wished his mind could recover as quickly.

As he stared at his image, he had an uneasy feeling he couldn't shake. Was it the fact that they were locked inside the office or the idea of going to the police the next day?

He walked into the kitchen and saw Clare sitting at the small table. She had helped herself to some milk and light yogurt in the fridge. The milk belonged to someone called "Marcia," and the yogurt container was labeled with the name "Janete." Henry matched the second name to a research assistant who had helped him find his way around the city when he first arrived in Manaus. He wondered whether she heard about what had happened to him and whether she thought he was guilty or innocent.

The kitchen was small, filled with light-blue tiles adorned with engraved flower motifs. The sink sat against the back wall, under a wide jalousie window with iron-framed louvers facing the back patio. To the right was the door to the backyard, also made of iron, and painted white.

Henry walked toward the door and went through the motions of trying to open it, just to see how strong it felt. He peeked at the patio outside, through a small, rectangular glass pane at the top. The yard was dark, but he could make out the ground, covered by Spanish tiles, and spotted a laundry tub, a small animal trap, and other assorted research equipment. The door felt heavy. It could not be pried open by anyone with less than Herculean strength, let alone by him.

The uneasy feeling returned. Then, the pieces starting to snap together in his mind, he found the source of his anxiety.

"I'm going to leave a thank-you note for Marcia and Janete," Clare remarked, oblivious to the thoughts furiously churning in Henry's mind. "Thank goodness they left some food in the—"

"We have to get out of here."

She stared at him with a mystified look.

"What?" she asked. "We just got here, and we are safe for now. Look at all these bars. No one can get in here."

"Or out."

He pulled the handle and tried to open the door to the patio to illustrate his point.

"We are locked in here."

He started to pace in the small kitchen.

"The only two ways out of this place are through heavy doors, which are locked and we don't have the means to open. All the windows have iron bars."

Clare looked unfazed, if a little confused, clearly questioning why they would need to get out before the next day.

"It's a trap!" he shouted as the full picture got clearer in his head. "She's locked us up in here so we won't run again."

"What are you talking about?"

Henry did not respond.

" 'I'll make some calls,' " he said to himself, quoting something that Oliveira had said before she left. " 'I know some people who can help you.' That's it! That's what threw me off."

"What do you mean?"

"That's the same thing she said this morning. She said she was going to make some calls and knew some people who could help us. Well, she had the entire afternoon to do it. Why didn't she call them like she said she would? If she did, why didn't she give us an update?"

"Maybe she just forgot or was just saying it to make us feel better. It still doesn't prove anything. That's a big leap you are taking."

Clare's appearance changed from confused to concerned. She looked at him. "Henry, I'm sorry, but aren't you being a little paranoid?"

"And she said she hadn't talked to the authorities yet!"

"Calm down!" she pleaded. "You are all over the place."

He finally paused, realizing he was shouting and

moving around frantically. He usually got excited and agitated when his mind was working on a new insight. It was how he processed his thoughts. But he could see he was scaring her. She was probably thinking he had lost it, wondering if she should worry about being locked in the office with *him*.

"I'm sorry," he said, quieting his voice. He took a deep breath and sat down at the table, across from her. "I'm just trying to work through this information, and it all leads to the same conclusion. She's involved in this."

He made an effort to speak slowly.

"Oliveira said she had heard from Marcelo at the research camp *yesterday*. He must have told her about the guys in fatigues holding everyone hostage. Wouldn't you be freaking out if your research camp was attacked liked that? Wouldn't you have called every contact you have to find out what was going on? So why *hadn't* she talked to the authorities yet?"

"You think she already knew what was happening?"

"Exactly. And our run-in with the local police has been bothering me too," Henry continued. "How did those guys find us in the hotel? We gave fake names at the reception desk, and nobody else knew we were there, except for your producer. She's the only one we've told where we were staying. How did the police find us so fast?"

"Well, it's the police. They knew we had to come to Manaus," she pondered out loud. "The police in São Gabriel could have contacted their colleagues here and circulated a description to all the hotels. Ours could have just reported us. Besides, we only gave Oliveira the name of the hotel at the very end of the meeting, so she could tell the driver where to take us. She couldn't have told them until after we left. How could they have mobilized so quickly?"

"Right. How could they have mobilized so quickly?" Henry repeated the question. "They couldn't! That's why we were picked up by the *civil* police and not the feds, who are the ones conducting the investigation. I'm guessing that after seeing us, Oliveira wanted to take control of the situation before we talked to more people. She and her associates were cooking up a story to frame us but couldn't get the Federal Police to act fast enough, so she used her connections to get the *local* police to detain us. I bet that whole story about a translator was made up. After the civil police had us in custody, they *had* to deliver us to the folks with jurisdiction over our case. Hence the transfer that gave us a chance to escape."

"But why bring in the consular service? To make it all look legitimate?"

"Probably."

The more he relived the events of the day, the more Henry was convinced he was onto something.

"There's more. The suspicion in her voice. I felt bad for resenting her when she was questioning us like that, asking if anyone knew we were here, and I bought into her story about how by helping us she could be endangering the foundation. I kept trying to see it from *her* perspective, with the information she had.

"But after she had talked to the camp manager and other people in the research camp, how could she doubt us? She knew what happened. She must have known we were shot at. So how could she be suspicious of us, despite what the police said? Unless . . ."

"She was trying to find out exactly what we knew and who we told," Clare completed his thought.

Henry saw the change in her expression. The validation scared him because he was secretly hoping she would prove him wrong. Each individual piece could be explained away. But when they put everything together, it became harder to believe Oliveira had no part in the conspiracy.

"So she wasn't suspicious at all," Clare continued. "She was making sure we didn't contact anyone else about this. And that no one knew we are here."

They tried the phone but couldn't make it work. Even local calls were still charged by the minute in Brazil; and Henry remembered that when he had worked out of the Fund-Ama office, all outgoing calls needed a budget code to be completed. Neither of them knew how to use the foundation's cumbersome phone system for reaching the operator to place a collect call. They decided against trying the local emergency number, assuming they could even get through, fearing they could not trust the police.

Henry inspected the doors and the windows again, looking for the one most likely to break with brute force, searching for any piece of equipment that could help.

"Wait." Clare stopped him. "There's one more thing."

Henry tried to listen but felt exasperated. There was enough information to convince them both of Oliveira's involvement. Now they needed to focus on getting out of there.

"She wouldn't be so concerned about extracting information from us and locking us up in here if she was just covering up for someone. That means there's something else. She knows what's going on there and stands to lose a lot if we find out!"

"Yes, we just established that," he said quickly. He did not mean to sound dismissive but wanted to concentrate on finding a way out of the building. He couldn't simultaneously dissect the situation further. But this time he was the one who didn't see the full picture.

"Is it really a coincidence that the research camp is close to the mine?" she went on.

Henry stopped cold in his tracks. She finally had his full attention.

It was, in fact, a *big* coincidence, considering Oliveira's apparent involvement. But he had been at the camp for a couple of years and could not fathom he had been working for the enemy all this time.

"That can't be," he tried to argue, as much against her as his better judgment. "That's a scientific research camp, established by some very prestigious organizations. You can't possibly think that—"

"I'm not saying the university or any of the scientists working there are involved. But do you know who selected that location and why?"

"It's a very biodiversity-rich area . . ."

"So is much of the Amazon, Henry. Why there?"

"It's not so simple. There are some parts of the region that are not as diverse. It depends on soil, human intervention, seasonal flooding, proximity to—"

She rolled her eyes and he interrupted himself.

He went over the rationale for choosing that particular area. The collaboration with the Baniwa community played a key role, he thought, but even if he was unconvinced that there was a connection, the idea wasn't so far-fetched. It was a very difficult place to get to, and there may very well have been other locations of equal scientific value that were logistically better suited for a research station.

"You are right," he conceded. "There could be plenty of other suitable areas."

He paused, letting the realization sink in.

"So, let's assume there's a connection," he continued. "How would the mining operation benefit from being close to the research camp?"

Then, he stopped. "We can continue this later. We need to get out of here before someone comes for us."

"You still don't see it, do you?" she asked impatiently.

He just stared blankly at her, not knowing what she was getting at.

"Oliveira, or whoever selected the location of the research camp, probably knew about the mine. If there's a connection between the two, there could be documents right here in this building that show it. Maybe a clue that can shed more light on what is going on over there, help us save Aidan and Liam, or even provide proof about what we found."

"Would she really leave us here if there was anything like that lying around?"

"Maybe not, but it's worth a try," Clare insisted. "If she's locked us in here, as you've convinced me she has, perhaps she doesn't care what we find. She doesn't think it will get out anyway."

"Only one way to find out," he finally concurred.

CHAPTER 24

THEY WALKED AROUND the house, trying to map where valuable clues could be. Each bedroom on the second floor was furnished for office work, with desks, shelves, and computers. Henry had used one of those desks when he worked out of Fund-Ama for a few days before heading over to the jungle. Oliveira's office was in the back, walls lined by beige and gray metal filing cabinets.

"This may take a while," Clare pointed out. Not being fluent in Portuguese, she couldn't be of much help. "I'll keep looking for a way to break out of here while you search for information linking Fund-Ama to the mine."

There were several file cabinets in each room. Henry moved quickly through them, scanning the folders. The files related to equipment, personnel, grants, foundations, universities, and lots of service contracts. The file drawers in all the offices were unlocked except for those in the director's office.

Henry turned to Oliveira's desk and started to search it. He remembered that her desktop computer synchronized with her laptop so she didn't have to carry it to the office every day. He turned it on.

"Nothing I can find up here." Clare walked into the director's office after looking at the rooms on the second floor first. "All I could see was office supplies, computers, and some gear for fieldwork."

Henry had seen the equipment piled up around the corners: measuring devices outfitted to support the rigors of humidity and heat, camera traps, and other small research equipment. None of these would help them break them out of the house.

She headed downstairs while Henry continued to look around Oliveira's desk, waiting for her computer to start up. The desk was simple, with a set of drawers on the right, two small at the top and a larger, file-size one at the bottom. He opened the first two and found only various business cards and assorted office supplies, including paper clips, a stapler, an eraser, elastic bands, and a collection of highlighters. He looked at the names on the business cards but did not recognize any.

The bottom drawer was locked.

Before worrying about how to unlock the drawer, he looked at the computer screen and saw that the device was password protected. He had no idea what to try, realizing he knew nothing about Oliveira's personal life that would be helpful, like the name of a pet, a child, or meaningful dates. He could spend all night trying and never guess it.

Clare came through the door, holding a flashlight and

a hammer in her left hand, with a crimson metallic tool-box hanging from the other.

Henry looked at her inquiringly.

"The pantry in the kitchen," she said, raising both hands to show what she had found. "Apparently, that's where they store everything. Mops, light bulbs, computer parts, and more office supplies. But nothing that will help us break out of this place."

"I didn't find anything in the file cabinets," he replied. "Her computer is password protected, and her bottom drawer is locked."

"Okay, let's switch. You try to find a way out of here, and I'll try to break that open," she suggested, pointing to the drawer.

Clare approached without waiting for an answer, placing the toolbox on top of some assorted paperwork and folders on the desk. The toolbox gave Henry an idea.

"Do they have a Phillips screwdriver in there? It's the one that has a cross—"

"I know what a Phillips screwdriver is." She mustered a faint smile, shaking her head in mocking disapproval. "Yes, there's one in there."

"Uh, great. I can remove the hard drive, and we can try to read the files later if we manage to get out of here.

"You know how do that?" She looked surprised. Henry did not seem the type who knew his way around inside a computer.

"Yeah, I used to put my own computers together. It's not that hard."

"But how will it help us? Isn't all the data stored online?"

"Yes, but there will still be a copy of the files on the

hard drive, at least the more recent ones. Otherwise, they would have to download each file every time they want to see it, not practical with all the heavy data sets and images they produce here."

"Okay, get to work, IT guy," she said, handing him the tool.

Henry turned to the computer, shutting it down and unplugging it. He pulled the tower from under the desk and sat cross-legged on the floor. Using the Phillips screwdriver, he removed the screws that held the case together and next pulled the side covers, revealing a metal skeleton with a plethora of wires and cables snaking over the green motherboard.

He identified the hard drive, attached to a bay in the front of the tower, and disconnected the two cables attached to it. Removing the screws that were locking it in place, Henry carefully slid the device out of the bay. He then grabbed an issue of *Science* magazine that was lying on top of the desk and yanked out some of the pages, wrapping them around the drive to safeguard it.

Standing next to him, Clare extended her arm, and he placed the hard disk on her hand. Henry seized a red cable used to plug the device to the motherboard, so he could connect it to another computer. He replaced the side covers and screwed them in place, pushing the computer back under the desk. When Oliveira tried to turn it on, she would not be able to tell right away what was wrong with it. It wouldn't amount to much, but it would be some time until her IT support opened the computer and she realized Henry and Clare had made away with her data.

Assuming, of course, that they could get out of the house.

While Henry was working on the computer, Clare had managed to pry open the bottom drawer, using the back of the hammer. He pored over the files and saw bank statements and other sensitive documents, but none of them jumped out at him as containing any information about the camp or the surrounding area.

Clare walked over to the other desk, across the room, and broke open its wide top drawer.

Before she could check its contents, the sound of a metallic clank in the quiet of the night caused her and Henry to jump at the same time, looking at each other with a nervous expression. The noise had come from the front of the house.

They were at the opposite side of the building, facing the backyard. Henry raced down the hallway and looked through the blinds toward the street. It was dark, and the view of the front gate was blocked by the roof over the garage; but under the dim streetlights, two men crossed the road and came toward the house. At least one more person waited for them at the entrance, inside the gate.

The two men were wearing jeans and short-sleeve shirts. One of them was a thickset, short, and square-faced man. Henry recognized the policeman they had escaped from just hours before.

"They're coming in!" he cried, running back to warn Clare. "How on earth are we going to get out?" he asked her, stopping in the middle of the hallway.

Henry held his head with both hands, his heart pounding. *What now?* he wondered. He bent his head backward, looking up toward heaven perhaps, but all he could see was the white hallway ceiling.

As he took a deep breath and exhaled in desperation, his field of vision caught a relief at the end of the ceiling, near the door to Oliveira's office. He narrowed his eyes to make it out better. It was a trapdoor to the attic.

"There!" He pointed.

Clare looked up to see what he was referring to. Henry walked right under it, keeping his ear attentive to any sound that would signal the approach of the men about to storm in through the front door.

He looked at Clare, who, like him, was staring at their only hope for escape.

"Can you get a rolling chair from there?" Without taking his eyes off the ceiling, he motioned with his head in the direction of the rear office.

She ran into the room, came back with the chair, and put it right under the trapdoor. She brought the hard drive and the flashlight with her and was also holding a long roll of white paper.

"What is that?" he asked, gazing at the roll of paper.

"A map. It was in the locked drawer, so I thought it might be important."

"Great," he said automatically, extending his hand so she could give it to him.

Henry usually treated maps with reverence, but this time he simply flattened and folded the roll, sliding it inside his pants, over his thigh. He also managed to fit the hard drive in one of his pockets and stuffed the flashlight over his crotch. Not elegant, but desperate times called for desperate measures.

They heard the door open downstairs, followed by steps coming into the house.

"They are in," Henry whispered. "You go first. Be as quiet as you can."

He held the rolling chair for her as she stepped on it and reached up to the trapdoor. She pushed it up and to the side, gently, to avoid making any noise. Dust fell on her eyes and into her mouth. She winced, as though fighting the urge to cough, and grabbed the trapdoor frame with both hands, looking down and giving a go-ahead nod to Henry. He hugged her legs and lifted her.

They were trying to be as silent as possible. As he brought his arms down after pushing Clare up through the trapdoor, Henry heard a light squeak of rubber against the hardwood steps. It was faint, but he had no doubt: the men were climbing up the stairs.

He stepped on the chair, each hand pushing hard against the opposite walls of the hallway, careful to stop the chair from rolling and sending him crashing down on the floor.

There was no time left.

Clare looked down at him from the dusty crawl space between the ceiling and the roof. Henry managed to balance himself on the wobbly chair while he grabbed the inside of the trapdoor frame with his right hand, his left still pressing on the wall. The edge was sturdy enough to hold his weight, he thought. When he had a firm grip, he released his left hand and placed it on the frame as well, ready to pull up.

The chair danced slightly.

He was facing the back room, where Oliveira's office

was. He looked at a shelf between the two desks and rehearsed the move in his mind a couple of times before pushing the chair with his feet in that direction.

Barely a split second went by between the time his shoes lost touch with the chair and the moment he bent his arms and shot up, his hands jumping swiftly to the sides of the opening as his hips cleared the hole and he brought his knees toward his chest. As he rolled into the crawl space, Clare immediately placed the square wooden cover on the frame, shutting the trapdoor.

Henry could not tell if the chair hit the target, but he was sure it went inside the room, leaving no indication they had used it to climb into the crawl space. He hoped the men coming up would hear the clunk of the chair bumping into one of the desks and look for him and Clare in Oliveira's office, then search the other rooms before figuring out where the two fugitives had escaped to.

Clare switched on the flashlight and started to survey the attic. Their pursuers would eventually realize this was the only place left to hide, so Henry and Clare had to find a way out quickly. The crawl space was dusty and gray, about sixty feet long and twenty feet wide. The cinder blocks that made up the walls were bare and exposed, as was the roof structure, a long, central wooden beam supported by two vertical columns, one in the front and another in the back of the house. Sloped beams spanned from the side walls to the central beam under the ridge of the roof. Flat red ceramic tiles fit together neatly on top of thin wood strips resting on rafters.

The flashlight was not very powerful, allowing them to see only one section of the attic at a time. As Clare moved the light around the space, they made out spare roof and bathroom tiles, a bag of cement, and other construction materials stored in one of the corners at the front side of the building. To the left were water pipes leading in and out of a small water tank. They saw nothing on the back side of the attic except for a perfect two-foot-wide spider-web, its resident nowhere to be found.

There were no windows or doors.

"I think the only way out is back through the trap-door," Clare said in an urgent whisper.

By now the men below must have finished canvasing the ground and top floors, finding no one. Henry and Clare could hear them talking loudly, wondering where the pair they came to apprehend had gone.

"Aqui em cima não tem ninguém. Como é que está a situação aí embaixo?" One of the two men upstairs shouted to his counterparts on the ground level. *No one up here. What's the situation down there?*

Henry heard a muffled response but did not understand it. Their time was nearly up. It would not be long before their pursuers came through the trapdoor.

He looked at the bare roof tiles and paused, keeping calm. After days of constant anxiety, Henry was getting used to the pressure. Having found a way out of several hopeless entanglements—including by his discovery of the trapdoor minutes ago, in the nick of time—he was still hopeful they could conjure up an escape from the attic too.

Out of instinct, and because he thought he should try every possibility, Henry pushed one of the tiles up slightly. To his surprise, it moved without any resistance. He tried another one, realizing that most of the roof tiles were not affixed to anything and that those nailed to the wood to anchor the others could be removed without much effort. The pieces were designed to fit together tightly and to resist water and wind from the outside, not pressure from below.

He quickly removed nine tiles, opening a space of about one and a half square feet. The gap between the wood strips on top of the rafters was not sufficiently wide for an adult to pass, but the battens were so thin that Henry could break them with his bare hands. Splitting the wood strips in a couple of places, he created enough clearance to let them through.

The planks snapped loudly, perhaps at a volume heard by the men below, but Henry and Clare didn't stick around to find out how far the noise could travel. He let her go first, then stowed away the flashlight and followed.

It was one in the morning, but their eyes were now adapted to the dark and they could see well, thanks to the streetlights.

They looked around, studying the scene.

"There!" she shouted, louder than she should have, pointing at the roof next to theirs.

Henry looked at the neighboring house. Unlike the wall facing the street, the one between the two houses did not have glass shards or electrified wire on top. They jumped over a three-foot gap and landed on the wall dividing the properties. It was about five inches thick, enough for them to find their balance. They crossed to the house that bordered Fund-Ama's backyard and climbed onto the roof, crawling along the tiles toward the street behind the foundation's headquarters.

Reaching the front, they discovered there was no way to get from the roof to the street. Down in the yard, a small mutt started barking furiously at them, a loud racket sure to wake up the entire block.

Henry was ready to attempt the ten-foot jump over the front yard—and the barking dog—when Clare pointed out that three houses down was a flat roof covering an enclosed driveway. If they could get there, the two of them could make it to the street without risking a broken leg.

They hopped from house to house until they reached the carport, and then climbed down the front iron gate. The night was silent, and they ran into the empty street in no particular direction, as far away as they could get.

CHAPTER 25

AN HOUR AND a half later, Henry punched the button of the intercom next to a dark gray iron gate. It was framed by a yellow wall that hid the front of a house on a quiet street. The wall ended where the next house began, and so it went all through the neighborhood, a series of wall-to-wall gates blocking the view to the small front yard that doubled as a driveway.

The top of the wall was covered with glass shards, an attempt to discourage burglars from jumping over into the property. The neighbor's protection was slightly more sophisticated, with the wall topped by electric wires. Other properties may have had spikes, but all had some security contraption to deter break-ins. Henry had always wondered how effective they were and was even more skeptical now that he knew his way around the typical Brazilian roof.

He tried the bell two more times before a raspy, sleepy voice came from the intercom.

"Pois não?" *How may I help you?*

He was relieved someone was home. He announced himself and apologized for calling so late. A couple of minutes later, they heard the click and clack of bolts being unlocked, and the door built into the gate opened.

A lean man with graying hair appeared. He was barefoot and shirtless, wearing only cotton pajama shorts.

He recognized Henry with a look of surprise and curiosity.

"Come in," he said, inviting the two visitors into his house, saving his questions for later.

They walked in silence through the dark, unkempt front yard. Henry noticed the overgrown vegetation, very different from what he would find back home. Instead of the ivies and berry shrubs typically found in the home gardens of his native Pennsylvania, bromeliads, ferns, and other tropical plants shared the narrow rectangle of soil next to the cement slab that served as the driveway, where an old Fiat Uno Mille with a sticker from the IBEA research institute was parked.

A small mango tree on the other side of the driveway blocked their view of the night's half-moon, the tree's fallen fruits dotting the ground, the sweet, pungent smell of rotting pulp faintly in the air.

Inside, the house was sparsely furnished. An elegant, but worn-out, dark-wood couch with beige pillows and a matching coffee table were the only features in the narrow living room. The white walls were bare.

The owner of the house seemed to notice what was in Henry's mind.

"I spend most of my time in the back," he mentioned

casually, leading them into the kitchen. "Can I offer you something?"

"Water would be nice," said Clare.

"For me too."

The host took a pitcher from the fridge and poured two tall glasses.

"Ice?"

They declined. The water looked cold enough.

Leaving the kitchen, the professor led them to a backyard as unkempt as the driveway. There was a small room and a bathroom at the rear of the property, a design common in Brazilian middle-class homes to accommodate the family maid, though most families adapted it for other purposes. In this house it had been set up as an office.

"I like working from here," he said. "I can see birds coming to feed off the fruit I put out for them."

The small room had a desk that was set against the window facing the yard. Two of the walls were covered by bookshelves; a two-seat couch rested against another wall, next to the door, with two posters above it. Henry read the captions: *Mamíferos da Amazônia* and *Aves da Amazônia*. The posters had drawings of animals of the region, one for birds and the other for mammals.

Henry and Clare sat down on the couch as their host excused himself to get dressed.

"How do you know this guy?" Clare asked when the man who had just welcomed her to his house left the room.

"He's a local professor and frequent collaborator with our research team. I met him when I first came to Manaus. His name is Egberto Rossi. We call him 'Berto.' "

Henry explained that while in graduate school he had

corresponded with the professor, and the two had become close when they met in person.

"Can we trust him?"

"Can we trust anyone at this juncture?" Henry asked, directing the question as much to himself as to her.

He spoke again after a short pause.

"Yes, actually. He helped me in the past when I was in a tough spot," Henry completed without elaborating.

"Besides, we had a very public falling-out a while back, so I doubt anybody could connect us to him anytime soon."

"A falling-out?" she asked incredulously. "And you still think you can trust him?"

"Yes, we can trust him. It was my fault, not his. It's a long story."

"I have time," she replied sarcastically.

Before she could ask the first of many questions that might have come to her mind in that short exchange, Berto came out of the kitchen door into the backyard, now in Bermuda shorts, a buttoned short-sleeve shirt, and sandals.

He entered the office and sat on the chair by his desk, looking at them for a moment before speaking. His tone was calm and matter-of-fact, neither welcoming nor hostile.

"It's been a while, Henry. Do you mind telling me how you found me and what you are doing here in the middle of the night?"

"You're in the phone book," Henry replied in response to the first question. "We managed to find one at a bar a couple of hours ago, right after we escaped from Fund-Ama. Teresa Oliveira locked us in there before some armed men came looking for us. There are people trying to kill us—we don't know who they work for, exactly—and we have nowhere else to go. We have no money—we walked over here, actually—and we're here because you are our last hope," he concluded dramatically.

It was out of character for Henry to be so short and blunt, but he was tired and wanted to get straight to the point.

The professor's reaction was muted, and Henry was not surprised. It reminded him of their many conversations where Berto would listen to the wildest theories with the same understated demeanor. It seemed dismissive to the casual observer, but Henry knew it was just the opposite. The professor had seen it all and had developed a habit of listening to anything without passing judgment until he had all the information he needed. It was one of the things Henry liked about him.

"I'm Clare." She cut in before Henry could continue, extending her hand with a smile. "I thought I should at least introduce myself before we spill out the details of our little saga. Thank you for taking us into your home at this hour."

Henry looked embarrassed for the omission. *Good thing she can make up for my lack of social graces.*

"It's good to meet you, Clare." The professor took her hand and shook it. "And you are welcome. I expect Henry has told you who I am. You can call me 'Berto.' Please go on," he said, turning back to Henry.

They had lost track of how many times they had told their story. With Clare's help, Henry summarized their ordeal as best as he could, focusing on the key facts. He made sure to mention their theory that the operation in the jungle involved someone in the high levels of the Brazilian government.

Henry was conscious that their premise regarding Oliveira and the suspected link between Fund-Ama and the mine was a hard sell. They were accusing an upstanding member of the local scientific community of criminal activity and conspiracy. The executive director of a respected organization had far more credibility than a foreign research student and a young journalist, even if the professor was sympathetic to their predicament, which was not a certainty at this point.

Berto did react with surprise at some of the most shocking aspects of their account, like their capture, the shooting of Powers, and their many escapes. But otherwise, he listened without interrupting or giving any indication of his thoughts.

As they finished recounting everything that had transpired, Henry couldn't help but think that their tale sounded too fantastic to be believed.

"That's quite a story. I'm sorry about everything you've been through," Berto said in a tone halfway between detached and sympathetic. "It's not hard to believe that there are illegal activities in the Amazon and that some paramilitary forces may be involved.

"But Teresa Oliveira . . . I've known her for a long time. She's a prominent scientist in Brazil, maybe the most prestigious in Manaus. Personally, I think she has more skills as a politician and activist than as a scientist, but that's not to her detriment. She's raised a lot of money for conservation and scientific research in the Amazon.

"She is also very politically connected. I don't agree with some of the policies she promotes, like restricting foreign research in the Amazon to give more opportunity to Brazilian scientists. I don't think that's in the best interest of scientific discovery or the protection of the rain forest. But despite my political disagreements with her, I've certainly never had any reason to believe she could be involved in anything remotely like this."

Henry remembered how difficult it was for him and his colleagues at the university to do research in Brazil. The paperwork and bureaucratic hoops they needed to jump through were maddening. That's why they had partnered with Fund-Ama. It was impossible for a foreign institution to do any research except in partnership with a local organization.

"Well, her *political* views," Henry observed, "are very self-serving. She gets a lot of money from foreign research institutions such as ours, thanks to all the restrictions on foreign organizations doing work in the Amazon."

"Ah yes. I don't disagree with that. But there are a great number of people who think that those restrictions are necessary to prevent the exploitation of our natural resources without sharing any of the benefits with our country."

Henry did not respond.

"But that's neither here nor there," the professor continued, realizing they had veered on a tangent. "We clearly have more pressing matters at hand."

He turned his chair to the window and looked out to his backyard.

"As we were saying," he resumed, "Oliveira is quite influential and has connections to politicians and government authorities. She is also a member of the current ruling party, with access to the highest levels of government. *If* what you are saying is true"—Berto made a point of emphasizing the conditional status of the premise at hand—"she could be acting on behalf of someone involved in the operation you stumbled upon. So as difficult as it is for me to believe her involvement, she does have the access and the means."

"I know our story seems far-fetched," Clare acknowledged. "But assuming you believe us, what do you think they could be doing over there?"

"Your theory is as good as any I can come up with," Berto answered. "I find it hard to believe they are going through all that trouble to extract iron ore. It is a widely available commodity, and they can't compete with the scale of a legitimate operation. But I'm no expert, so that may very well be what they are doing. Whatever they are extracting from that mine, whether iron or some other mineral, could be conceivably being sold to fund revolutionaries in other countries. The Venezuelan government is not so secretly trying to subvert governments all over the Americas. The Brazilian administration has not publicly endorsed or condemned these actions, but some of the president's close advisors are said to be sympathetic. So it makes sense that they would try to help in this way."

"You mean the Brazilian government may be helping Venezuela fund guerrillas across the Americas?" Henry asked with incredulity.

"We are obviously speculating, based solely on the facts that you conveyed. Perhaps there's another side to the story that is not so sinister. But as long as we are considering the possibility, we can't ignore the fact that the current administration is close to insurgents in Colombia and has in fact granted asylum to some of them. I surely hope that as more facts emerge, there will be a simpler and less disturbing explanation for all of this."

"It's late," Berto observed, closing the discussion. "You need some rest, and I need some time to think about all of this. With a clear mind and some perspective, perhaps tomorrow we can find a way to help you."

They nodded. It had been an exhausting stretch, and they had to get some sleep.

"You can stay the night of course. We'll pick it up from here in the morning."

∽

Clare lay next to Henry in a twin bed in the professor's guest bedroom. Henry had offered to sleep on the couch downstairs, but she said she didn't want to be alone. Neither did he, though he was too proud to admit it.

The room seemed rarely used, with just a bed and a nightstand, the white walls disrupted only by the natural-wood window shutters.

Propped up on some pillows against the wall, Henry lay awake next to Clare, not moving, afraid to disturb her sleep. His eyes adjusted to the dark, he watched her belly go up and down, breathing slowly and deeply. She looked at peace.

Her face was turned toward him, and he watched the freckles on her nose, spreading over to her cheeks and forehead before fading away near her hairline. She was close enough to him that he could see the pores and light hair on her soft skin. Her slight imperfections only made her more beautiful.

He closed his eyes again and took in the night's moist, warm air, realizing it contained her body's scent. He felt embarrassed, as though he was taking something without her permission.

His affection for her bothered him. He didn't know exactly what is was but felt guilty for thinking of her that way while she was grieving and vulnerable. He wouldn't dare take advantage of her in those conditions. Not that he would have the nerve to approach someone like her in normal circumstances anyway.

He closed his eyes and let the events of the past few days shuffle in his mind, like random excerpts from a movie. The image of Bill's still body in Clare's arms came into view, followed by her catatonic expression the night they slept by the river. His mind replayed the conversation with Oliveira before she locked them in the Fund-Ama office, then he saw the escape from the police car and heard the sound of bullets whizzing by his head in the forest as loudly as if it was happening again.

The flashbacks made him increasingly anxious, until his mind zeroed in on the glorious sunset over the jungle, hours after escaping from the Pitiri Station. He felt the warm, thick air fill his lungs again and saw the bright orange-and-pink colors projected on the shifting clouds in a striking array, so beautiful no photograph or work of art would ever do it justice. It had given him hope and strength then, and it did so again now.

His thoughts came into sharper focus. He knew what he had to do.

CHAPTER 26

CLARE WOKE UP wrapped in faded blue sheets, a warm breeze blowing through the louvers with a mix of the earthy scent of the rain forest and dusty city smells. She felt slightly disoriented, taking a moment to realize where she was. She had spent each night in a different place for a week now.

It was late morning. The sun was up and the day was hot and humid, a notch above what it had been during the night.

She looked around for Henry but did not worry when she didn't see him. After everything they had been through together, she trusted him. Perhaps he had been in the jungle for too long, or maybe he was just an introvert, but at first she had found him distant and awkward. She was used to men with big egos who were forward and keen to show her how smart they were, whereas Henry was shy and reserved. She had come to appreciate that about him.

There was something peculiar about his past. She

knew no one would abandon the prospect of an academic career for a job as a research assistant in the middle of nowhere. It may be interesting and adventurous, but it would lead to no degree and do nothing to advance his prospects as a scientist. What had made him leave his PhD program?

She brushed her thoughts aside and got up. Her bare feet touched the hardwood floor, and she walked out of the bedroom into a short hallway. To her left, the door to the bathroom was open.

After freshening up, she went down the steps, wearing the same oversized T-shirt and shorts she had slept in, borrowed from Berto.

She found the professor bent over the kitchen table, his eyeglasses resting on the bridge of his nose, extending his neck to read the local newspaper.

Sitting in his chair, he jumped with surprise as she walked up.

"Oh, hello," he said with a smile. "I didn't see you come in."

"Sorry, I didn't mean to startle you."

"It's all right. I don't usually have company. I also tend to tune things out when I'm reading."

"Sorry," she said again. "Where's Henry?"

"He just left. Went to get us breakfast."

"Isn't that risky? Someone could see him and call the police."

"We checked all the news this morning. There's nothing about you two."

"That's a relief. I was imagining a citywide manhunt."

"Based on your story," Berto noted, "the very reason

people are after you is to keep a conspiracy under wraps. It would achieve the exact opposite to make it into a public pursuit."

"Yeah, makes sense," she agreed, pulling up a chair and sitting down at the kitchen table, diagonally across from him.

"Henry said you are a professor at IBEA," Clare said, changing the subject.

"Yes. I teach and do some research. Mostly theoretical stuff. It's been difficult to get enough funding to do field studies, so I focus on research I can do from here." He waved his arm to indicate the room. "I miss the fieldwork, but it's probably for the best. My old body doesn't take as well to the rigors of the jungle as it used to."

Berto turned back to the newspaper, and she sensed it was a sensitive subject, wondering if his lack of funding was connected to Henry's past troubles. That's when her journalistic instinct took the better of her.

"Professor?"

He looked up over his glasses, his head still facing the newspaper.

"I need to ask you something."

Berto put down the paper and waited for her to speak.

"What happened to you and Henry? He said you two had a falling-out. I can't help but think it's somehow related to the end of his academic career."

The professor slowly removed his reading glasses and put them on the table.

"It's a long story. Politics, mostly," he said calmly, shrugging noncommittally.

"Would you mind sharing it with me?"

"Have you heard of Professor Wallace Sayre from Columbia University?" he asked.

"No."

"He famously said, decades ago, that academic politics are so bitter because the stakes are so low." He chuckled.

"I'd heard that thought but never knew who said it," she replied, thinking he may be trying to evade her inquiry. "So what does that have to do with you and Henry?"

"Very well." He paused, sitting up straight. "First you have to appreciate how strict the environmental regulations are in Brazil. This is out of fear—not entirely irrational—that a foreign company will develop a drug or a new product based on an active ingredient from a plant or animal found in the Amazon and sell it without paying royalties to the communities or scientists who first discovered it. As well as to the government, of course. No one can collect anything from the jungle without a permit. If the police or officials from the environmental agency find you with a seed or leaf that you picked up because you liked it, they can throw you in jail. I'm not exaggerating; this has happened to people I know."

"Henry?" she asked.

His head moved slightly, but she couldn't tell if he was nodding or had just ignored her. She didn't press.

"The whole thing is all the more fascinating because the same politicians behind these laws to"—Berto raised his hands and made the quotation-mark sign with his fingers—" 'protect' Brazil's natural resources are often connected to the loggers and farmers who are actually plundering the forest. It's very effective. They profit from the forest destruction while posing as protectors of the

Amazon against the foreigners and scientists that are"—he repeated the quotation gesture—" 'stealing Brazil's natural resources.'

"And NGOs and other foreign donors eat this up—or at least pretend to, flooding the country with money for all sorts of *sustainability* projects while the destruction goes on pretty much undisturbed. They hand out millions to the government and quasi-government organizations under the excuse that Brazil has tough environmental regulations and the pretense it is cracking down on the destruction of the rain forest. In reality, the authorities are just rounding up owners of exotic pets and throwing them in jail."

"I see." She leaned forward with interest.

"When these laws passed in the mid-to-late nineties, most people were optimistic that it would help reduce illegal deforestation. Scientists continued their research as usual, with a few formalities added here and there. But the reality is that the laws are so strict and complicated that no scientific project is one hundred percent legal. So you can understand . . ."

"Is that why foreign universities partner with local organizations?"

"Precisely. Henry's advisor—or former advisor, I should say—and his research team are essentially buying protection from Fund-Ama against any corrupt government official that may decide to throw the book at them, either for a bribe or political gain. If anything goes wrong, the researchers can point to their Brazilian partners and claim they were relying on the locals to make sure everything complied with all regulations. Besides, the bureaucracy is so slow that it takes forever to get a permit, especially for foreigners. But Oliveira is well connected and can accelerate the process with a single phone call. Fund-Ama's coffers are filled with foreign cash because there's no other way to get a project going.

"The complexity of the regulations and the difficulty of getting the permits open the door for corrupt government officials and politicians to collect bribes and score political points when needed. A few years ago, when the law finally started to be implemented and the deforestation of the Amazon was at record highs, some groups started a witch hunt against anyone who could be perceived as stealing Brazil's natural resources. It was a brilliant way to show they were doing something, allowing the money to continue to pour in, while the actual deforestation continued.

"There was already great resentment in Brazil against foreign corporations coming here and developing products based on chemical compounds found in our native species, without any benefit to the country. Sometimes the *discovery* is common knowledge in local forest communities, which don't get a dime from the millions in profits they generate. And when the companies patent those native substances, the same communities can't use them without paying royalties. One company in Japan went so far as to trademark the *name* of a popular fruit and threatened to sue anyone who used it commercially. Have you heard of *cupuaçú*?"

"Really? Someone tried to patent that?"

"Yes. That name is so commonly used here in the region that it's like someone trying to trademark the name for the banana. But the main trigger for what happened was the case of a pharmaceutical company that developed a blood pressure medicine from the venom of a Brazilian snake and made more than a billion dollars in profit without paying a cent in royalties. Most of the initial research on that had been conducted by Brazilian scientists working at local institutions, so you can understand their outrage.

"Capitalizing on this scandal, prosecutors were keen to show they were tough on environmental crimes and started to arrest scientists over trivial things, like bringing a plant to a lab without a permit. A friend of mine was jailed because she was maintaining a rescue shelter for wildlife without all the necessary permits. She had applied three times for those permits and had been waiting for a response for years. Her situation was perfectly legal, mind you, because the law allowed her to run the shelter while the permits were pending. But government officials needed a high-profile case to distract the media and foreign donors from the fact that the new environmental laws did very little to stop actual deforestation and smuggling of wildlife."

"Where do you and Henry come in?" Clare asked, showing her impatience at the long-winded introduction.

"Sorry, I guess that's enough background," Berto replied. "I was helping Henry with his research project. He belonged to one of the most prestigious tropical ecology programs in the world and was a very promising PhD candidate. One of the brightest I've met.

"After his first stint at the Pitiri camp, he was under a lot of pressure. Field research is expensive. His scholarship required him to publish results frequently; and if he didn't finish his program in time, he would lose his funding, including his tuition fees and the stipend he lived on. He had collected some samples of plants and animals and applied for the permits to send them abroad for analysis, but the process was taking forever. Oliveira was asked to intervene; but it was during the height of this major witch hunt, so she said it wouldn't do much good.

"I advised him to apply for another permit, to bring the samples to my lab at the university. Yes, you do need a different permit for that, in case you are wondering. But the bureaucracy is so maddening that you are not allowed to apply for two different permits. So Henry became impatient and decided to take matters in his own hands, trying to take the samples out of the country before the permits were granted. One of the local researchers found out about it and warned the authorities, for no reason but jealousy. The police stopped Henry at the airport and caught him red-handed."

"Oh no! Was he arrested?"

"No. He was detained, but the charges were later dropped."

"But he lost his career over it," she completed.

"Essentially, yes. He was caught up in the middle of the witch hunt. A foreigner trying to smuggle samples of the rain forest out of the country made for an easy target. The university could not afford to keep him on as a PhD student, lest all scientists affiliated with the program be barred from continuing with their research. Henry was forced to resign; but they let him continue as an assistant, managing the research on behalf of other scientists, including the project he started. While his position is funded by the university and he reports to his former advisor, he is employed by Pitiri, so there are no formal links to the research program he used to be part of."

"So how did you get at the forefront of the scandal?" Clare asked.

A voice intervened, startling both of them.

"He took the fall for me so I could escape jail time and have a shot at rebuilding my career."

Clare was so absorbed in their conversation that she hadn't noticed Henry come in. He held a brown bag with their breakfast, the aroma of fresh bread taking over the kitchen.

"Henry!" she gasped, blushing. "I'm sorry. I didn't mean to . . ."

"It's okay," he said. "I was going to tell you sooner or later."

"I wasn't quite that noble, to be frank," Berto continued.

"What do you mean? You said you had advised me to leave the country with the samples, even though it was entirely my decision, my mistake. You lost your lab over this!" Henry cried out.

"It wasn't just because of what I did for you. I was trying to help other people at the same time. You see"—he looked at Clare—"there were many decent people, scientists and friends alike, getting into trouble because of their frustration with the bureaucracy or other ridiculous regulations. I thought my prestige and position would allow me to push back on what I saw as an overreach and grossly disproportionate punishment. I ran the biggest tropical research lab in Manaus and had hundreds of thousands of dollars in research funds. I thought all of that would protect me. Some hubris on my part . . ."

Berto let that linger for a moment.

"That's where the petty university politics come into play," he continued. "A colleague had an eye on my lab and my position. When she saw the opportunity, she jumped at it. She denounced me for being the ringleader of a gang smuggling precious natural resources to greedy multinationals. It was all fabricated, of course, but since I was taking responsibility for what Henry did as well as for several other charges of irregularities that others were facing, it was a credible accusation. My intervention backfired badly.

"It didn't matter that nothing ever came out of it; the damage was done. In a sense it worked out, though. Once Henry's advisor and other researchers disavowed me, I became the focus of the story, and that made it easier on everyone I was trying to protect."

"I was never comfortable with that," Henry said.

"I remember. You wanted to take responsibility for what you did, which only endeared you more in my eyes and strengthened my resolve to help you. But remember that, at the time, we thought the whole scandal would blow over soon, so I was happy to take the blame and pretend I had a big falling-out with you and your team over it. It didn't exactly go as planned, but I'd happily trade my own career prospects for those of all the people I helped."

"So," Clare tried to summarize the story to confirm her own understanding, "one scientist threw Henry under the bus, while another called the authorities on you to get your lab and your position at the research institute."

"Hardly the stuff worth ruining someone's life over," Berto concluded. "But such is the way of the cutthroat academic business."

"Don't be so modest," Henry said. "You could have recanted and saved your career. Instead you gave me and others a shot to save ours."

"And look how well it turned out for you!" Berto exclaimed.

"Can't argue with that," Henry answered, reciprocating the professor's sarcasm with an ironic smile. "But you saved me from some jail time and gave me another chance. I had to leave the PhD program, but they still let me work for the team as a research assistant."

"Doing all the work and taking none of the credit. You know they didn't do this as a favor to you, right?"

"Yes, but I'll take it. I'd rather see my research through without getting the credit than let it go to waste."

"It wasn't all because of me, you know," Berto replied. "You were well liked by the people who worked with you, and everyone knew you weren't stealing anything to sell to some evil corporation, just trying to get on with your research. The permit delays and the overreach were causing a lot of frustration among many researchers. Your detention may have played well among some of the more nationalistic local scientists, but it infuriated a great many more."

"What happened after you said it was your idea for Henry to take those samples out of the country?" Clare asked.

"Like I said, the frustration was growing. If Henry had been prosecuted, there would have been a backlash from a lot of scientists. Not only that, the trial could have potentially exposed that some government officials were delaying the permits on purpose in order to ask for bribes. So when I told the investigators Henry acted at my recommendation, the government had a good excuse to drop the charges and avoid the potential embarrassments a trial might have brought. They found a fall guy to parade in public. It was always about the politics.

"Acting on the accusation from my colleague at IBEA," Berto continued, "the police raided my lab and found several samples of animals, plants, fungi, and other organisms. They were all part of my research, of course, and I had published numerous studies based on them. But it was enough to start an investigation that made my life miserable for a while. In the end, all they could show was that I gave some bad advice. I was reprieved, and they couldn't even find grounds to fire me from IBEA. My credibility was destroyed, obviously, and I lost my funding and my lab."

"I wish we had stood up for you," Henry said.

"That may have made you feel better, but it wouldn't have helped me. Your advisor and colleagues knew it, and that's why they didn't intervene. Trust me, we talked about it.

"None of us ever expected it would go down so badly for me. When it did, there was nothing anyone could do," Berto went on. "By the time I realized I had misread the politics, it was too late. There's no point in second-guessing that decision. It was the right thing to do. Watching you and all those other people fall might have protected my career, but I wouldn't have been able to live with myself. I did it as much for me as for you and them. I paid a steep price, but a clear conscience is well worth it."

CHAPTER 27

BERTO BREWED A pitcher of strong coffee, using a cone filter. They drank it with sandwiches made of fresh French-style buns, thin cheese slices, and *requeijão*, the traditional creamy cheese spread that is popular all over Brazil.

After finishing their meal, the three of them brought their coffee across the small backyard into the professor's office.

"Should we start with the hard drive you took from Teresa's computer?" Berto suggested.

"Yes," Henry answered, ready to start. "Can I borrow a screwdriver?"

He opened the professor's computer tower and located the light-gray cable connecting the motherboard to the hard drive. It was flat and a couple of inches wide, with two sockets, one for the master drive, currently in use, and another for a secondary device. He connected the stolen hard disk to the open slot and plugged it into the power source, not bothering to screw it to the drive bay.

The computer's operating system recognized the new hardware automatically. Henry opened the file-explorer application and anxiously clicked on the newly installed device.

> *You do not have permission to access this folder.*

"No!"

"What is it?" the professor asked.

"The files are protected. I can connect the cables and set up the drive, but I can't access the data."

"Isn't there a *back door* or something?" Berto asked, the uncertain tone in his voice indicating he may not know exactly what it means.

"I'm sure there is," Henry replied. "But it goes beyond my computer skills. We're stuck," he declared.

"That's it? There's nothing you can do?"

Henry just raised the palms of his hands.

Berto looked pensive for a moment. He asked, "What time is it?"

"Eleven nineteen." Henry glanced at the clock on the lower right corner of the computer screen. "Why?"

"I may know someone who can help."

Berto picked up the phone on the desk and made a quick call.

"Let's start with the map," he said when he hung up.

They spread the large chart on the desk and crowded over it, carefully studying its features. It was a simple, high-level map, with blue markings showing the water bodies and thin, black contour lines representing the area's predominantly flat topography. Occasionally the lines would come closer together, revealing the rock formations that sprouted out of the forest.

The area of the cave was one such formation. Henry thought it would be the easiest element to find and looked for it first, following the blue line marked as the Içana River. Right where he expected the cave to be was a symbol consisting of a horizontal *Y*.

He checked the key at the bottom and found it meant either a mine tunnel or cave entrance.

Henry noted a few other symbols scattered across the map. South of the cave and slightly to the west he found a hand-drawn marking that showed the location of the research camp.

"It's an old survey map," Berto noted. "Probably commissioned by the government or a mining company looking to identify opportunities in the area. This may be one of the first maps showing the cave. Pitiri was drawn by hand later on, see?" He pointed to the same hand drawing Henry had spotted.

As the professor finished speaking, Henry noted the symbol of two pickaxes crossed like an *X*, north of the cave.

"Here," he shouted excitedly. "This is the site!"

Clare and Berto looked. The mine's location looked fairly close to the research camp but was separated by two sets of very close contour lines delineating the two ridges Henry and the two filmmakers had ascended to get to the mine and back.

Next to the legend at the bottom right corner of the

map, Berto pointed to a name in bold black letters: "Mineradora da Floresta S.A."

"I recognize this name," the professor said. "It was one of the big state-owned mining companies in Brazil several years ago. I'm pretty sure it's no longer in operation. They were big in the nineteen seventies and eighties but faded away after the transition from the military to the civilian regime."

"So somehow Fund-Ama got ahold of this map," Clare noted. "Does this show they are connected to the paramilitary that took us, or at least to the mine?"

"Probably not," Henry replied. "They could argue they just needed a good map of the area."

"Actually, that wouldn't make much sense," the professor corrected him. "Brazil has a mapping agency that has high-quality maps with many more-meaningful geographic and ecological features than this one. But as far as I know, they don't include mining sites. The only reason Fund-Ama would need an old map like this would be to find those sites. Everything else is more reliable and readily available on government maps."

That sent a chill up Henry's spine. The map indicated a connection between Fund-Ama and the mining operation. Or at least a suspicious interest in mining.

"But all this proves," Berto continued, "is that Fund-Ama is interested in mining surveys. There could be a reasonable research angle to this."

"Perhaps," Clare said firmly. "But they wouldn't lock us up in their office and try to kill us over a research angle."

She let her point linger for a few moments and then asked:

"Do you believe us now, Professor?"

"Well, this certainly seems to support your story."

∽

The doorbell rang, preventing them from speculating further about the meaning of the map.

The professor excused himself to check the door, returning with a guest.

"This is Ciro, one of my neighbors." He introduced a young man carrying a laptop.

"Nice to meet you," Ciro said with a heavy Brazilian accent, pronouncing the *t* like *chee*.

His skin was too pale for a kid growing up in the tropics, and Henry assumed he spent most of his time indoors. With a circular face, long hair, and large glasses, Ciro was the caricature of a computer geek.

Henry introduced himself and showed the error message. He started to speak Portuguese, but Ciro wanted to practice his English.

"Can you make this work?" Henry asked.

"As long as it's not encrypted," he answered. "In this version of the operating system, it typically isn't. It's not hard to bypass this type of security."

"Great, let's try it."

Berto and Clare left Henry and Ciro to deal with the stolen hard drive.

"May I?" Ciro asked, pulling up the chair.

Henry waved his right hand toward the computer, and the young Brazilian took a seat. Ciro went to an internet forum dedicated to computer security, which Henry quickly saw was a euphemism for hacking, typed a few search words, and started reading some postings. Henry tried to follow but got lost in the computer jargon.

Ciro read through different instructions, nodding occasionally and mumbling a few words in his native language.

"Piece of cake," he said proudly, after just a few minutes.

He accessed the menu and opened a new window, where he typed a few commands that Henry did not recognize. A black screen came up, and Ciro started furiously typing some advanced computer code.

A few minutes into the black screen, he went back to the operating system and clicked on the icon designated for the stolen hard drive.

The folders opened without a glitch.

"Done," Ciro said. "Like I thought, not encrypted. I just had to change some of the settings. The operating system now thinks all the contents of this hard disk were created under the owner's profile. You should be able to access all the files unless they have a password."

"And if they do?"

"Tell Berto to call me. Each file type has a different level of security, so I'll have to take a look on a case-by-case basis."

"Thank you, Ciro. This is a big help."

"Let me do a couple more things to help you find whatever you are looking for."

With a few more clicks, the young Brazilian opened Berto's email client and set up a new account linked to the file on the Fund-Ama hard disk. He closed the email program and then downloaded new software.

"Here you go," Ciro announced. "You now have access to all the messages and files on the drive. It stores only the most recent emails, a few weeks' worth. I also installed a program to let you search the contents of all the documents. Just click here to start searching." Ciro pointed to an icon on the screen.

"This is perfect," Henry said. "Thanks again."

"You are welcome."

"I take it you're Berto's free IT support?"

"For sure!" Ciro laughed. "But that's nothing compared to what he does for me and my mom. Berto paid for my computer and also arranged for me to audit some computer classes at the university. That's the least I can do for him."

"He's a good man," Henry replied, thinking of all the professor had given up for him. "Thanks again for all your help, Ciro. It was great to meet you."

"You are welcome," he said for the second time, taking his leave. "Good luck with everything."

Ciro walked out, and Henry saw Berto put his hand on the young man's shoulder in a paternal way as he said goodbye, thanking Ciro with a warm smile.

Henry turned back to the computer screen and crouched over the fourteen-inch flat-panel monitor, studying the file structure on the stolen hard drive. He browsed through the folders and tried to familiarize himself with the logic behind them. The names were in Portuguese, which slowed him down a bit, but after a few minutes he found his bearings.

He started navigating through the files and realized he was looking at Oliveira's personal documents. He checked the properties of the hard drive and discovered it had 4,844 files, including emails and other file types in several different folders.

This may take a while.

He tried looking through the folder names to see if there was anything related to a mine or the research station. He opened a few files but didn't find anything of interest.

Henry searched for some key words with the new software installed by Ciro. He started with the names of the film crew and his own, finding a few messages related to the visit to the station for filming a documentary but nothing beyond that. The words for *death*, *accident*, and *trouble* in Portuguese did not get any meaningful matches either.

Something finally came up when he tried the combination of the word *urgent* in Portuguese with the date of the incident at Pitiri. There was a single message marked with a red flag and the subject title "Precisamos Falar." *We Need to Talk.* The body of the email had one sentence:

"Me ligue com urgencia."

Call me with urgency.

Henry looked at the date-and-time stamp. It was from the same day Bill Powers was killed.

"Unbelievable!" he cried out loud, getting the attention of Berto and Clare, who had since returned to the professor's office. "She lied to us! She heard about it as soon as we escaped."

They got up and leaned toward the screen.

"Look at when this was sent." Henry pointed at the email. "It's around the same time we escaped from the camp."

He saw a gloomy expression come across Berto's face as the professor read the message.

"That's not the worst of it," the professor said. "I know the recipient."

Henry looked at the name: "Dirceu Vargas." He didn't recognize it.

"He's a senator and a close advisor to the president," Berto noted somberly.

⁂

The magnitude of their situation weighed heavily on Henry. They had suspected the conspiracy may go that high, but the confirmation unsettled him. The more evidence they uncovered, the more he feared they would never leave the country alive. They were fighting not just a ruthless and well-connected criminal gang, but top members of the Brazilian government with possibly the country's whole security apparatus behind them.

It only reinforced what he had already decided the night before.

Clare and Berto must have taken notice of the resolve in his expression, because they were staring directly at him, waiting for him to say what was on his mind.

"I realized something last night," Henry said, responding to their inquiring looks. "I've been dreaming of exploring the Amazon since I was a kid. I came here to realize that dream. It was everything I thought it would be and more. I may have lost my shot at an academic career, but I won't let anybody take away whatever is left.

"I'm going back to that mine," Henry declared. "I'm going to find out exactly what they are doing, get proof of it, and then I'm going to blow it wide open. I'll tell the whole world about it."

"You expect to take on an entire army, win, and just waltz back in one piece? This is crazy!" Clare cried out, her voice growing louder.

"Crazy would be to let these people get away with what they did. How many more times do we have to escape before we are *actually* safe? Unless we confront this head-on, every night for the rest of our lives we will be going to bed afraid someone is coming for us. I'm done running away. It's time to go on the offensive."

Clare and Berto stared at each other.

"What other option do we have?" he continued. "My past mistakes alone automatically discredit me in the eyes of any authority. We don't have our passports, so we can't get out of the country. What else are we going to do?"

"We can go to our embassies and get a new passport," Clare replied. "No one can touch us there."

"Do you think the people from the embassy will just believe our story? With the police after us, backed by a senator who is a close advisor to the country's president?"

"I called my father and my producer while you were checking out the hard drive," she countered. "They are reaching out to a lot of people. We'll have authorities from Australia and the UK involved. And aren't your colleagues back home bringing in the US government as well? We are not alone in this."

Henry didn't listen.

"Sunlight is the best disinfectant," he paraphrased

former Supreme Court Justice Louis Brandeis. It resonated with him now more than anything else. "Our best protection is to get evidence and go public with this story. As long as it remains buried, we are in danger."

Clare did not reply, perhaps because she knew she wasn't getting through to him. Or maybe he was getting through to *her*.

"It's also unexpected," Henry continued. "They expect us to be in hiding, not trying to fight back."

"I still don't understand how you can hope to take on professional soldiers." She sounded alarmed.

He stared at the map spread over the desk, a plan forming in his head.

"I don't have to take them on. I just have to find out what they are doing and bring back some proof. I know the terrain like the palm of my hand and can find my way around the jungle as well as anyone. But regardless of my chances, I can't just wait here to find out what happened to everyone over there."

He saw her look away from him and knew she felt guilty at the thought of leaving Aidan and Liam to their own devices until the authorities decided to step in.

"You'll be safe here with Berto," Henry concluded as he realized there would be no more pushback. "No one knows where we are. You can continue to work with our colleagues and the authorities. That will be a big help."

"Are you joking?"

He looked at her, confused. Of course he wasn't joking. Was she not taking him seriously?

"If you are going back, I'm coming with you."

CHAPTER 28

I T WAS A short-lived discussion.

"I can't just sit here waiting to hear news about Aidan and Liam," she said with a finality that did not leave room for argument. "Besides, I'm the reporter. If we are going to expose this conspiracy, you're going to need my help."

They didn't waste any more time debating it. Henry knew not to prolong a discussion he couldn't win. Instead, they started preparing for their return to the jungle.

Berto drove them to a local camping store, where he bought flashlights, ready-to-eat meals, a portable water filter, hiking clothes, two backpacks, and a couple of knives. A separate trip to the supermarket yielded more food, light raincoats, and a few extras. After getting supplies, they made a stop at IBEA, and the professor checked out one of the institute's satellite phones under the pretense of a last-minute field survey.

Back at the house, Henry and Clare also took Berto's

five-year-old point-and-shoot camera. Although ancient by the standards of digital technology, and lacking the latest bells and whistles, it had the two features they needed most: it was equipped with a good zoom lens and ran on AA batteries, an important design when hundreds of miles away from the electric grid with no place to recharge.

Henry lined the inside of the backpacks with a garbage bag to add an extra layer of protection against the ever-present element in the rain forest: water. Staying dry in the jungle was one of the keys to survival.

The blankets and extra clothes went in the bottom of the bag, with heavier items, such as food, up in the middle, close to the back for better balance. Berto's old GPS, a compass, the camera, a knife, the first aid kit, and the plastic raincoats were stored in the outside pockets for easy access.

He recalled the anticipation and excitement of getting ready for a camping trip or a new expedition, noting the contrast with how he felt now. He was tense, his stomach heavy. Though he had eaten little at lunch, he still wasn't hungry by dinnertime.

Berto walked into the room, carrying something packaged in an orange felt cloth.

"Take this," he said, unfolding the fabric.

It revealed a .38-caliber revolver, a Brazilian-made Taurus with a long barrel and capacity for six bullets.

Henry took a step back, reluctant to accept the offer.

"I hope to God you don't have to use it," the professor insisted, grabbing Henry's wrist and putting the weapon in the younger man's hand.

"But considering where you are going and the people you are facing, it's better to have it than not."

◆

As Clare and Berto were getting ready to go to bed, Henry sat in front of the professor's computer, composing an email to his former advisor and a few other colleagues. He explained in detail everything they had discovered and provided all the evidence he could, including a copy of the email he had found on Oliveira's hard drive and a picture of the map. Henry was careful not to mention Berto's involvement. He feared that if their plan failed and word got out, the professor could become a target.

He also omitted that he was going back to the jungle with Clare. Not knowing how far the conspiracy extended, they had decided to keep it a secret until their return. The note ended saying that they were hiding in a safe place near Manaus and would be in touch after they talked to lawyers and had a plan to prove their innocence.

After clicking "Send," Henry felt a sense of relief. If anything happened to him, there would be an account of what he knew and who he thought was responsible. But he wasn't ready to turn in just yet. There was one more thing he wanted to do. He needed to find out whatever he could about what was actually being extracted at the mining site.

He logged in to the university library. The school had cut formal ties with him after the scandal but allowed him to keep his library account. He still needed access to all the publications and databases the university subscribed to in order to carry on the research for his team. Like most of his colleagues, in the first semester of his PhD studies Henry had learned that pretty much every piece of information ever to be digitized and placed online could be found in one of those databases.

Even though he had exhaustively studied the fauna, flora, climate, and geology of the region, he was surprised to find out the diversity and scale of the mining activity in the Amazon. There was a long list of minerals regularly extracted from under the rain forest: bauxite, kaolin, fluorite, iron ore, copper, potassium, tin, leucite, tungsten, manganese, gold, gypsum, columbite, and chromium, most of which he had never heard of before.

There was also a great deal of illegal mining going on, feeding a robust market for contraband minerals. One of them in particular caught Henry's attention: columbite-tantalite, an ore containing a metal used in the components of a wide variety of electronics, from cell phones to guided missiles.

The connection to potential weapons-building materials took him in a new direction. It made much more sense that the conspirators were secretly exploiting a valuable mineral commonly used to build military weapons than extracting iron ore for sale. Could this be what was behind the operation he had bumped into? It would explain how aggressively those responsible for it were coming after him.

He wondered if he could find anything related to Mineradora da Floresta S.A., the company that had produced the map he and Clare had stolen from Fund-Ama, and whether it had been involved in any such mining. What he discovered was even more alarming.

Unearthing an investigative report based on a declassified file from the National Security Agency from the late 1970s, Henry learned that the company hadn't been an ordinary mining enterprise. It was created during the military government in Brazil, as part of its nuclear program. Its mission was not to exploit iron or even other ores that could be used for military ordnances, but uranium. The key ingredient for nuclear-power plants and atomic weapons.

The discovery made him nauseated. *This just keeps getting worse.*

Along with Brazil's nuclear-power ambitions, Mineradora da Floresta S.A. had been shut down after the transition to civilian government back in 1985. But illegal mining of uranium ores was still rampant in the Amazon, he learned, especially of thorianite, a black heavy mineral commonly sold in the highly illegal and secretive international nuclear market. Some reports postulated that many of the sites originally opened by the company were now the source of much of the thorianite trafficked by international smugglers.

Remembering the military ID he had found, Henry looked next for a link to Venezuela. It didn't take long to find several papers speculating about the existence of a Venezuelan nuclear program. Going deeper, he immersed himself in the world of wild conspiracy theories, some suggesting a secret connection to other countries, but there were far too many to sort out the credible from the crazy.

As he wrapped up his searches, Henry was left pondering the extent of his findings. Was the mine that they had found extracting thorianite? If so, could it be feeding a secret Venezuelan nuclear program? And if some of the conspiracy theories he had found were correct, could there be even more countries involved?

He was determined to find out.

∽

Jolted by his discovery, Henry knew he wasn't going to be able to sleep anytime soon. Realizing how high the stakes were and how dangerous was the task he had set for himself, he wanted to call his family. He wanted to say that he missed and loved them before he embarked on what could very well be a one-way journey, but he didn't want to put them in the situation of waiting days on end for news of him, not knowing if he was dead or alive. If the worst happened, better that they get all the news at once.

Instead, he wrote his parents and two sisters a long update about his research and his mundane thoughts on life in the field, and included how much he missed them and appreciated everything they had done for him. It was a positive note, sharing his experience in the Amazon rain forest, the realization of a lifelong dream.

Should he never come back alive from the jungle, it was a nice last communication to remember him by. It was close to midnight when he finished. The writing had been calming and cathartic, and Henry was finally ready to go to bed.

CHAPTER 29

THE SINGLE-ENGINE CESSNA 210L cruised leisurely across the morning Amazon sky. Henry
had his back to the pilot and looked intently
out the rectangular window, opposite Clare on the seat
athwart. He normally enjoyed looking up at the sky
during a flight, but today his view was blocked by the
wings on the top of the thirty-year-old aircraft.

The engine's noise made it difficult to carry on a conversation, and the choppy air tossed the small plane up
and down and from side to side. Henry had once read
that it didn't matter how old an airplane was, only how
well it was maintained. That was of little comfort as they
bounced at twenty thousand feet in the dynamic tropical atmosphere.

Berto had taken care of the flight arrangements, dropping them off at the Aeroclube de Manaus at daybreak.

"You are going to land at the research camp of a collaborator of mine. His name is Mateus Toshiaki," he had

explained. "I emailed him, saying a writer from a German magazine is coming to interview him as part of a story on scientific research in the Amazon. He will be very excited, since most of his funding comes from German organizations, just like Pitiri's is connected to Americans. He is also a rival of Oliveira—they hate each other—so it's unlikely that he'll know anything about you, especially being out there, isolated in the jungle. Just make sure you leave the camp before he comes back from his daily rounds; otherwise, he'll want to practice his German with you."

"How will we ever repay you?" Clare had asked as they parted ways, with a look of deep appreciation. "A chartered flight does not come cheap."

"You and Henry coming back in one piece would be enough compensation. I'm an old man with no family. I don't spend or need much money, and this won't make me any poorer. Besides, the flight is not as expensive as you may think."

He paused and let out a broad, impish grin before continuing. "Trust me. You'll realize it when you see the plane."

She smiled back and reached out to give him a long hug.

The flight path followed the Rio Negro, going northwest over the left bank and then straight west after crossing the river just before its southward bend toward Manaus. Despite everything that was on his mind, Henry was soon in awe of the view from the rough sky, filled with bright, scattered clouds. Shortly after takeoff he and Clare were gazing at the glorious chain of four hundred green islands dotting the river, the Anavilhanas, stretching for miles on end just north of Manaus. The Amazon tributary was so wide and large that it accommodated another, even bigger archipelago farther up, a seven-hundred-island wonder known as Mariuá.

Henry was marveling at this second, dreamlike island formation as they approached the small town of Barcelos, a hidden ecotourist gem that served as the gateway to Brazil's deepest cave and a myriad of waterfalls. The sight of verdant patches on the dark waters of the Negro River was breathtaking, the islands so lush that Henry—knowing just one of those little islands had more species of plants and animals than all of Scandinavia—could feel the life pulsating from under the emerald canopy thousands of feet below.

The old Cessna's flight range was sufficient to take them to the research station, but not long enough for the return trip. Since there would be no fuel available at their destination, the pilot made a stop at Santa Isabel do Rio Negro, an isolated town of about twenty thousand sprung out of an old settlement opposite the river's largest island.

They were back on their way in less than half an hour. As they charted the midmorning sky, the plane went over the equator, crossing into the northern hemisphere. It would take another couple of hours to reach their final stop, a research camp situated in the same gigantic indigenous reserve as the Pitiri Station. It stood on the margins of a small river southeast of the cave they had visited a week earlier.

The aircraft landed on a dirt runway, greeted by a handful of children in what was seemingly the standard welcome at these isolated outposts.

Not a bad way to arrive anywhere.

As the pilot taxied toward the end of the strip, they could see the short path to the small village that housed the few workers who kept the camp humming.

They were received by the camp manager, who introduced himself as Jonas, not bothering to give his last name, in good Brazilian fashion. He was tall and athletic, with long, straight hair and a short beard, and welcomed the visitors cheerfully, though his immediate attention seemed more focused on Clare than on her colleague.

Their cover as journalists was immediately threatened when Jonas greeted them in German. Henry thought of replying in Portuguese, but it wouldn't take long for the camp manager to realize his accent was American.

Clare stepped in, speaking before Henry.

"Hi, I'm Clare," she introduced herself. She must have noted the way Jonas looked at her, because she immediately extended her hand to avoid the customary kiss on the cheeks and to set her boundary.

"I'm *Herr* Foster's colleague," she explained cheekily. "I'm sorry; I don't speak German. Can we use English, please?"

Jonas seemed disappointed and slightly surprised but carried on with a heavily accented English, asking them to wait for Dr. Toshiaki to come back from his field observations. Henry responded, with a fake German accent, that being familiar with the scientist's research, he and Clare would be eager to meet Dr. Toshiaki later, but right now they needed to get going.

Striking up a conversation with Clare, the camp manager appeared to brush off any suspicion she may have triggered by not speaking German.

"I'm from Rio," he volunteered proudly. "Have you been there?"

Henry welcomed the distraction. She was good at small talk and would manage to keep Jonas's attention away from Henry and the fact he didn't work for a magazine.

They talked about Rio de Janeiro for a while, Clare saying she had always wanted to go, being a beach girl from Australia herself. She teased Jonas that the waves were surely better in her own country, though, and he laughed.

Henry felt a smidgen of jealousy, forcing himself to brush it off.

Clare finally managed to steer the conversation toward the cave, explaining they were planning to visit for a few days, before the interview with Dr. Toshiaki.

"I don't recommend doing that," Jonas warned in his broken English. "There has been a recent situation with the death of a foreigner a few days ago. Very dangerous at the moment."

Clare froze. Although it was easy to see the alarm in her expression, Jonas probably took it as a natural reaction to what he had just told her.

"What happened exactly?" Henry asked, curious to know how much of the incident had reached Jonas and his colleagues.

"I don't know the details. We heard that there was a confrontation involving a gang of foreign smugglers and that one of them was killed. But it seems some of them escaped, so it's not safe out there."

Smugglers? he wondered to himself, perplexed but realizing that, after being accused by the Manaus police of murdering Bill, this should not have come as a surprise.

∽

Arguing that they needed as much daylight as possible for the trip to the cave, Clare apologized for not waiting for Dr. Toshiaki. They'd be back in a couple of days for the interview, she explained.

They left on a boat Berto had asked for in advance. The professor must have a very good relationship with his collaborator, Henry thought, for the request to have been accommodated with less than a day's notice.

Henry took command of the launch and headed upstream, due north, the current growing stronger as they advanced. Approaching the massif range to the north, the terrain sloped gently, and the forest gradually closed in on them as the river narrowed.

It had taken them a plane and a boat ride to get there, but they still saw some huts on the margins along the way, deep into the jungle and as far away from the comforts of modern society as anyone could get.

Henry navigated with confidence, the charts fresh in his memory. Rather than keeping north toward the cave, as the stated purpose of their visit would have it, he turned left at a small tributary. They had no intention of going back to the natural wonder. Their destination was the Pitiri Research Station.

Soon the waterway started to transition into rapids. The small motorboat almost capsized while Henry tried to steer through the myriad of undercurrents pushing them in different directions. They were reaching the point where it would be impossible to continue by water.

Before he could decide to stop, Henry saw a wall of water and rocks ahead, a drop of about three feet blocking their way forward. He turned around and noted a small clearing on the right bank, probably used before by others who had arrived at the same dead end.

Henry and Clare would have to go by foot from here on.

He drove the boat into the bank, lifting the engine's propeller and leaping out as they came to a stop. Clare helped him pull the shell away from the water as far as they could. He then tied it to a tree and bookmarked the location on the GPS. If they did not come back this way, he would let Jonas know where they had left it, so some-one could come get it before the next rainy season, when the heavy floods would wash it away.

The afternoon was already coming to an end, and night would fall quickly. They marched through the forest, in the direction of the research station, until there was hardly any daylight left, when they set up the tent for the night.

Dinner consisted of ham and cheese sandwiches with chocolate milk from a kid-sized carton. The child-ish indulgence helped lighten the somber mood as they sipped from the straw in the cartoon-decorated box, under the faint glow of a flashlight.

"Good call on the chocolate milk," Clare said as she savored it, with an amused look at Henry's carton, deco-rated with a pink monkey character from a TV show she didn't recognize.

"Life in the jungle makes you appreciate the little

things," Henry observed with a contented smile. "Before I came here, I never imagined a candy bar could bring a man so much joy."

He saw her smile, but it faded away quickly.

"I didn't mean to pry earlier about you and Berto. I know it's none of my business. I'm sorry about the way things turned out for you with your academic career."

He shrugged as if it was no big deal, though he knew he couldn't hide the fact that it was.

"I just can't help my curiosity sometimes," she continued. "Like when I insisted on going to the mine," she added with a measure of guilt and regret, looking down. "I wish I hadn't pushed everyone to go."

"Don't do this," he said firmly. "You couldn't have known. None of us could. And you didn't exactly force anyone to go. We all wanted to."

He actually admired her inquisitive nature. It reminded him of his own need to know everything.

"As for my own *fall from grace*," he said sarcastically, forcing a change of subject, "I've made my peace with it. My dream was to come down here and see the Amazon for myself, really *experience* it, not to become a stuck-up university professor. I won't deny that I got caught up in the whole thing, dreaming of running my own research team one day. But the reason I ended up here had nothing to do with academic vanity. Anyway, it seems so trivial compared to what we're going through now."

"What *was* the reason?" she asked.

"The reason?" Henry asked, confused.

"You mentioned that the reason you came down here wasn't academic ambition. What was it, then?"

"I just *had* to," he replied after a pause. "Like I said before, I've been in love with it since I was a kid. There's a mystique about it that kept pulling me in when I was growing up. Every time I saw something about the tropical rain forest, I was drawn to it. Like that *curiosity* of yours, I suppose . . ."

He gave her a teasing look, and she smiled warmly.

"I think the turning point came during my junior year in high school. My interest in the Amazon was steadily growing, but it might have gone away, just like a lot of other things did. One day my biology teacher, the same one I told you about, seeing my fascination with the rain forest, handed me an old tape and told me to watch it. It was a TV series from the 1980s, about an expedition to the Amazon River. After I watched it, I felt like a fire lit under me, cementing my desire to come down here. I wanted to do exactly what the guys on that show were doing."

"What was the show?"

"It was called *River Explorations*, by a French explorer . . ."

"Jacques Cousteau!" she cried excitedly.

"Are you a fan too?"

"Are you kidding me? His shows were one of the biggest influences on my career. I watched all of them with my dad, back in Australia. I wouldn't have become a nature journalist if it wasn't for him. Our own show is hugely inspired by what he did."

"So we both owe our career choices to a skinny Frenchman with a red knit cap."

"I guess we do."

"To Jacques Cousteau!" he cried, raising his little milk carton in the air.

"Cheers," she replied, laughing heartily and toasting to the late explorer.

CHAPTER 30

AFTER A SEVERAL-HOUR hike from their overnight campsite, Henry and Clare had approached the research station cautiously, steering clear of the fields and trails, keeping to the denser part of the forest to avoid being spotted.

When he looked at the research station from under the cover of the vegetation, not far from where Bill had been shot, Henry was surprised to see two of his fellow researchers sitting on the porch of the main building, chatting casually as if nothing unusual had transpired just a few days earlier.

Things had apparently gone back to normal.

Marcelo was certain to contact the Fund-Ama chief if he knew Henry and Clare had come back, so Henry chose to see the only person he trusted—the man who had assisted in their escape.

When they came to his door, Chico responded with an expression of surprise and fear, gesturing for them to get inside and briefly stepping outside to check whether anyone had seen the two visitors come into his house.

His wife and two daughters were sitting at the table, their lunch interrupted by Henry and Clare's arrival. Ana Maria beamed with widening eyes as she saw Henry, but her smiled faded when her father addressed the visitors in an angry tone.

"You can't come into my house like this," he scolded them.

Turning to his wife and daughters, he asked them to go to the bedroom.

Ana Maria looked at Henry apologetically as she complied. He gave her a warm smile and a friendly wave to let her know it was all right.

Chico's small house had only two areas: the bedroom, where the whole family slept together, and a combined kitchen and living room. An image of Mary hung prominently next to a cross on the dark-wood wall opposite the main doorway.

The furniture was old and sparse, sitting directly on the dirt floor. The inside was dark even during the day. Like other houses in the region, it was lit only by the natural light coming from two small windows and the gaps between the wood planks that made up the wall.

"I'm sorry to intrude like this," Henry replied. "But you are the only person I trust around here. I promise that we won't stay long and no one will ever know we came by. I will die before I put your family in any danger. You know how much I care about them."

He paused, hoping the farmer would recognize that his oldest daughter was almost like a little sister to Henry.

"I just need to know what happened after we left," he continued.

Chico remained silent, staring past Henry at the image of Saint Mary behind them.

"What happened to the other two foreigners who came here with her?" Henry asked, pointing at Clare. "I'm pretty sure they were being held captive when we escaped."

Without acknowledging the question, Chico walked back through the door and stepped outside again, looking carefully in all directions. Shaking his head nervously, the farmer also proceeded to shut the faded pink curtains, making the inside of the house even darker.

He finally spoke again, waving his hand at the kitchen table as an invitation to sit with him. "Please promise me that after today you will not come back here. And that you will not say anything about this conversation to anyone."

Henry was taken aback by the finality of the request but understood. "You have my word."

"A couple of days after you two escaped, the men left and took your friends with them. I don't know where they went or came from. The police arrived later on the same day, with Gederval."

Henry recognized the name. He had met Gederval de Abreu, one of Oliveira's deputies, a few times at the foundation's headquarters in Manaus.

"The police took the dead body and started their investigation," the farmer continued.

"They questioned everyone while Gederval told us that the foreign visitors were not here to make a film but to collect plants and animals and send them to another country without paying any money to our country and that"—he stared straight at Henry to finish the sentence—"*you* were helping them."

Chico's tone was detached, not accusatory. It was an outlandish accusation, and Henry wondered if the farmer or anyone else in the camp believed the story. Mistrust of the police or any form of government authority ran deep in Brazil. Resentment of foreign companies taking advantage of the local knowledge resonated with Brazilians, but surely most reasonable people realized those elaborate conspiracies were unnecessary in light of the rampant corruption of government officials?

Still, it was a clever plot, Henry admitted to himself. Gederval de Abreu and Oliveira were capitalizing on his past mistakes and the country's exaggerated fears of the theft of its natural resources. The charges against him would fit like a glove, considering his record. It had not been that long since Henry had been detained at the airport trying to leave Brazil with illegal samples of the country's flora and fauna. He had learned at the time that the Brazilian environmental-crimes law was so strict that while someone accused of *murder* could post bail, those charged with an *environmental* crime could not. The accusation alone could land them in jail.

Interestingly, the charge that he and Clare had murdered Bill Powers was absent from the story. Perhaps because the people in the camp had witnessed what happened. Or maybe it just didn't occur to those behind the conspiracy to frame Henry and Clare for it until later.

"And how about the armed men who took two hostages at the camp? How did the police explain that?"

"They were trying to stop you and the others, we're told."

Henry gave a nervous laugh.

"Chico," he said, making eye contact, "I understand if you are suspicious of me. But I promise you, none of it is true. I think you know that. I did not know Clare or any of her colleagues until *Marcelo* told me to go meet them up at the Baniwa village. I didn't even want to be their guide."

The farmer said nothing. Henry suspected he just wanted the conversation to end.

"Those guys that came here and took the two foreigners," Henry continued, "they don't work for the Brazilian government, and they most certainly were not here to fight biopiracy. They were after us because we saw that they have something going on in the old iron mine, which I'm pretty sure has nothing to do with iron. Whatever it is, it's something bad, worth *killing* for. I'm not sure what, exactly, but that's why we came back. To find out what they are up to. If all we wanted was some stupid seeds, we'd be long gone."

Again, the man across the table didn't react. Henry let his words sink in for a moment, then asked another question.

"Did you ever see those men before?"

"No," the farmer replied. "That was the first and last time."

"What did the police say about the two people who were taken?"

"Nothing. We all assumed that since they were committing a crime, they would just be handed over to the police."

"I know this looks bad, Chico, but I beg you to believe me. And I promise I will never come back here and bother you or your family again. I just need to ask you one last favor."

The farmer gave him a nervous look.

"Please don't let anyone find out we came back. I promise on my life that no one will ever hear from either of us that we had this conversation."

At this point Henry had seen enough of Brazil to know how skeptical most people were about the police or any figure of authority. With widespread corruption, few people had any faith in the honesty of the *autoridades*, as they were called. He counted on that distrust.

"Can you please promise me that, Chico?"

∽

"Are you sure you can trust him not to tell anyone we came back?" Clare asked after hearing Henry's summary of the conversation.

They had started to make their way through the forest toward the mine.

"I'm not one hundred percent sure of anything these days. But of all the people I met in this camp, he's the one I trust the most. We wouldn't have made it out of here without his help, remember? If he talks, there's a chance his role in our escape will come out. He won't risk that."

"What about the girls?"

He paused. They were the weakest link.

"We'll have to hope they listen to their father. We only need a day or two. I don't think it's too much to expect they can stay quiet for that long. If Chico is concerned about word getting out that he talked to us, he'll probably make it very clear to them they shouldn't say anything about our visit."

"I hope you are right."

"I'm more worried about their safety than ours. We may find a way to leave the country for good, but they will still be around. I'd hate to think something could happen to them because they helped us," he noted somberly. "One more reason to blow this conspiracy wide open, forcing the army or the police to kick those thugs from Fund-Ama and the mine out of the area."

Henry easily found his way around the familiar surrounding terrain. They had left Chico's farm shortly after midday, heading due south and carefully avoiding any paths or trails. It would take an hour longer to go around the perimeter of the camp instead of heading straight north, but it was the safest option.

The march was brisk and quiet, the silence helping them save energy and reducing the risk of someone spotting them.

A few miles north of the camp, a tropical storm came on, bringing strong winds and delivering a thunderous lightning spectacle. The green jungle canopy shook violently at times, absorbing the fury of the elements. The same tree cover that blocked the sunlight, preventing the growth of vegetation on the forest floor, also protected the ground dwellers.

They made good time despite taking the long way. At dusk the terrain became steeper, indicating the beginning of the massif formation containing both the cave and the mine.

Pressing on after nightfall, Clare and Henry stopped for water and a quick snack at the top of the slope leading down to the cave entrance. The full moon had ended only two nights before. With their eyes adjusted to the darkness, they found the moonlight that penetrated the leafed jungle ceiling, although faint, was enough to illuminate their way without the need for a flashlight.

Passing the entrance at the bottom of the valley, the two hikers ignored both the cave and physical exhaustion to continue for another few hours, finally stopping on the slope halfway between the cave and the mining camp.

Henry set the tent next to a fallen tree, where the clearing allowed the surrounding vegetation to grow denser and provided cover from any patrols that might pass nearby during the night.

Knowing both he and Clare were riddled with anxiety, Henry realized a good night's sleep was unlikely despite how tired they both were. But sleep or no sleep, a few hours of rest was critical before continuing to the mine, where they planned to arrive ahead of the first light, for reconnaissance and to find a way to get to Aidan and Liam—assuming, of course, that the two filmmakers had been brought back there, as Henry and Clare suspected.

They changed into clean shorts and shirts, hanging their clothes, dampened by sweat and rain, on a branch of the fallen tree. It felt good to get their tired feet out of their boots. They were now dry but sore from the long day's walk.

Henry took a last look around and crawled inside the tent. Clare was getting some sandwiches out of the backpack, the flashlight at the lowest possible setting to avoid giving away their location.

She looked pale and shaky in the dim light, and Henry guessed that despite her initial fighting attitude and readiness to come all the way back to find her friends, the magnitude of what they were about to do was dawning on her.

It was hard on him too, though he tried to hide it. Without exaggeration, the next day would be the most consequential of their lives. To his surprise, as anxious as he was while thinking of all the bad things that could happen tomorrow, he wasn't dwelling on them with extra concern. Instead, his mind was racing through various scenarios, imagining how different events could unfold and planning the best ways to deal with them.

"How are you feeling?" he asked, sitting down cross-legged opposite her, keeping his voice as low as he could.

"Not hungry, that's for sure," she replied, handing him a ham and cheese and taking one for herself.

"Me either. We need to eat something, though."

"I know." She nodded, taking a bite.

She tilted her head, looking at his eyes in the dim light. "How about you?"

"I can't say I'm not scared," he answered honestly. "But there's a part of me that can't wait to get there tomorrow. I'm tired of thinking about how this is going to play out."

"I know what you mean. I want to get this over with, one way or another."

She turned off the light and they ate in the dark, in silence.

One way or another. He wondered what she meant by

it. Though he couldn't see her, he could vividly picture her sitting across from him with the anxious expression she wore before turning off the light. He could hear her irregular, nervous breathing.

He shifted his position, and their bare knees touched.

"Sorry," he said.

"It's okay," she replied softly, putting her hand on his leg.

Without thinking, he covered her hand with his, holding it tightly.

"What do you think is going to happen tomorrow?" she asked.

"I don't know," he answered. "But after all we've been through, I think we are prepared to handle whatever comes our way."

"I'm nervous, Henry. I've been trying to put on a brave face since we left Manaus, but I'm really scared about tomorrow. How can you stay so calm?"

"Calm?" he said, hoping she could picture his smile. "I just hide it better, I guess."

"Does that mean it's obvious how frightened I am?"

He didn't know how to answer that.

"Come here," he said, pulling her toward him, trying to soothe her.

She accepted his embrace, resting her head on his chest. They stayed silent for a few moments, but he could tell by her heavy sighing that she was not feeling any more peaceful.

"Tell me something interesting about the Amazon."

"What do you mean?"

S. J. Philips

"Anything. Just to get our minds off of this. What's the most fascinating story you heard around here?"

He thought for a moment.

"It has to be the legend of the pink dolphin."

"Tell me!" she said eagerly.

"Well, according to the tradition, during the full moon the pink dolphin turns into a tall and handsome man, dressed in white clothes and wearing a big hat to disguise the blowhole on the top of his head."

"Is that right?"

"He walks around, visiting the local villages, where he approaches young women with his enchanting ways and seduces them, convincing unsuspicious girls to come with him to the bottom of the river, where they make love."

"How do they make love at the bottom of the river?"

"Hey, I'm just telling the story. If you buy into a dolphin turning into a man, surely you can accept that he can make love to a woman at the bottom of the river?"

"Sorry. Go on."

"The next morning, they part ways. He turns back into a dolphin, and the girl returns to her community."

"Is that it?"

"Pregnant."

"Seriously?"

"Yup. When a woman gets pregnant without being married or when the father of a child is unknown, people blame it on the pink dolphin."

"How convenient."

"The dolphin is quite admired around here, actually. People say that dolphins help the fishermen with their catch and can also guide them to safety during a bad storm."

"Yeah, I've heard that before."

"Anyway, if you ask me," he continued, "this legend seems like a great excuse for dads to warn their daughters to stay away from handsome strangers."

"It does," she agreed. "But most of us girls won't heed our parents' advice on this. Legend or no legend."

He became aware that he was stroking the back of her head as it rested against him, playing with her hair. She raised her head. It was too dark for him to see her expression, but he felt her face get just a few inches from his, so close that he could smell her now-familiar scent and feel the warmth of her cheeks.

Henry's heart accelerated, and suddenly he wasn't in control anymore, leaning down just enough to bring his lips to hers. As their mouths touched, Clare put her hand around the back of his neck and pulled him toward her, turning his gentle approach into a passionate kiss.

CHAPTER 31

A FEW HOURS BEFORE sunrise they had everything packed. Their boots hit the ground, lit only by moonlight.

Henry remembered the terrain, a sloping relief dotted by tall trees with buttresses as tall as he was, but he checked the compass and GPS from time to make sure they were following the fastest route.

The backpacks felt lighter without the tent, cooking utensils, and extra clothes, left tucked under a patch of bromeliads in the clearing where they had slept. Today they would carry only the essentials.

As he walked toward potential death, all Henry could think of was Clare. Had that been just a spur-of-the-moment thing? Would they be together after this was over? The irony did not escape him. He was worried about his love life on the dawn of what could be his last day on earth.

I can't think about this now.

He consulted the GPS again, reviewing his bearings. Drawing a line in his mind, he recalibrated the route, turning slightly to the left after going around a mound of termites.

Clare followed in silence. They kept marching at a quick pace, deliberately not talking, avoiding not only detection but discussion of what had happened.

The trek took shorter than anticipated, and they arrived at the site well before dawn. The dim moonlight worked to their advantage, the darkness providing cover to move around the camp's perimeter and find a good place to observe. It would be safer to turn north as they approached the bottom of the valley, but the relief flattened in that direction, making it a poor vantage point to survey the compound. They walked southeast instead, settling for a spot on one of the steeper parts of the slope, the same area where the two of them and Bill had spent the night after escaping from one of the tents below. The location afforded a broad view, protected by the dense vegetation.

The camp was quiet and completely dark, with no one stationed around the perimeter. It made sense, since there was no path or access trail and it was impossible to cover the entire camp or predict where an intruder would come from.

This gave Henry pause. Why had his group been surrounded so quickly when they first arrived here? Was it possible that the armed men that captured them had been tipped off? They could have received word from the research station's manager, either a general warning that there would be people in the area or, if Aidan and Liam had arrived at Pitiri early enough, the exact number of people on their way there. It was also possible they had made too much noise approaching the mine. It didn't matter now anyway.

Henry and Clare stood on the southern edge of the camp, scanning it with their binoculars. They could distinguish the outline of a few structures, their pupils well adjusted to the night. Without tree cover blocking the moonlight, they could see the features of the valley better than the inside of the jungle.

Directly in front of them was the head of the landing strip. A few dozen yards to the left of the runway was a large structure that seemed to serve as a deposit for heavy equipment and assorted boxes, covered by a bulky camouflage tarp.

Beyond the tarp, a lit cigarette near a row of tents in the northwest corner of the camp gave away a sentinel, unconcerned about being spotted and likely bored out of his mind after the long night shift. Henry touched his face, right where he had been hit with the heel of an assault rifle inside one of those same tents. The pain was gone, but the memory was still vivid.

To the east of where they stood, on the far side, was a wood cabin isolated from the other structures and raised a couple of feet off the ground. Henry knew this design was intended to avoid damage from flooding and crawling wildlife. As in the community center at the Pitiri Research Station, it was critical to protect sensitive gear and documents. He guessed the cabin served a similar purpose and must be the command center of the operation.

A bright light abruptly went on next to the equipment site. Henry and Clare were startled, but the sentry near the tents didn't seem bothered by it.

Henry was curious, wondering whether it was a silent call for the soldiers to start getting ready for the day. But nothing happened after a minute or two, and he brought his attention back to the camp.

Now that they had time to observe the site in detail, Henry realized how big it was. He tried to study the deposit at the head of the runway, helped by the artificial light. There were dozens of boxes, additional equipment he couldn't quite recognize, and a large excavator.

His eyes focused on the last item. He wondered how a machine weighing at least a few tons got to the middle of a valley with no roads or waterways.

It must have been airlifted here. These guys have resources.

After the initial reconnaissance, there was little to do but wait for daylight. Henry started plotting how to photograph the entire site. He analyzed the perimeter, looking for the best spots to approach without being seen. The hardest part would be stealing his way to the deposit under the tarp. He would have to wait for just enough light to be able to take pictures, but not so far into the day that the soldiers would be up and wandering about.

He felt good about his strategy. No one was expecting them, and he knew that he could move quietly through the forest, reminding himself he had been quite successful in getting close to animals with much better hearing and olfactory senses than possessed by any of the men guarding the complex. At the very least, it gave him confidence to think he could pull it off.

The sentinel lit up another cigarette as the horizon

started to brighten. Henry looked at his watch. It was close to 6:00 a.m., and daylight would soon arrive.

Henry's eyes fell on Clare, who was gazing studiously at the site. She wore a ponytail but had missed a few hairs, which dangled fuzzily around her ears and temples.

He was staring mindlessly at the freckles across her nose when he heard a distant noise coming from their right. It was faint but growing perceptibly louder.

She turned to him and they exchanged a puzzled look, trying to identify what it was.

As it became louder, they recognized the unmistakable sound of a jet engine before they saw an aircraft approaching from the east, still under the cover of the night as the sky grew brighter behind it. It was then that Henry realized there was another light at the opposite end of the landing strip, about a mile down. The floodlight was not a signal to the soldiers in the camp, but a beacon to guide the plane's approach.

The jet landed clumsily on the grassy runway and produced a deafening noise as it reversed the engines to slow down. It proceeded to the end of the strip, the turbines still roaring. A soldier left one of the tents and, when the engines died down, moved to the plane, carrying two large wood blocks and placing one ahead and another behind the aircraft front wheel. Henry concluded this must be routine, because no one came outside to check what all the noise was about.

The plane was all white but for orange stripes toward the bottom and a black registration number on the tail. It was about the size of a regional jet, though it looked wider. The front door on the left opened, unfolding toward the ground. The stairs extended until they reached the grass; and a short man, dressed as a pilot, stepped outside the plane, pulling the embedded rail upward. A tall man wearing fatigues and a crew cut emerged from the plane, helping a slim old man with a thin mustache walk down the steps.

The guard who had put the wood pieces next to the tire waved once. The two men nodded and walked to the main cabin, while three soldiers from the compound joined the pilot and the guard in using long poles to cover the plane with an enormous camouflage canvas. Henry did not have time to pull out the camera, and dawn was likely still too dim to take pictures anyway, so he wrote down the registration number.

The floodlights were off and the camp was quiet again, except for the cacophony of birds chirping and other animal chatter filling the air. It was a familiar noise for Henry.

He studied the camp under the emerging daylight, zooming in on the area under the tarp covering the boxes and the construction equipment. The excavator was yellow, he could see now, and there were more supplies next to it: shovels, carts, wood beams, and gray boxes with yellow markings on the side, which Henry couldn't distinguish from a distance.

He spotted a big blue tractor he had not noticed before, next to the yellow excavator. A gazebo south of the storage pavilion contained dark blue drums that he guessed stored fuel for all the heavy machinery. There didn't seem to be enough fuel for the jet. *They must have come in with enough for the return trip, just like the plane that brought us.*

Morning arrived quickly, the light now bright enough to take pictures. He made sure he got several shots of the tarp-covered plane, its shape still discernible despite the disguise. He also documented the equipment storage area, trying to capture every item. But he needed to get closer to capture the details and the inscriptions on the boxes and, most importantly, their contents, which he suspected to be the key to the entire mystery.

While Henry took pictures, making sure he recorded multiple images of the entire camp and everything in it, Clare watched the compound with her binoculars. She tapped Henry's shoulder and pointed at the tent row on the northwest perimeter, where they could see a man keeping guard, sitting on a bench and holding the barrel of a machine gun, its butt resting against the ground.

"It looks like they could be holding people inside that tent," she said in a low whisper, barely audible in the jungle's morning racket. "It has to be Aidan and Liam!"

A flicker of excitement crossed her face.

"We need to find a way to get to them," she continued.

"I know."

"Any ideas?"

"Let's observe the camp a little longer," Henry replied. Rescuing Aidan and Liam would be a tall order. But he knew they had to try. "We need to wait for an opportunity. Maybe when the plane takes off. Or we wait until it's dark again."

"I agree," she said. "We can't afford to be hasty. We should wait for the right time, like when we escaped from those two cops."

Henry hoped they'd be as lucky again.

"I have to get to that supply deposit and look closer," he said. "I want to photograph every detail. I might even find something that can help us get Aidan and Liam out."

"Like what?"

"I don't know. We'll see," he answered. "Guns, explosives?"

"I'm coming with you," she declared.

"No," he responded in a firm whisper. "This is the most dangerous part. We can't both be captured. Besides, one person moves more stealthily than two. And no disrespect, but I've been sneaking around in the jungle for a bit longer."

She opened her mouth to answer him but didn't.

He continued. "If I'm captured, you need to try to get to the American embassy and tell them everything you saw. Can you do that?"

"Okay," she replied automatically.

"I have to go now. Before the whole camp is awake."

"How long will you be?"

"A couple of hours, I think. I need to move slowly. You should be safe here."

CHAPTER 32

HE STARTED WEST, so he could cover the busiest part of the complex and get to the deposit before the compound started humming with activity.

As he moved on the steep slope around the western perimeter, his first stop was opposite the entrance of the mine. He pointed his camera to the opening, partly concealed by the vegetation growing around it, and eagerly fired the shutter. The tunnel was in an almost vertical incline, large enough to fit the excavator he had seen earlier. Rather than removing the entire topsoil to get to the mineral, as Mineradora da Floresta S.A. had done back when it was exploring the site, today's illegal excavations occurred under the surface. It was costlier and more dangerous to the workers but avoided detection by satellites.

He circled over the top of the entrance and found himself at the northwestern end of the complex, where the slope started to moderate. At a slight elevation, halfway between the tents and the mine entrance, his position was at the shortest possible distance between the edge of the vegetation surrounding the camp and the pavilion with assorted equipment.

Focusing binoculars on the deposit, Henry noticed the boxes, some of them still open. He assumed they contained the big prize, the source of all their trials and adversities. The mineral that was the real reason for the existence of the site, which had never been an iron mine in the first place.

Thorianite.

Eight to ten percent uranium and sought by rogue states the world over.

But Henry needed to get to the boxes to confirm. He wanted to feel it, grab it, and squeeze the dense, heavy mineral, the cause of all the violence he had seen.

Brazil had been a signatory of the nonproliferation treaty to stop the dissemination of nuclear weapons, along with almost every other country on the planet. It could not legally mine uranium-rich minerals without close supervision of international monitoring bodies. Neither could Venezuela, Brazil's northerly neighbor and the country that issued the military ID Henry had found in the stolen backpack.

So what was going on here? Was Brazil facilitating the transfer of the mineral to Venezuela? Were the two countries secretly collaborating in the development of nuclear weapons in breach of the international agreements they had signed? Whatever it was, Henry felt a chill at the thought of the lengths both countries would go to in keeping this operation a secret.

As he prepared to cross the open field to get to the boxes, he saw the two men that had disembarked from the plane come toward the pavilion. The older one was holding a clipboard, observing his surroundings and making notes. They were followed by another soldier and the Portuguese-speaking man that had questioned Henry, Clare, and Bill a week earlier, who Henry assumed was the leader of the operation.

Henry would have to come back and try again later.

Until then, he needed to be content with taking a step back and using the camera to record all the activity, trying to get close-ups of the men as they walked into the deposit. He also took close shots of the excavator and tractor, the shovels, the boxes, every detail.

He could now read a few of the larger signs. Some boxes covered by plastic contained a notice that said *Material Explosivo.* Explosives. He still couldn't discern the markings on the boxes he suspected of containing the thorianite. From a distance, they looked like some sort of ancient script, as they had when he saw the boxes during his detainment a week before.

Henry continued moving and turned right a few dozen yards ahead, heading east over the northern edge of the mining complex and reaching the tents that served as the quarters for the soldiers. They were rectangular, made of green canvas, about thirty-five feet long, he guessed. The westernmost tent was a little smaller, in the shape of a square. It was the same one where he had been held captive and where he and Clare suspected Aidan and Liam were being detained.

He wondered how the two hostages would be faring after a full week. *Probably not well.*

On the front side of the tents, there were several people walking around in fatigues, a few of them shirtless as they prepared for the warm day.

The section of the tent back wall they had cut with a knife to escape a week before had been stitched together with a thick brown string. Perhaps during the night he could cut through the same wall again to rescue the two filmmakers, though if he found a soldier inside guarding the prisoners, they would all be toast.

He looked down at the camera. The battery indicator showed that the charge was at 75 percent, and the memory card was half full. Plenty of room and juice for more images.

About 120 yards farther, he stood directly north of the camp's main cabin, some 200 feet from his position. Through the back window Henry could not see any movement inside, only a large radio transmitter on top of a desk. If he managed to get inside, he could probably find some incriminating documents, but he knew it was too risky to try. There was no way to approach the cabin without being seen.

Continuing east, away from the camp's buildings and around the airstrip, there was little to record. When he got to the end of the runway, he estimated it was almost a mile long. After going around the eastern border of the complex, Henry started heading back to Clare.

Having satisfied himself that he had documented everything he could, their original vantage point would be a good place for recording the plane being loaded with the boxes.

They would then wait for darkness, when the camp should fall quiet, to collect some samples of the thorianite and try to rescue Aidan and Liam. That would be the hardest part. How they would do it—and then get out of there—he didn't know yet, but Henry was happy with how the first part of the day had unfolded.

Gone for almost two hours, just as estimated, he had circled nearly the entire camp, the terrain becoming progressively steeper again on the way back. He put the camera away in his backpack and hurried his pace, anxious to share his observations with Clare.

Henry was no more than ten minutes away when he heard someone shouting in Spanish. From the slope he looked down toward the noise and saw three men crossing the landing strip to the camp's headquarters, escorting someone at gunpoint.

It was Clare.

CHAPTER 33

Q UEASY AT THE sight of Clare being taken across
the runway, Henry turned around in desperation, tightening his right fist. He raised his
hand to punch the trunk of a tree right in front of him but
found enough self-control to stop himself from ramming
his knuckles on the bark. He looked up and clenched his
teeth, fighting the urge to scream in rage.

He squatted on the jungle floor, holding his head in
disbelief. *That was a good spot to hide,* he told himself. *If
only I had been faster.*

Realizing that despair would be of little help, he put
himself together, regaining his composure. Standing up
and looking through the forest at the compound, he saw
the patrol approaching the main cabin with Clare. Her
capture had caught the attention of the entire camp, and
Henry saw the soldiers shouting and whistling at her. He
scanned the complex quickly, searching for something,
anything that could help him rescue her. His eyes stopped

at the equipment site to his left, and an idea started to form in his mind.

Turning his head back to the right, he saw Clare being escorted up the steps of the elevated cabin. Then he raced carelessly to the same spot where he had stood just two hours earlier, at the western end of the mining complex, the shortest distance between the forest and the equipment pavilion. This time there was no one in sight.

He looked at the three hundred feet of open field he wanted to cross and hesitated, his heart beating so fast he could feel it pounding inside his chest. Almost paralyzed by fear, it occurred to him that he had felt like this several times in the past few days. It was a familiar feeling by now. He let out a nervous laugh.

Panic was trying to get the best of him again. He was not a trained soldier like Bill, just a biologist from Pennsylvania. How could he take on an army of trained fighters by himself?

He couldn't, of course.

But there were only two options available to him. He could try to save her and die in the attempt, or he could run away with the evidence he had obtained so far, which he was confident he could accomplish. The men would soon learn she was not alone and would come looking for him, if they weren't already, so he had to decide fast.

It was such an easy choice that he laughed nervously once again, wondering why he had been wavering at all.

All the camp's attention seemed to be turned on the main cabin, where the attractive female prisoner had been taken. The men were caught up in loud chatter, with the soldiers trying to figure out who had been brought in and what was going to happen to her. Except for a few sentinels at that central area and one guarding the tent at the far end of the camp, the men congregated around a long table in front of the row of tents, a curious look on their faces, gathering in small groups to speculate.

Henry waited until he thought no one was looking his way and raced as fast as he could across the gap, toward a set of tightly arranged boxes that blocked the view from the rest of the complex. He cringed, expecting a shout or, worse, a shot that would cut his dash short. It took about fifteen seconds to find cover behind the boxes, though it felt like more.

Did I make it? He shook his head in disbelief. *Maybe this will work after all.*

Provided he had not been spotted, his position was now well protected. He was surrounded by boxes and had a good view of the situation, through the small gaps between the different piles of boxes and assorted materials.

Studying the area around him, he realized he was surrounded by explosives. If just one shot came his way, he feared the whole place might light up. Another rush of panic started to flood in, but he brushed it aside quickly. Taking a deep breath, Henry noticed that not all the boxes were marked with the explosive sign; some were marked with the ancient-looking script he had seen earlier, from a distance.

He approached an open box and found the dark gray gravel resting in it. Henry reached inside, grabbing a handful of the loose, rounded fragments of rock. It looked just like the photos. *So this is the thorianite.* The mineral felt heavy. He let the material slip through his fingers, back into the box, and rubbed his hands against each other to shake off the dust, reaching for the lead pouch he had brought with him.

While safe to manipulate briefly without protection, thorianite emitted some radioactivity that could cause harm with longer-term exposure. When Henry had shared his findings about the likely purpose of the mine with Berto and Clare, the professor gave him an old lead pouch used to protect film cameras from airport X-ray machines.

"It's not like I'm ever going to need it again now that we've all gone digital," Berto had said. "This should make it safe to carry the mineral around for a few days, though I'd still keep it away from your privates."

Henry grabbed a couple handfuls of the thorianite and filled the pouch, putting it in the knee pocket of his cargo pants. Then he pulled out the camera and took several close-ups of the mineral and the equipment surrounding it.

As he focused the camera to capture the markings, Henry realized it wasn't some bizarre ancient script he was looking at, just plain warnings in an alphabet that looked like Arabic. Next to it, among other symbols, he recognized a flag that had featured prominently in the news for some time and in some of the reports he'd seen two nights before. It belonged to a country that had for years been suspected of trying to develop nuclear weapons and supporting terrorist groups. It was the flag of the Republic of Alashrar.

Henry finally put the final piece of the puzzle in place. The radioactive minerals were not going to Brazil or Venezuela.

They are going to Alashrar, he realized with horror.

Brazil and Venezuela could be pursuing a nuclear weapon that they may employ for leverage but never use. But the country the boxes were destined for could very well drop the bomb on one of their enemies. Worse, any nuclear device it developed could easily end up in the hands of terrorist organizations that would not hesitate to use it.

CHAPTER 34

NOW CAME THE hard and dangerous part. And the least likely to work.

Peering through the gap between the boxes, Henry closely watched the movement around the camp. The men were loitering around the long table in front of the tents, about seventy yards from his position, divided into different groups, eating and talking loudly. Still abuzz at the capture of a new prisoner, their attention was turned to the main cabin in the opposite direction of where he stood.

This may be his only window for action, he thought. Soon the novelty of the new captive would wear off, and his position could be compromised when someone inevitably came over to the equipment yard or spotted movement there.

Three soldiers stood as sentinels at the bottom of the steps leading up to the cabin's elevated porch. He shuddered at the thought of what they could be doing to Clare inside.

At the tent where he guessed the two filmmakers were kept, a sole guard sat on a bench by the entrance, holding a machine gun. Cutting the wall of the back of the tent to get Aidan and Liam out still looked like the best option, even if another guard waited inside. He would have to be prepared for it.

Rescuing Clare would be harder. Maybe he would come up with a good idea, but for now he knew there was no telling how the situation would unfold. If he had learned one thing throughout this whole ordeal, it was that, regardless of how brilliantly he planned everything, he would have to improvise at some point anyway.

The setup of the equipment worked to his advantage. The tractor was parked next to the excavator, which provided cover from most of the camp. It was attached to a metal cart he assumed was used to haul the minerals to the pavilion, where they would be boxed for transportation. He concluded that the boxes would be loaded on the plane, for he didn't see another way to take the material to its destination.

Henry turned to the boxes of explosives and opened them.

Not even as a child on the Fourth of July had he ever blown anything up. When other kids had been playing with fireworks, he was toying with little insects and plants, already nurturing the biologist in him. But he knew the basic physics of it, aware that different explosive charges required different amounts of energy to ignite them. Today he would put his scant theoretical knowledge to the test.

There were different types of explosives, he noted. Some were tightly packed in red plastic, like big sausages the size of his forearm. A second set could be mistaken for bags of coarse salt. The two bags were each labeled in English, in large caps, as "ANFO Blasting Agent," the standard explosive of the mining industry everywhere, a mixture of ammonium nitrate and fuel oil. Another variety he recognized easily as dynamite, attached to one another in packs of six sticks.

He glanced back at the camp, where all the attention was still on the arrival of the new captive. Henry then found, sitting next to the explosives, a set of bags with what looked like wires. He pulled one, deducing they were bomb fuses, and noticed they were attached to a metal capsule. The back of the package read "Waterproof Safety Fuses with Detonator," along with lengthy disclaimers and safety instructions.

Can it be this simple? he asked himself, wondering if all he had to do was attach the fuses to the dynamite and blasting agents.

He would soon find out.

The boxes with explosives were too heavy for him to carry a full load, so he emptied them to half capacity. There were about fifteen feet between his position and the cart attached to the tractor. Hoping that the excavator parked at the side provided enough cover, Henry picked up the first half-full box and flexed his legs slightly, setting himself in a starting position for the short run. Peeking at the sentinels in the distance, then at the men congregated near the table outside the tents, he dashed out while they all looked in the opposite direction, focused on the action at the main cabin.

He made it to the tractor without being spotted and proceeded to spread the hot dog–looking packs on the metal cart.

Carefully scanning the camp again, he waited for a suitable opportunity to run back to the boxes under the tarp. When he got there, Henry picked up a box with the second type of explosives. He repeated the maneuver, dropping the saltlike ANFO bags on the cart and getting back undetected again.

In his last run, he brought the dynamite and the fuses with the detonator. That would have to do it, he thought, reluctant to push his luck a fourth time. He arranged all the different kinds of explosives on the cart, packing them tightly. Untying the safety fuses, six or seven in total, he stuck the blast capsules randomly in the different explosives, just as he had seen in action movies. He assumed that if he succeeded in detonating at least one of the charges, the others would go off too.

Approaching the excavator, he noted the fuel-tank cap but couldn't find a hose to siphon out its contents. Looking around the camp, Henry noticed a fuel drum across the gap between his position and where the explosives were stored. He would have to dash back and forth through the open space a fourth time.

Luckily, Clare's capture continued drawing everyone's attention.

The drum was well hidden from the rest of the camp, behind the pavilion, but he still needed to find a way to get the diesel out. Without a hose, he could try to make a hole in the midsection, but that would create too much noise and draw unwanted attention. His boldness growing, he pushed the top hard. The drum wobbled but stood upright. In his second attempt, Henry shoved it with all his strength and the barrel tipped, making an audible thud on the soft grass, though not loud enough to be heard beyond a couple dozen feet. The fuel started to spill.

He felt guilty at the idea of causing his own little fuel spill in the Amazon rain forest, but time did not allow him to dwell on it. Grabbing a large plastic bucket, he filled it with the dark gold fluid leaking out of the drum. He also foraged around the site for nuts, bolts, tools, and any metal scraps he could find.

Just before he prepared to run back to the tractor, it occurred to him that while he had seen diesel quickly ignite in action movies, he wasn't sure it would be so easy in real life. Looking around the pavilion, his eyes fell on a set of containers kept away from the explosives, on top of a sawhorse table, with a series of safety warnings in both English and Spanish. Drawn to a label that said "Danger: Highly Combustible Material" in bold letters, he seized a gallon of benzine.

Getting back to the cart for the final time, he showered it with diesel and benzine, topping it all off with the metal pieces he had gathered.

He found a small wood beam next to the boxes and jumped on the tractor seat, hidden behind the excavator, quickly studying the pedals and the instruments on the panel. The keys were in the ignition at the right side, close to the throttle lever. He stepped on the clutch a few times and played with the gear stick and the steering wheel to get a feel for it.

Henry apprehensively looked back and forth between the forest and the camp. There would be no turning back after this. He acted quickly, mostly to avoid thinking too much and getting cold feet.

The tractor engine growled as he turned the key.

Henry stepped on the clutch and engaged the first gear. He pressed on the gas pedal all the way, having no idea how fast the tractor would go, and released the clutch. The engine screamed louder, and the tractor started moving.

As he passed the excavator, Henry saw two soldiers getting up from the table and starting toward the equipment yard, springing into action after hearing the engine noise. A tall man with a shaved head was shouting orders at them while they ran with their machine guns.

Steering in the direction he wanted the tractor to head, Henry used the wood beam to lock the wheel in position and then put a toolbox on the gas pedal to keep the tractor moving. He jumped out to the right, running for cover back at the tent with the explosives as he heard one of the soldiers yelling at him.

While it was too late for them to stop his immediate plot, he had been spotted. It would all be for nothing if he was captured.

The camp's attention had now shifted from the main cabin to the uproar around the equipment site, where a driverless tractor moved away from the pavilion with a cart full of explosives in tow.

The pair of soldiers stopped for a brief moment but

reacted quickly, splitting so one could run to the tractor and the other after Henry.

Timing was critical now. Although Henry saw one of the men coming his direction, he waited in position with a clear view of the tractor and cart, protected by the boxes of mining equipment. He saw the other man running toward the cart but knew the soldier wouldn't get to it soon enough to stop it. The few moments it had taken the men to realize what was happening was all the time he had needed.

When the tractor was at the right spot, Henry pulled the revolver the professor had given him, aimed carefully at the metal cart, and started shooting at it.

At the sound of gunfire, both soldiers immediately fell to the ground, looking for cover and buying Henry some precious extra time to finish the job.

He unloaded all six bullets from the Taurus at the cart, getting at least a couple of them on target. The sparks from the bullets hitting the metal caused the benzine and fuel to ignite, spreading fire over the explosives. The flames triggered the detonator attached to the fuses, causing a series of explosions, one after another, each louder and bigger than the other.

The fuses did not pack enough energy to set off the more stable and powerful ANFO blasting agents, but those attached to the dynamite sticks were more than sufficient. The blast from the dynamite, in turn, released enough energy to make the other explosives blow up with even more power just as the tractor was gliding under the left wing of the airplane.

Henry marveled in disbelief at how well it was all working. He had timed it perfectly.

Before he could fully appreciate the damage, an even louder explosion projected flames hundreds of feet into the air, throwing debris all over the camp. As he had hoped, the plane, loaded with enough fuel for the return trip, detonated like a massive firebomb.

CHAPTER 35

THE COMPOUND SHOOK with the explosion, turning into complete chaos. Soldiers scrambled all over the place, and the already-steamy heat was now many times worse due to the burning aircraft.

Henry ran as fast as he could back to the compound's perimeter, escaping to the thick of the jungle, surprised by the scale of the blast and pleased with the mayhem he had caused.

Despite his success in creating a diversion, he wasn't sure what to do next. And he knew the soldiers would be coming after him.

Looking from the edge of the camp, Henry saw three men escorting Clare away from the cabin. Other troops were trying to fight the fire with dirt, their effort wholly insufficient. As sophisticated as the operation was, they did not have the resources or contingency plans to deal with a fire of that magnitude. He could tell they were improvising and realized for the first time that the camp had no running water.

Clare was being taken in the direction of the tent he assumed was holding Aidan and Liam, so Henry followed the edge of the camp to get closer to it, keeping inside the forest for cover. There would be another patrol searching the perimeter for him, he was sure, but he had to take his chances.

Two soldiers now guarded the entrance of the smaller tent. One of them saluted the men approaching with the female captive, her hands tied behind her back, looking scared and outright confused by the chaos around her but in control of herself. One of the sentinels and two other soldiers walked inside, while a third held her by the entrance, Henry watching attentively from his position behind the dense vegetation.

A moment later Aidan and Liam emerged from the tent.

Henry was relieved to see confirmation they were still alive, but even from a distance he could tell that the pair was not faring well. They looked skeletal and pale.

Clare shouted something to them, and Aidan and Liam seemed briefly heartened by the sight of their colleague, if perplexed by the giant ball of fire burning not far away. But any encouragement they may have received from the presence of Clare faded quickly, as they were again subdued when one of the soldiers poked Aidan's back with the tip of his gun and ordered all three to walk. One of the sentinels joined the trio that had brought Clare from the cabin, and each of the prisoners was taken by a man in fatigues, with a patrol leader following behind.

They went around the tent, leaving the other sentinel behind, and started in the direction of the forest. Henry continued to follow a couple of hundred feet away, wondering what could possibly be in the forest to justify taking the prisoners there. He had covered the entire perimeter earlier and did not recall anything around that area. Had he missed something?

Then he realized in horror that there was in fact nothing back there. He felt his chest collapse when he realized what was happening.

They are going to be executed.

His heart pounding, he wondered how he was supposed to stop four trained soldiers with machine guns. He still had the .38-caliber revolver, though he had not thought of reloading it after the explosion. It would be no match against professional soldiers holding machine guns anyway.

The soldiers stopped a few yards before the edge of the forest. They lined up the prisoners and made them get on their knees, facing the trees, with their hands tied behind their backs.

Around the compound, Henry saw the troops flock to their positions in the wild confusion he had sown. They seemed unaware of what was unfolding behind the tents in the northwest corner of the mining complex. The structures provided cover from the rest of the camp, allowing the execution to proceed without the display of a spectacle that would distract the men from their jobs.

Henry moved a few yards to position himself behind the executioners, making sure they had their backs to him. Then, out of urgency and sheer desperation, he jumped from the edge of the camp into the clearing, racing as fast as he could in a suicidal move toward the prisoners, across the open field. It was reckless, but he had the element of surprise on his side.

Amid the loud noise of troops shouting and the crackling fire, each of the soldiers stepped behind the captive he had escorted and waited. At the patrol leader's order, they pulled the guns hanging from the straps over their shoulders and switched the safety locks off, holding their weapons firmly and waiting for the countdown.

Henry still had to cover about forty or fifty yards. Despite the heavy hiking boots, the uneven soil, and an effort to keep his steps as quiet as possible, he was running as fast as he ever had in his life.

"Prepare!"

Each man raised his weapon slowly and pointed it at his assigned victim.

The weight on his feet did not slow Henry down. He was approaching fast from behind, the soldiers so focused on their job that they did not look away from their targets.

"Set!"

Their fingers moved to the triggers.

When Henry got about fifteen yards behind the soldiers, they all turned their heads at the sound of his galloping, muffled by the grass and until then obscured by the background noise around the camp. The patrol leader also looked back in surprise, stopping his countdown.

Henry let out a scream of uncontained rage as he covered a few more yards in a fraction of a second, then jumped toward the executioners, feet forward. When the men finally reacted, turning their guns to the wild creature charging them, Henry was already in the air, too close for them to stop him. He struck two soldiers at the same time, each with the sole of one boot. His left foot hit first, striking the side of the rib cage of one of the troops, while his right boot hit another in the jaw.

Powered by Henry's acceleration, the kicks brought the two men down, but the third countered quickly, aiming his gun at Henry and readying the shot while the patrol leader reached for his own weapon.

The captives had turned around too. Clare reacted the fastest, getting up with one quick jump and running back to slam her body against the man about to shoot Henry, making him miss by inches.

The scene unfolded fast. Weakened as they were, Aidan and Liam managed to get up at the same time, no doubt fueled by the adrenaline rushing through their blood, and raced in the direction of the patrol leader, who had drawn his gun and pointed it at Henry. They sprang toward him while he locked his aim. When he noticed the attack by the two long-held captives, it was too late to react. Liam had gotten close enough to headbutt him in the nose, bringing him down before he could decide whether he should pull the trigger or fight the assault.

With the wind knocked out of them, the two men Henry had kicked were slow to get up, but the soldier knocked off balance by Clare recovered swiftly, violently shoving her to the ground and raising his gun at her. Back on his feet, Henry charged him, taking the soldier down before he could fire and viciously punching his face until he was unconscious. Clare folded her legs tightly and slipped her tied hands under her feet, to the front of her body, just as the two men kicked by Henry started to get up.

Aidan and Liam, though depleted, were holding down the troop leader, Aidan pushing his knee against the soldier's chest while Liam choked the man with his right shin. But their opponent was strong and their grip was loosening.

Clare stood and raced to the two men slowly getting up, seizing one of their guns. When she reached for the second rifle, the owner grabbed her forearm, pulled her toward him, and punched her. It caught her only half strength on the left cheekbone, but it was enough to cause her to lose her balance and fall back on her bottom. The soldier must have been still disoriented from the kick on the jaw, because instead of immediately going for the AK-103, he faltered, fighting to find his balance before charging her.

Clare, in turn, did not hesitate. With her wrists still tied together, she held the gun with both hands near the trigger, pushing it against her body to keep it steady. She pointed at his chest and pulled the trigger as the soldier moved toward her, hitting him with a spray of bullets. The man jerked backward and fell on his back.

The other soldier was now standing, if a little unsteady, and finding his footing. At the sound of the shots, he instantly raised his hands, staring at Clare with a fearful look, and then shook his head with an expression of despair that begged her not to shoot him.

"Don't move!" she shouted, pointing the weapon at him while she remained sitting on the grass, not trying to stand with her hands tied.

Seeing Clare in control of the situation, Henry rushed to the aid of the two filmmakers trying to hold down the patrol leader, who was about to extricate himself from his two debilitated assailants.

Henry took his gun and aimed it at his head, telling him in Spanish to stand up and move toward the soldier Clare had at her mercy.

The other two soldiers lay still on the ground, one made unconscious by Henry, the other critically injured by Clare.

Putting some distance from the two men they had captured, Henry reached for a knife in one of his pockets and approached Clare to cut her plastic handcuffs.

"Are you okay?" he asked, inspecting the left side of her face, which was starting to bruise.

She looked at him and nodded. He extended his left hand, helping her stand while his right hand pointed the assault rifle at the two soldiers.

"I knew you would come!" she cried as she pulled down his head with both hands to kiss him.

Aidan and Liam looked puzzled, though that had been far from the biggest surprise of the morning.

Henry put his left arm tightly around her, relieved she was okay, then asked her to watch the prisoners. He next turned his attention to Aidan and Liam, cutting their handcuffs.

Aidan managed to put his hand weakly on his rescuer's back and utter a heartfelt *thank you*.

"Yes, thank you," Liam joined in.

"Don't thank me yet," Henry responded. "We still need to get out of here."

The tents and the noise had provided cover up until now, but someone had certainly heard the shots, even with all the noise around the site and despite the burning airplane a few hundred yards from them. There was no time for any further acknowledgments or pleasantries.

"We need to leave, *now*!"

Henry took off his backpack, realizing he'd had it on him as he performed his stunt. He kneeled as he put it on the floor and took a small rope, motioning to the two soldiers still standing to extend both hands to him. Quickly studying the two men lying on the ground, he decided that neither would recover in time to stop them from escaping. The one shot by Clare may not recover at all. He moved to the edge of the forest and tied the other two to a tree.

"Let's go," he commanded.

CHAPTER 36

ENRY LED THE group north, pushing at a hasty pace despite Aidan's and Liam's poor conditions. The farther they got from the mining compound, the better their chances of escape. He knew the soldiers would come after them in full force and without mercy. In his possession was proof of an international conspiracy to develop nuclear weapons.

"I know you have questions," Henry said as soon as they started to move through the forest. "But right now, we need to keep quiet and move fast. We are still in danger, and you can't afford to waste any energy."

He should be feeling good about how incredibly well everything had turned out, but it was far too soon to declare victory. They were still in the jungle, with no means to get out and an army in pursuit. As fantastic as the rescue had been, the sinking feeling that it was too good to be true and the fear of what could still go wrong kept his focus razor sharp.

Half an hour in, walking due north, Henry checked his GPS and compass, then turned northeast. Their best chance to get away was by means of a major river to the east, but he assumed it would be the first place their pursuers would check. While it would take longer to get to the river his way, with only minutes on the troops it would be better to reach the bank farther away from the mining compound, reducing the risk of running into one of the patrols that would now be combing the forest for them.

The undulating terrain sloped gently upward, coming out of the compound and flattening after a few miles. Based on the maps and what he knew of the geography of the area, Henry expected it would remain like that all the way to the riverbank. The adrenaline rush wearing off, Aidan and Liam started to slow down under the weight of a week of captivity and malnutrition.

Henry kept pushing the pace until Aidan stumbled, coming to a stop and leaning on a tree as he grasped the bark with both hands for support. He was breathing fast, looking down to the ground and barely managing to stand on his own.

It was dangerous to stop—a patrol was certainly coming in their direction. But seeing Aidan's and Liam's conditions, Henry had no choice. Trying to disguise his anxiety, he helped Aidan sit down and gave him and Liam an energy bar, fruit, and water, hoping it would afford them some strength to continue for a while longer.

Aidan opened his mouth to say something, but Henry harshly cut him off before he could utter a word.

"Save your energy. We'll need it to get you out of here."

He suspected Aidan was about to tell them to go

ahead and leave him behind, but Henry had not gone through all this trouble to let that happen.

Aidan's skin was as white as snow, and his eyes were lost in a blank stare.

"The first thing you need to know is that we are not leaving you behind, no matter what. I know you feel like crap, but I need you to pull through. Your life and everyone else's"—he waved his hands, gesturing toward Liam and Clare—"depend on it."

Clare ate an energy bar and had some water. Henry drank some but saved the food for the others. They didn't have a lot of it, and he thought the filmmakers would need the calories more than he did.

The brief stop and the food gave Aidan and Liam a little bit of extra energy to carry on, but Henry knew it would not take them much farther. He hoped it would be enough to get everyone at least as far as the river's edge, now that the terrain had flattened, where he hoped they could find a boat before the troops found *them*.

They resumed the march and walked for another hour and a half, the fear of meeting a patrol surely burning in everyone's heads. Henry pushed them, keeping an eye on Aidan and Liam, worried they would be forced to stop any minute because the two could not continue.

He thought they had succeeded when they managed to reach the river without further incident. But after they finally stopped, Aidan collapsed to the ground.

Clare rushed to her colleague, and Henry helped her prop Aidan up against a tree. The ailing filmmaker felt cold to the touch, conscious but pale and disoriented. Clare gave him some water, but it did not help. Without warning, Aidan turned away from her and threw up. Henry had pushed him too hard.

"He can't go on," she cried. "What are we going to do?"

Liam was in better shape but not by much. At least he could stand on his own and had not vomited. Henry feared he had saved the two men only to force them on a march that would kill them by exhaustion or dehydration.

"There's nothing to do but wait for a boat and hope the patrols don't find us," he said, hoping for another miracle.

He looked at the sky and saw heavy, laden clouds starting to gather. A big storm was coming. Henry and Clare had left most of the food and gear behind to make the backpacks as light as possible, holding on to a few plastic bags but no rain jackets or spare clothes. With the heavy rain, no boat would hear or see them at the margins, making it an almost certainty that the soldiers marching up the edge of the river would find them.

❧

Back in the mining complex, the compound chief joined the unit's lieutenant in front of the tents to map all the possible escape routes, dispatching teams to each one of them. A group of four men was sent east in a straight line, toward the nearest river. They were told to split in two once they got there, one pair covering the margin in each direction. If the fugitives made it that far, the river would block their escape, and one of the two units should eventually find them.

Broken into pairs to cover as much ground as possible, the troops were assigned targets: the Pitiri camp, the cave, the other research stations in the area, and the Indian settlements. After all possible destinations were covered, additional teams were sent randomly into the forest, casting a wide and tight net.

Unless the fugitives were able to flag a boat quickly, which was unlikely, the river created a formidable barrier that would contain them within the search area. With two of the fleeing group in poor health, the patrols should reach the river and all other possible destinations before the fugitives could slip through.

Leaving nothing to chance, the compound boss got on the satellite phone, calling his immediate superior. He gave Teresa Oliveira a quick update on the situation and advised her to start working with her government contacts in case the fugitives made it to the nearest village along the river or beyond.

The troops proceeded to scour the jungle, leaving no stone or branch unturned. They knew the terrain well and moved quickly and quietly, ears and eyes attuned to any noise or clue to help them find the fugitives.

Their order was to take no prisoners.

CHAPTER 37

"TAKE OFF YOUR clothes."

The abrupt order was so absurd that it sounded like an inappropriate joke at the worst possible time.

Clare and Liam stood still, with a puzzled look, not understanding the bizarre demand.

"What?" Clare asked, realizing Henry was serious.

"They are coming for us," he replied. "If we stay here, those men will find us. They must have reached the river downstream already and should be following it up the margins, searching for us. They will be here soon."

This being a major waterway connecting Brazil to Colombia, a boat or barge would eventually come by. The question was, What would get there first: transport or an enemy patrol? But even if he managed to hail a boat, the soldiers could still stop it, making the four of them easy prey. Henry decided their best bet was to get in the water.

"We have to get across," Henry explained.

"Are you serious?" she asked.

The river was at least a hundred yards wide, and the current looked dreadfully strong. Trying to swim to the other side with two debilitated people did not seem like a good choice.

"Aidan may not be able to walk, but he can hold on to a floating device," Henry explained as he moved around, looking for something. "We can't carry him, but if we get him in the water, we can pull him."

"What are you looking for?" Clare asked, sounding unconvinced.

"A fallen log or anything we can use as a float."

He saw her take a hard look at the river.

The current was strong enough to drag them, preventing any swimmer from going on a straight line, but not so powerful that it would drown them—at least not right away, assuming Aidan and Liam could hold on and nothing else went wrong.

"As much as this may not be a *good* choice," Henry said, "it's the best one available."

"Better than waiting around, I guess," she said, joining in the search.

They found a fallen tree. It was too heavy to carry to the river, but they managed to break away a large branch from the decaying trunk and bring it to the bank.

"What if there are cascades and rocks along the way?" she asked.

"It's a risk," he said coldly. "But according to the maps, most of the rougher terrain is upstream and to the west."

Clare turned to Aidan and put both hands on his shoulders, in an encouraging gesture.

"Hang tight, mate. I need you to hang tight. We'll get you out of here."

He managed to hold her gaze, a positive sign. But he looked defeated.

"You guys just hold on to the branch, and we'll do the rest," she argued, responding to their obvious skepticism. "If anyone can get us to safety, it's Henry. You have no idea how many tight spots he got us out of in the past few days."

"Is that why you gave him a smooch?" Liam asked, managing to produce a smile. It was followed by an aching cough.

"Shut up and save your energy," she answered with a grin. Aidan didn't appear to be in good-enough shape to laugh with them. "I trust him completely, and so should you. He saved our butts, didn't he? Just do what he says and we'll be okay."

"Yes, ma'am," Liam mumbled feebly, managing to muster some sarcasm.

Her words may or may not have worked on Aidan and Liam, but Henry got a boost out of her little pep talk. He was far from ready to give in, but as doubts about the river crossing started to creep into his head, hearing Clare express her faith in him helped his confidence grow, along with the determination not to disappoint her.

Aidan and Liam looked gaunt as they stripped down to their underwear.

"You sure we can't go in with our clothes on?" she asked self-consciously in her sports bra and hiking briefs.

He had held her in his arms just the night before but realized he had never seen her like this. She was physically stronger than her tall, slender frame indicated, her muscles toned but not bulked up. The memories from the night before flashed in his mind, but he quickly cast them aside.

"We can. But we will float better without them. Besides, we don't want to get our clothes wet. With the high humidity, it will take forever for them to dry; and there are far too many diseases around here that could develop on wet skin, some probably still unknown to modern medicine. You and I can make it, but in their condition, I don't know about Aidan and Liam."

He collected all the clothes and used them to wrap their gear, with special care to keep the camera and the other sensitive equipment well protected, putting everything in the trash bags he had brought with him precisely to guard their belongings from water. To increase flotation, he filled the rest of the bags with leaves gathered from the ground, then doubled them up with another layer of plastic and put everything in the backpack, which went inside yet another trash bag to make it as waterproof as he could.

"Do we have to worry about any creatures in the water?" Clare asked. They were about to get in the river practically naked.

Piranhas, anacondas, alligators, stingrays, electric eels, and candirus, the legendary little fish that can allegedly find their way through a man's penis into the urethra. The list was quite long, but the chance of an attack was small. Henry and his colleagues at the research station had frequently gone for a swim in these waters without incident. The acidic black-water rivers, such as the one they were about to jump in, were not as rich in scary creatures as the muddy rivers that flowed from the Andes in the west.

But the risk was not negligible, and the answer he gave was not reassuring.

"I'll take my chances with any of them over the people coming for us."

He paused and looked at the sky. The laden clouds had gotten heavier, and the storm seemed about ready to start, making their attempt to cross the river even more dangerous.

"I'd worry more about the river itself. And the weather." Henry pointed upward. "But it's still our best option."

They waded tentatively at first, sliding their feet on the muddy banks to avoid stepping on stingrays. The riverbed dropped quickly. Soon their toes couldn't reach the bottom, and their bodies were submerged, with only their heads above the water.

Wrapping their arms around the tree branch, Aidan and Liam leaned their chests on it while Henry and Clare pulled it with one hand each, the other holding on to the backpack filled with their possessions and the leaves implanted for buoyancy. Kicking the water with their feet, the two powered the improvised human raft slowly across the river.

The current was dragging them faster than expected. With the rain already coming down heavily in the jungle upstream, the river flow had grown progressively stronger. The wind picked up as well, and waves started to knock them around. After several minutes they had managed to get only a couple dozen feet away from the edge of the forest, and Aidan was struggling to hold on.

Henry started to second-guess the decision to get in the water.

"You have to get back there and help him!" he shouted to Clare. "Don't worry about swimming; I'll take care of it. Just make sure they are both holding on!"

He wasn't a particularly strong swimmer but had enough stamina to manage it. His biggest concern was the waves. If they separated Aidan or Liam from the tree branch, the two would certainly drown.

Progress was painfully slow. Not halfway across despite all his exertion, Henry found more reason for concern as he thought of their pursuers patrolling the riverbank. Floating down the river so near the edge of the forest, they increased the chances of meeting a patrol following the margins upstream in their direction. If one of the troops spotted the fugitives in the water, they would shoot to kill. At that proximity, the swimmers would be quite literally like fish in a barrel to soldiers carrying assault weapons.

If the risk of drowning in the rough water, a possible attack by piranhas, alligators, or both, or the increasing chance of being shot at were not reason enough to panic, with the arrival of the storm they faced the added danger of lightning. Not only did holding on to a tree branch in the open water make them more vulnerable to a strike, but even if not hit directly, they could be electrocuted or knocked unconscious by a discharge nearby.

Just as Clare got between Aidan and Liam, the storm started, lashing them violently. The raindrops hit their faces like pellets, the water got even rougher, and the current grew faster. Henry realized that trying to get across was futile. He stopped swimming and turned to his companions, helping them hold on tight to each other and their floating devices, while the surging river carried them downstream.

The downpour continued heavily as they hung on for their lives. Henry looked around and could barely see beyond a few feet ahead, a heavy sheet of water surrounding them. He was no longer sure of their position and had no idea where they would end up.

But instead of panicking, he grew confident. If he couldn't see the riverbank, the soldiers looking for them would not be able to spot them either. Provided it didn't kill them, the storm may very well turn out to be their salvation. He lost track of time and the distance they were covering, trusting the river to deliver them to safety.

Henry now concerned himself only with keeping them all together, letting the storm follow its course and take them where it may. As they drifted down to their unknown destination, he grew more certain they would make it out of the jungle alive. He wondered if the storm had also passed by the mining complex and put down the fire. It didn't matter anymore. The aircraft had been destroyed, and he had gotten away with the evidence he had come for.

CHAPTER 38

I T WAS LATE in the afternoon when the storm finally passed. It had been a struggle at first, but once Clare and Henry had given up trying to swim and worked solely on keeping everyone together, they had settled in their positions and were able to just ride it out, like a plane in heavy turbulence.

They had been dragged far downstream from where they entered the river. When the current slowed down, well after the sky had already cleared, Henry and Clare finally managed to get them all the way to the left bank and out of the water.

He quickly led them away from the margins, making everyone walk for a few minutes, until he found a suitable place to stop. When they did, he pulled the bag of dry clothes out of his backpack and, discarding the leaves, carefully unwrapped the gear and distributed the garments to their rightful owners.

The effort had been strenuous, but not as bad as a

fast-paced hike in the jungle's heat and humidity. Aidan still required attention. He felt cold, so Clare helped him dry off with Henry's shirt and got him into his clothes. The warmth of the tropics and some rest would hopefully take care of the remainder.

Propping Aidan up against the backpack, Clare gave him some water but no food, lest he should get sick again, proceeding to clear the ground and helping set up camp for the night.

"Do you think we are safe now?" Liam asked, speaking for the first time since getting in the water.

"For now, yes. I'm not sure where we are, but that means the people looking for us have no idea either. We are across the river and far downstream from the mine. I doubt that any patrols will get here. But there is still the matter of leaving the country, which will be the hardest part. The people behind this have ties to high levels of the Brazilian government."

He looked at Clare, who was again tending to Aidan. Relieved that the imminent danger had passed, Henry wanted badly to embrace her.

"But before we deal with *that*"—he snapped out of his thoughts, getting back to the task at hand—"we need to get out of the jungle."

"How?" Liam asked.

The night was starting to fall. Getting on a boat to a city would be too dangerous, their pursuers sure to monitor the ports and expect them in any of the urban centers.

Henry pulled the satellite phone from inside the bag. It had stayed intact and dry, along with the rest of their gear, thanks to his overzealous packing.

"How about I call us a limo?"

◈

Henry walked back to the river to get better reception. Arriving at the bank, he pulled out the GPS, checked the coordinates, and made a call.

"We got them, Berto," he blurted out as soon as the professor answered.

"Henry!"

"They were being held in the exact same tent we were. Aidan is in bad shape, but I think he'll make it. Liam is doing better, as good as you can for someone in captivity for a week."

"That's good news. How are you and—"

"It's thorianite!" Henry cried, anxious to tell everything he had discovered. "Like we thought. I got a sample of it and pictures of the whole camp. And the people working there also."

"Perfect."

"It's going to the Republic of Alashrar," Henry went on. "I saw the flag on the boxes, ready to go on a plane. They have markings in Arabic all over them."

"Farsi," the professor corrected him. "It's similar; but like the Iranians, the Alashraris speak Farsi, not Arabic. I suspected Alashrar may be involved."

"How so?"

"Buried in the mountain of conspiracy theories you downloaded to my computer the night before you left, there was a reference to an Israeli government report claiming Venezuela was supplying the Republic of Alashrar with uranium. It took me a while to sort through all the noise, but it made sense. Venezuela's nuclear capabilities are way behind."

"Well, now we have proof."

"I reached the American consulate officer you met."

"Angelo Knowles? What did he say?"

"He didn't want to talk to me at first," the professor explained. "Like I was wasting his time. Typical bureaucrat. But when I told him you had found evidence of an operation to supply Venezuela—and maybe Alashrar—with uranium, I got his attention. Since 9/11 no American official will dismiss even the wildest theories about national-security threats without at least a cursory look.

"I gave him the coordinates of the Pitiri Research Station as well as the position of the mining camp. Knowles said that everything would be shared with the relevant agencies through a program called the Nationwide Suspicious Activity Reporting Initiative. Then he hung up."

"And that was it?"

"I thought so," Berto replied. "But yesterday a couple of tough-looking guys with military haircuts came knocking on my door."

"What?"

"They said they got my name from Knowles. I called him and he confirmed. Funny, he wouldn't tell me who those guys were or who they worked for, only that I should tell them everything I knew and that they could help you."

"Who do *you* think they work for?"

"Some intelligence agency or another," Berto replied. "Or maybe the military. It's not surprising that the US government would have some of those folks down in the Amazon."

"Seems straight out of a spy movie."

"This whole story does. Let's just hope it has a happy ending."

Berto went on. "Anyway, the guy who seemed to be in charge—he said his name was Ronan West—explained that the information I gave Knowles was passed to a variety of agencies and ended up catching the interest of one of their colleagues."

"Oh."

"The guys seemed intrigued by the fact that the site was operated by Mineradora da Floresta back at some point. They even asked about the Venezuelan ID you found and how we suspected the mine was extracting thorianite. They wanted to know about every detail. I told them everything."

"Did they explain to you why they were so interested?"

"I asked, but all they said was 'I cannot comment on that.' So many times, I could have turned it into a drinking game. That's how I knew I was talking to the government."

Henry laughed.

"It was a bit infuriating, but I let it go. I figured this West gentleman is our best shot at getting help from the US government. Or from any authority at all."

"I think you are right," Henry agreed.

"And it worked. Because they seem very interested in whatever evidence you can share. West said he wants to see you as soon as you get to Manaus."

∽

Berto called Ronan West right after he hung up with Henry.

Unbeknownst to the professor, US officials from different agencies had come across the existence of the mining compound through their intelligence-sharing network. Combining it with other reports that monitored the collaboration between Venezuela and the Republic of Alashrar, intelligence officers had made the connection to that regime's nuclear program. An analyst from the Bureau of Intelligence and Research, the State Department's division tasked with gathering information to support American diplomatic efforts, had quickly realized the finding's implication for an upcoming urgent vote at the United Nations.

The UN Security Council would soon vote to impose crippling sanctions on the Republic of Alashrar, an attempt to stop progress toward the development of an atomic bomb that would at best destabilize the entire Middle East. And would at worst fall into the hands of terrorists.

But Brazil and Mexico had just announced a deal that would supposedly ensure any nuclear technology Alashrar developed could be used only for peaceful purposes. American diplomats, as well as some of their counterparts in other countries, were certain that the agreement would accomplish just the opposite, despite any good intentions Brazil and Mexico may have.

A few of the key members of the Security Council, however, needed to be convinced before they agreed to the sanctions that would cost millions of dollars in lost business to their countries. The evidence gathered by

Henry, proving the existence of the compound, was the last remaining hope to persuade them in the vote that was less than forty-eight hours away.

"You are sure Mr. Foster has photographs of the site and samples of the thorianite?" West asked.

"Yes, I just talked to him," Berto confirmed. "And he has some pictures of the people working at the camp. Maybe your team can identify some of them."

"We need to see these photos."

"Of course. We will hand them over to you as soon as everyone is safely out of the country."

"We don't have time for that," West stated firmly. "I need them urgently. This is a matter of national security, Mr. Rossi."

"We want to help, Mr. West. If not, I wouldn't have contacted your colleague at the consulate. But surely you must agree Henry and the film crew's safety is also a priority? If what I told you about the involvement in this conspiracy by top officials of the Brazilian government is true—and the fact we are having this conversation is evidence that it is—we need to get my friends out of Brazil as soon as possible."

"I will try," West conceded. "But I need those pictures by tomorrow. Otherwise, it will be too late, and there will be nothing I can do to help them."

CHAPTER 39

THE MORNING AFTER their improbable escape from the mining complex, Henry walked back to the riverbank and called Berto again. The professor gave him a set of coordinates, and Henry plotted the course on his GPS, leading the filmmakers on a three-hour hike, this time at a slower pace to avoid overtaxing Aidan and Liam.

Coming to an abandoned airstrip north of where they had spent the night, with small shrubs growing across the landing path, they waited.

"Can Berto really pull this off on such short notice?" Clare asked forty minutes after their arrival, sitting impatiently in the shade at the edge of the neglected runway.

"Of course. He's pretty resourceful, don't you think? When I gave him our location yesterday, he already had a plane on standby to send to the closest landing spot he could locate. This is it."

"How did he find this so quickly?"

"Satellite maps. He has access to very recent images through IBEA."

"And it just so happens that there are runways scattered all over the jungle?"

"I don't know about all over, but there are quite a few. The drug cartels and contraband runners have to move their merchandise somehow."

Henry saw the look of concern on everyone's faces.

"I don't think there's a big chance we'll run into them. If a particular strip is used often, the government will shut it down. That's why there are so many."

That seemed to assuage their fears some, and his as well, though not completely.

"There it is." Henry pointed, after a ninety-minute wait. "It's the same plane that brought us back to the jungle three days ago. You recognize it?" he asked, looking at Clare.

The aircraft bounced around during the approach, landing awkwardly on the grassy runway overtaken by the growing vegetation.

The pilot walked out of the Cessna 210L and greeted the four exhausted would-be passengers with water and food. He also carried some medicine to help Liam and Aidan weather the flight back to civilization.

The trip was uneventful save for the heavy turbulence and a refueling stop. Landing at the Aeroclube de Manaus early in the evening, the travelers were whisked away by Berto in his beat-up Fiat Uno and taken to the house of one of his friends. A shower, a warm meal, and a comfortable bed awaited them.

A doctor was called to come see Aidan and Liam,

both of whom were debilitated but, luckily, in need of only rest, fluids, and good nutrition.

Berto had also invited another guest, a reporter from one of Brazil's largest newspapers. She had arrived that same day, on a two-and-a-half-hour flight from Brasília, the nation's capital, eager to break the story.

The professor's young neighbor, Ciro, came by too, bringing a laptop and a printer to make multiple copies of all the photos from Henry and Clare's jungle excursion. Following instructions from Ronan West, Ciro helped Henry upload all the data securely to a server where the information would start to be immediately analyzed.

After a quick shower and a bite to eat, Henry got right back to business, working with Berto to divide the thorianite samples into smaller batches, which they placed in lead pouches, putting together several packages of the evidence for distribution. They planned to disseminate it as widely as possible, making sure their findings could not be suppressed.

✺

It was well past midnight when Henry watched two small SUVs park in front of the unremarkable house in a quiet neighborhood of Manaus. The men inside matched the description of the guys the professor had mentioned: tall and muscular, with crew cuts. The drivers stayed in the vehicles. Two other men exited, standing guard while another member of the team walked to the door. Though they were all wearing plain clothes, the confident and rehearsed way they moved led Henry to assume they had military training.

"Time to go," Berto said to Henry as the man knocked. "That's West."

The professor went into the bedroom and woke up the three guests, who had fallen with abandon on their beds, giving in to physical and mental exhaustion and crashing into sleep.

Henry had not slept, choosing to power through his fatigue to retell his tale in meticulous detail to the Brazilian reporter.

"This gentleman was sent here courtesy of the US government." Berto pointed to Ronan West, who looked annoyed at the revelation, as the professor addressed the still-disoriented filmmakers walking red eyed into the living room. "Not that he would admit it. If anyone asks, he and his buddies are civilians sent here by a concerned citizen who just wanted to help."

Henry was at the same time impressed and terrified that the American government could deploy a team so quickly in this isolated city.

When the two SUVs arrived at the Eduardo Gomes International Airport in Manaus, they drove straight to the tarmac, bypassing the airport check-in, security lines, and border control. A private jet was on standby.

Henry did not dare ask how they managed to get access to the restricted area, guessing a good deal of deception and maybe a bribe had been involved.

Inside the airplane, a lean-built man with graying blond hair sat at the front with a thick, brown accordion folder on his lap. He typed furiously on his cell phone, a box full of assorted files and a laptop occupying the seat next to him.

As the ragged foursome boarded the aircraft, he looked up from his phone and studied them briefly. Standing and showing his badge, he introduced himself as Senior Intelligence Officer Dwight Chancelor, from the NSA field-operations team.

It was the first confirmation that the people they had been dealing with were in fact from the US government, Henry thought, relieved to finally shed his small concern that this could be just a trap.

He shook the intelligence officer's hand and, at Chancelor's request, handed him a pouch containing one of the batches of thorianite. The official thanked him, passing it to one of the three other officers on the plane. That agent seemed to have some expertise on the mineral, for he proceeded to his seat and opened a briefcase with a magnifying glass and several instruments, promptly starting to analyze it.

Before the plane took off from Manaus, Chancelor explained that Henry and the three filmmakers would be debriefed and exhaustively interviewed individually by himself and his colleagues. The newly arrived passengers were then asked to sign a legal document formally waiving any legal representation in connection with their cooperation and agreeing to fully and truthfully answer all questions.

They were free to refuse and stay in Brazil, Chancelor clarified, in which case he would notify the Brazilian authorities. Hesitating but obviously desperate to leave the country and put their nightmare behind them, none of them declined to sign it.

⤚

With the vote at the United Nations taking place in a few hours and dependent on the veracity of the evidence brought by Henry and Clare, there would be no time to relax and enjoy the flight. Each member of the group was immediately separated from the others, and the questioning began as soon as the doors closed.

Henry was assigned to Chancelor, the most senior of the officers. The agents had a keen interest in Clare as well, since she and Henry were the ones who had uncovered the conspiracy. They were connected via satellite link to a situation room at the NSA headquarters in Fort Meade, Maryland, where a team of analysts pulling an all-nighter were painstakingly examining the evidence uploaded a few hours earlier and sending their observations and questions to the officers on the plane.

After landing at a military base at an undisclosed location a few hours from Manaus, all of which were spent under detailed interrogation, Henry, Clare, Aidan, and Liam were held for debriefing an additional two days, still not allowed to see or speak to each other and kept under tight surveillance.

Despite obtaining all the intelligence they needed during the flight, the officials wanted to double-check and document everything they had learned. Henry and the film crew were released only after signing confidentiality agreements and long, formal sworn statements summarizing their entire experience, from landing in the Amazon to coming back to Manaus on the flight arranged by Berto. The US government had made the most out of the arrangement, extracting every ounce of information their four new assets had to offer.

✧

Henry saw Clare—for the first time since they had been separated—when they boarded a military transport to Miami. Escorted by army personnel throughout, they did not have a chance to talk privately.

From Miami, each was put on a commercial flight back to their homes. Henry headed to Philadelphia, while Clare boarded a plane to Australia. They said their good-byes awkwardly at the airport terminal, promising to stay in touch.

As he looked out the window of his plane during take-off, Henry wondered how he would adjust to a normal life after everything he had been through. Would he have nightmares about Bill Powers dying in Clare's arms for the rest of his days? Would he forever be looking over his shoulder, living in fear that someone would seek revenge against him for revealing the conspiracy? And what would he do now that his career as a tropical ecologist was essentially over?

But the biggest thing on his mind had nothing to do with those questions. Mostly he wondered whether he would ever see Clare again.

CHAPTER 40

WHEN THE AMERICAN ambassador finally confirmed the vote was going ahead after several hours of delay, some of her counterparts couldn't hide their annoyance. Even a few of America's closest allies seemed to be running out of patience.

"This is a waste of time," said the British ambassador in a last-minute meeting before the vote. "With the news about the agreement, it would be premature to impose crippling sanctions at this time. We are not prepared to endorse an embargo if there is a chance that this new framework will ensure that the nuclear technology will be used only for peaceful purposes."

The American diplomat nodded, took a deep breath, and handed a manila folder to each of the permanent Security Council members.

"As Your Excellencies can see—" She started to explain, pointing at the materials just placed in front of them. The ambassador was nervous, but her countenance was confident and seemingly unperturbed by the protests of her counterparts.

The documents in the folders were still warm, fresh off the printer. A team of NSA analysts had worked overnight at warp speed to confirm that all the evidence was accurate and to put the package now in the folders together.

"—we just obtained hard evidence of an illegal uranium mining operation in Brazilian territory, run to benefit the very country the United States is today recommending for sanction. What you see in the photos, which our intelligence services have been able to confirm as authentic, is a thorianite mining camp operated by the Venezuelan military in a remote area of the Brazilian Amazon forest."

Jaws dropped, eyes rolled, but everyone leaned forward. The US ambassador had their full attention.

"Our source on the ground obtained a copy of a Venezuelan military ID belonging to one of the soldiers in these photographs. The document is now presumably in the hands of the local Brazilian police. Our analysts have confirmed that, despite the absence of a flag, the uniforms you see match the design used by the Venezuelan army. You can also see that the weapons they are holding in the photographs are the AK-103, standard issue in their country's military. Your Excellency should be able to recognize it quite easily," she said, staring at the Russian ambassador. "They are made in your country."

She was being undiplomatic but wanted to make

implicit that the US was ready to implicate Russia by association if needed.

"We have already shared these photos with all your intelligence agencies, along with the coordinates of the site, so that your own government officers can check these facts for themselves."

The expression of annoyance and surprise on the ambassadors' faces transitioned to one of acute interest.

"We also checked the registration number of the airplane you see in the photos. While it's covered by a camouflage tarp, the tail number was recorded by one of our sources, who is now in protective custody of the United States government. The aircraft used to belong to a private individual with suspected ties to terrorism. According to intelligence shared by our Russian colleagues"—the ambassador acknowledged her counterpart again, waving her right hand casually in his direction—"it is now in use by the same regime we are today trying to prevent from building nuclear weapons.

"I also point to the photos of the boxes labeled in Farsi with the caution they contain thorianite, a mineral from which uranium is commonly extracted to be enriched and weaponized. I'm sure you can recognize the Republic of Alashrar's flag and military symbols next to the labels. These boxes were about to be loaded on the plane before it was destroyed by a fire. Our intelligence officers are also in possession of some samples of the mineral shown in the photographs, taken directly from one of these boxes. Our experts have confirmed it's thorianite. We can share these samples with your own intelligence services for verification.

"Please also refer to the photograph of Fazil El-Ghaz-zawy, also known as 'The Engineer.' " She drew their attention to the image of the thin old gentleman with the pencil mustache. "He is a Saudi scientist who all our intelligence services have long suspected to be helping the Alashrari regime develop a nuclear bomb. He is shown here inspecting the facilities at the mine just two days ago."

She could tell during her presentation that the room had turned. The ambassador then presented the last piece of evidence.

"And now take a look at the last image in the folder." She held it up, showing it to her fellow diplomats. "This is a high-definition satellite image of the site. You can make out the airstrip and the mining camp, despite great efforts to disguise it. We ourselves didn't find it until the location was known to our intelligence."

She put down the image and concluded:

"Now, if one of you can help me understand why we should give credibility to a deal brokered by the Brazilian government while this whole operation is going on in their own country?

"And how can we believe the regime will abide by this so-called *momentous* agreement when they have been obtaining uranium in breach of the international agreements they committed to?"

A couple of countries briefly tried to question the authenticity of the evidence, asking for a delay in the vote and time to review it. But the ambassador pushed back forcefully, saying they had all played enough games. Her counterparts backed down after she also mentioned that her office had already been contacted by several international news organizations in possession of the same evidence after a Brazilian newspaper had broken the story an hour ago.

The Chinese ambassador was the first to change his tune and condemn the agreement with great outrage, calling it malicious, irresponsible, and lacking in credibility.

The sanctions were approved unanimously.

✖

Back in Washington, watching the vote on a secure feed in his office on Twenty-Third Street, Andrew Everett, the veteran diplomat who had dedicated his career to fighting the proliferation of weapons of mass destruction, celebrated by jumping and punching the air.

This was a temporary measure, he knew, but an important one nonetheless. Not only would sanctions delay the development of the nuclear program, but discovery of the mining operation would further hurt the program's progress by depriving the regime of a major source of uranium.

His work would go on. In fact, it never stopped. But for now he could finally go home in peace. He looked up to the ceiling and thanked, out loud, the tropical ecologist and his companions who had unwittingly helped prevent the latest plot toward nuclear proliferation.

CHAPTER 41

BY THE TIME Henry read about the UN sanctions against the Republic of Alashrar, it was already old news. The media had moved on to the latest scandal, involving an American politician.

Henry had arrived in Philadelphia a few days after the vote, planning to stay with his parents while he figured out what to do with his life now that his dream of exploring the Amazon had been cut short.

His first call was to Berto. Thankfully, no one had learned of the professor's involvement. Henry invited him for a visit, receiving a vague promise that the professor would try. If Henry ever got back to Brazil, he thought, it would be to see the man who had made it possible for him and Clare to expose the conspiracy and live to tell the tale.

Henry's name had stayed out of the papers, but he

couldn't help wondering what would happen if he ever returned to Brazil. Pleased as he was that his exposure of the mining compound had resulted in sanctions to delay nuclear proliferation, the result of his efforts had been mixed. Hardly any of the perpetrators had faced justice.

Following the scandal of the secret smuggling of nuclear materials right under his nose, the president of Brazil, bowing to pressure from the opposition, called for an aggressive investigation. The Brazilian army raided the mining complex, razing to the ground what little had been left behind by the Venezuelan troops and burying the mine.

Ramito Torres, the thin-bearded man who was the chief of the compound—Henry had come to learn his name through the media—was the only person ever to be arrested. He confessed to the illegal mining and helping the Venezuelans but refused to implicate anybody else, seemingly content to be the scapegoat for the entire debacle. His loyalty allowed Fund-Ama's director, Teresa Oliveira, her associates, and a number of officials in the federal administration to avoid investigation.

Despite facing no charges, Oliveira's involvement had been reported in the news, causing Fund-Ama to lose all its funding and consequently fold. Henry found only a modicum of consolation in the fact that at least she didn't get to keep her career while he lost his.

To the relief of Henry's research team, the Pitiri Research Station was quickly taken over by another Brazilian organization, making it possible for the ongoing scientific studies to continue. The largest impact on the several projects underway was the loss of Henry, who, despite offers to remain onboard, had decided it was not a good idea to stay in Brazil. With his departure, the studies would be significantly delayed, but they would go on.

What bothered him the most was the impunity around Bill Powers's death. The detailed testimony of several different people about what had happened did little to identify who had actually pulled the trigger or who had ordered it, though Henry was quite sure it was a Venezuelan soldier and the mining-compound chief had played a role in it. And while Henry would eventually pay a visit to Powers's parents to tell them what had really happened, the murder would remain officially unsolved, with no one held accountable. The only closure the family would ever have was the return of Bill's remains, so they could at least have a proper burial.

But as Henry mulled over everything that had happened, it became clear that even if the outcome of his efforts was far from satisfactory, he was lucky to be alive. He owed it to himself to move on.

He drove down I-95 to the airport in his old and rusty Ford Ranger pickup truck, which had been gathering dust in his parents' garage since he had moved to the jungle.

His heart was pounding with anticipation.

Henry was aware that he and Clare had known each other far too briefly to drop everything and spend time together. But despite their short relationship, they had both jumped at the idea the moment it came up.

What else would they do anyway? Henry's career had been derailed for a second time, and Clare was far from ready to go back to work. His salary at Pitiri had not been much, but with hardly a chance to spend any of it out in the jungle, he had enough to make ends meet for a while.

They had talked about driving west to see some of the national parks and sleep outdoors under the Grand Canyon's starry sky. Or maybe they would go to New York or Washington, DC, to see the sights. He didn't really care one way or another.

Henry had no job, no career, and no prospects. But the odds he had beaten in the Amazon jungle were far worse than any challenges he may have ahead of him.

The smile on her face when she saw him waiting at the terminal confirmed she was all he needed right now. She raced to embrace him, holding him tight and then pulling back just enough to give him a long kiss.

The End

Made in the USA
Monee, IL
02 December 2022